Count Maffei

Brigand Life in Italy

A History of Bourbonist Reaction

Count Maffei

Brigand Life in Italy
A History of Bourbonist Reaction

ISBN/EAN: 9783741189586

Manufactured in Europe, USA, Canada, Australia, Japa

Cover: Foto ©Andreas Hilbeck / pixelio.de

Manufactured and distributed by brebook publishing software
(www.brebook.com)

Count Maffei

Brigand Life in Italy

BRIGAND LIFE IN ITALY.

VOLUME I.

BRIGAND LIFE IN ITALY:

A HISTORY OF BOURBONIST REACTION.

EDITED FROM ORIGINAL AND AUTHENTIC DOCUMENTS.

BY

COUNT MAFFEI.

IN TWO VOLUMES.

VOL. I.

LONDON:
HURST AND BLACKETT, PUBLISHERS,
SUCCESSORS TO HENRY COLBURN.
13, GREAT MARLBOROUGH STREET.
1865.

LONDON :
PRINTED BY MACDONALD AND TUGWELL, BLENHEIM HOUSE,
BLENHEIM STREET, OXFORD STREET.

A VOI

MIA BUONA MADRE

DEDICO QUESTO LAVORO

IN ATTESTATO

DI RIVERENTE E CALDISSIMO AFFETTO.

PREFACE.

Tne enemies of Italian unity have done so much
at all times to mislead public opinion on the reactionist movements which have agitated the Southern provinces of Italy—happily now so far subdued
as to permit of the facts connected with them being
spoken of with perfect frankness and impartiality—
that I thought a work containing a truthful history
of brigandage in the ex-kingdom of Naples would be
at the same time useful and interesting.

My object in undertaking this task not being that
of winning a literary success, for which, unfortunately,
I have no title whatever, but only to enlighten public
opinion, I thought I could not do better than begin
my work by acquainting English readers with the
narrative of M. Monnier, who, an eye-witness for the
most part of the time, related the history of the first
period of the Neapolitan troubles with an accuracy
and conscientiousness which are not to be found elsewhere ; and notwithstanding the alterations and notes
I have been obliged to add, I contrived, as much as

I could, to leave it in its genuine character—happy
to have thus an opportunity to pay a due homage to
M. Monnier, as a token of the gratitude that every
Italian owes him for his sympathies to our cause.

I have then continued the history of these sad
annals from the point left by M. Monnier up to the
present day, availing myself of every investigation
that has been made on this subject—of every official
document that has been published, and chiefly of the
admirable report made by my learned friend Commen-
datore Massari, presented to our House of Deputies, on
the investigations accomplished by the special Commission charged by the Italian Government to report on
the causes of brigandage, and to express their opinion
as to the best practical means of assuring its destruction.
In this part of my work I have laid bare the state
of misery and degradation in which the kingdom of
Naples was left by five generations of Bourbons, and
have exhibited, in its minutest details, the complicity
with the intrigues of Francis II. of that single Government which still remains in Italy as the representative of its long servitude—a complicity to which
that harassing agitation, from which our country has
so much suffered, was chiefly due.

In the second volume I have also been able to
introduce a report kindly sent to me by General
Pallavicini, on his last brilliant expeditions into the
most infested parts of the Southern provinces, and
have concluded by some remarks on recent poli-
litical events, and the progress that has been made

by the young kingdom of Italy. Deprived of any
other merit, my desire has been solely to offer a conscientious work, in which I have not only followed
the best authorities on this subject, but have also been
guided by the experience acquired during a long
residence at Naples, at a period when its real condition was as little known to the civilized world as if
it had been cut off from the rest of Europe by a
new Chinese wall.

To the public of England I hope this work will not
prove totally unprofitable. It will furnish them with
data by which they will be enabled to form an opinion
upon a question regarding which the most contra-
dictory judgments have been expressed, not only
by the enemies of Italy, but also by persons not
unfavourably disposed towards the cause of national
unity. It will show them that the disorders of the
South of Italy do not contain in themselves the germs
of serious disagreements with the rest of the Peninsula,
for the loss of its former autonomy. It will perhaps
destroy that strange confusion of ideas so charitably
kept up by the legitimist party, in order to give to
the movement in the old kingdom of Naples the
character of a civil war, and point out by whose
hand the reaction was kindled. Whatever may
have been written on this subject, in order to exhibit prominently, by an accurate description, not
only the evils arising from many years of a corrupt
and immoral rule, but also the connivance of
the Pontifical Government with the intrigues

of a prince deposed by popular indignation—thus showing the evident contradiction in which the abuse of temporal power places the Holy See with the sacred mission of peace it has to perform on earth —an unprejudiced exposition of Neapolitan brigandage will not, I trust, be found inopportune at the present moment. In fact, on the eve of the departure of the French from the Eternal City, and when clerical intolerance is so audaciously throwing the challenge to the civilized world, it will perhaps be of great use to know the real state of things in Italy. In correcting the erroneous ideas that have prevailed on this subject, the public will be enabled to form an impartial judgment upon the motives which have inspired the present policy of France, and on the spirit which will dictate the future attitude of the Italian Government, in the new phase that the fulfilment of the convention of September is about to create. Should I succeed in attaining this purpose, I shall certainly render a great service to the cause of my country, and this will be my excuse for making the attempt.

A. MAFFEI.

49, Grosvenor Street.

CONTENTS

OF

THE FIRST VOLUME.

CHAPTER IV.

CHAPTER V.

CHAPTER VI.

CHAPTER VII.

CHAPTER I.

CHAPTER I.

THE ancient Môle of Naples, before the fall of the Bourbon Government, was the rendezvous of the *lazzaroni*, who, after their day's work, were in the habit of assembling there for the enjoyment of repose, to perform their devotions, and to amuse themselves. When they were not sleeping in the sun, in their large osier baskets, they would collect around some wandering priest or some itinerant Pulcinella. But when the Improvisatore came upon the scene, brandishing his staff as an emblem of command, the Pulcinella and the priest immediately lost their audience. Children quitted their play ; the fisherman stood up with his basket on his shoulder ; the girl hastened from the water's edge ; the *marinarella* came running up with her chair and distaff ; and all this noisy crowd, as if calmed down by enchantment, pressed around the wonderful story-teller, hanging with eager attention on his words ; whilst behind them, and beyond the forest

of masts rising out of the harbour, was seen the
double summit of Vesuvius, immoveable, and, as it
were, attentive to the scene, the smoke continuing
unceasingly to ascend from it.

What, then, did this singer of stories relate?
Frequently the narratives recorded in the poems
of Ariosto, but oftener the adventures of renowned
brigands, the valorous deeds of Titta Grieco, of the
Spicciarelli, of Angelo del Duca, Bartolomeo Ro-
mano, or Pietro Mancini.   The crowd listened with
open ears, their eyes fixed upon him with almost
painful interest, uttering shouts of admiration as they
heard of each new murder committed by one of the
heroes I have named.   The people of Naples, in common with many others much more civilised, have this
characteristic—they like stories where there is a good
deal of blood and murder.   The nation, however, is
showing signs of improvement; it is becoming enlightened, and the day is approaching when the Improvisatore will hardly be able to collect the credulous
audiences that once assembled round him.   As to the
brigands who supplied him with the subjects of his
tragic stories, they also will soon have disappeared
in their turn.   The three years just elapsed
have seen brigandage, in its ambition to assume
a political rôle, attempt a task which has led it
on to its destruction.   Repressed at first by the

energetic employment of military force, it now sees
its total ruin accomplished by the happy concurrence
of moral and material progress.

In order to know what brigandage was under the
ancient régime, it is not necessary to go to the Môle
of Naples. Many of those strange stories which the
inexhaustible genius of the Improvisatore enriched
with a thousand attractive details, have been preserved
by the printing press.   These are in general those
poems in lines of eight syllables, which, violating all
the laws of syntax and of prosody, are written in a
double language, half Italian, and half *patois*, which
certainly no foreign readers could understand. I take
one of these poems, the first that comes to hand, the
adventures of Agostino Avossa.   It will be sufficient
to give an idea of ancient brigandage, and also of
those open-air epopees which have long delighted the
idlers on the Môle.

The poet commences, in the manner of the classic
authors, by *proclaiming* that which he is about to
sing.   Never, he says, will there be anything worthy
of comparison with the adventures of his hero.   Then
comes the habitual invocation, addressed not to the
deities of Olympus, but to our Lord Jesus Christ.   He
next tells us that Agostino was a native of Naples,
the son of a rich butcher.   He possessed two dogs,
which he brought up with great affection.   A great

lord, named *L'Erario* (the Fiscal—the authorities are
always made to play the odious part in popular
poetry), one day meeting Avossa, said to him : " My
friend, give me, if you please, one of your dogs for
my hunter." Avossa refused. " That dog," he replied, " is the very heart of my life ; take my life, if
you please, but that creature is mine." Some days
after, in obedience to the orders of the great lord, the
two dogs were killed. This act of the Erario, in the
language of the Neapolitan people, is called a *tradimento*, an act of treachery. The *tradimento* is
followed by the *vendetta*, vengeance. In the opinion
of the lazzarone, the *tradimento* is infamous, the
vendetta noble.* Avossa avenges himself by killing
L'Erario; after which deed he becomes *fuorgiudicato*—
that is to say, bandit, outlaw, and takes to flight. He
lives first at Rome, where he continues to follow
the occupation of assassin, but having destroyed
two of his enemies, is obliged to quit the Eternal
City. He returns to Naples well provided with ammu-

---

* Under the Bourbons the plebeian had no faith either in
commissaries or in magistrates ; he took justice into his own
hands. When he had performed an act of justice, that is to
say, committed a murder, his whole caste applauded him as a
man of courage. Neither a criminal trial nor the bagnio
was any stain to him. A convict who, after he had been at
liberty for more than eight months, still wore his red jacket,
being asked why he did not get quit of it, replied that it was
still good for wear.

nition; and, necessarily halting at some monastery on his way, is well treated by all the monks, who, we know not why, have, under every régime, invariably protected the bandit.

Agostino Avossa shortly after becomes enamoured of a young girl of Borgo di Loreto. The two are so devoted to each other, that they appear like husband and wife, which in that country, where everything assumes a singular aspect, is regarded as the very extreme of passion. Avossa often leaves the holy place in order to visit his beloved. Warned of this fact, the *corte* (for so the Government is named in the poems of the Môle) sends four captains and forty soldiers to seize the bandit. From that moment the entire life of this remarkable man is a succession of astonishing acts of prowess. He kills one of the soldiers of the detachment, and leaps out of a window; he pursues three sbirri, brandishing his musket as they fly, and forces his way into a convent by breaking in the door. To the trembling monks he says—"Fear nothing; you surely know me—I am Agostino!" The monks, re-assured by the name, give him shelter; but the *corte*, that is, the armed force, appearing on the scene, the fugitive is taken prisoner. Conducted to the prisons of the Archbishopric, the people collect in numbers to see him, exclaiming that this man alone filled the world with his fame. Scarcely have

the doors of the prison closed upon him, ere Agostino
discovers that two other prisoners desire to accomplish his death (by a *tradimento*); he kills them (that
is a *rendetta*).   "As Judas betrayed Jesus for a little
money, so did these two traitors desire my death,"
said Agostino, to the priest of the prison, who was
waiting for him to sit down at table.   " Now let us
dine."   But the *corte*, on learning these new deeds of
prowess, is so barbarous as to confine the hero's
feet in fetters.   He breaks them, bursts through the
walls, and is on the point of escaping once more,
when he is unfortunately re-taken, and cast into a
dungeon of the Castle of St. Elmo.   Avossa, not
discouraged by so slight a *contretemps*, suborns a
Swiss sentinel who was on duty at the fortress, and
one morning makes his escape with him.

We see that these desertions, so frequent at the
present day, date from a distant period.   The people
find them perfectly natural.   The moment he is free,
what does the brigand do ?   He goes to Bosco, to the
house of one of his friends, another priest, who presses
him in his arms, covering him with kisses and tears.
"My dear, blessed son (*caro figlio benedetto*)," says
the priest to him, with pure love (*con puro amore*),
"think on thy life."   After this first visit, Agostino
sets off to see his kindred and friends, receives arms,
money, and munition, and is again roaming in the

mountains. Attacked by the Royal troops, he per-
forms prodigies of valour. He precipitates himself
at last from the summit of a rock, and, after several
successive falls, lies prostrate at the bottom of the
abyss, covered with bruises, but still living. Betrayed by a peasant, he is taken, bound, and conducted by coach to Naples. The corporals, the
soldiers, discharge their muskets in testimony of their
joy; while the people show their regret by tears.
The court of justice assembles, and the sentence of
death, which is pronounced, is almost immediately executed in the presence of a mourning crowd.

This popular narrative, selected from among a
thousand, shows the remarkable prestige by which,
some years ago, the bandit was surrounded. He was
regarded, not as a malefactor, but, like the corsairs
of Byron, as a romantic being in a false position.
Loved by the women, blessed by the priests, he was
received with acclamations by the people. Even at
the present day, in many parts of the country, coarse
lithographs display, on the white-washed walls of the
peasants' cottages, the valorous deeds of Mammone
or of Fra Diavolo. The bandit, who was merciful
to the poor, and attacked only the rich, found everywhere accomplices and adherents. Sometimes, when
dying of hunger, he was succoured by the indigent,
his brethren. It occasionally happened even that the

country people practised brigandage as a trade, and
made no secret of it in presence of the military
authorities.   A Neapolitan prefect (Stendhal relates
the fact) found fault with a peasant for not paying
his taxes.   " What can I do ?" replied the peasant ;
" there is nothing doing on the high road—I am out
on it every day with my gun, but no one passes.   I
promise, however, to go every evening, until I have
picked up the fifteen ducats you want."   Not un-
frequently, after several years passed in such an
irregular life, the bandit returns to his village, where
he lives with impunity on his *rentes*.   In the evening, when he takes his seat in the village street, to
enjoy the fresh air, all the young girls and children
of the place gather round him when he is disposed to
relate the adventures in which he has been engaged on
his various expeditions, which he calls his campaigns.

   Such is a general picture of what brigandage is in
the eyes of the people ; but in order that we may
more perfectly understand its history, which it is my
intention to record, it is necessary, in the first place,
to have some idea of the race by whom Southern
Italy is inhabited.

   The Neapolitan character has been the subject of
various judgments, almost all of which have been conceived in a hostile point of view.   It has been too much
the tendency of writers to form their opinions of

the mass from certain unfavourable examples ; and therefore the Neapolitans have been badly or imperfectly appreciated.

There are in that country two classes, distinguished by strongly-marked peculiarities—educated persons and the *vulgus*, or the low, ignorant, and uninstructed. I do not speak of the aristocracy, for at the time when the Revolution took place it was not to be found in Naples. The individuals of whom that body was composed were nearly all at Rome, and in Paris. Nor do I say anything of the illiterate *bourgeoisie*, for such a class has no existence in the country.

No part of Italy is more full of promise than the territory that constituted the late Kingdom of Naples. The learned show, by their number and importance, what the future of that country will be, when, having once passed out of its present transition state, it shall have been for some time under the government of moral and just laws, that offer no impediment to the progress of the people. Naples has already—even in the most unfavourable circumstances—given to Italy the greatest number of men distinguished in every department of learning. Even before the Revolution its political exiles held a leading position among the men of worth and mark in Italy. It was among the ranks of the Neapolitan proscripts that the most eminent doctors and lawyers were found. They

crowded the Government offices; they filled every
important place in the universities; and in private
life they were the men most universally esteemed.
The generally high standard of character by which
they were distinguished must, in particular, not be
forgotten.

In Naples, as in other places where great revolutions have occurred, it may be that some who stood
high in the opinion of the people, or who had risen
to influential posts in the Government, afterwards fell
in the estimation of those by whom they were once
so highly regarded; but at the same time it must
not be forgotten that for twelve years, in the land of
exile as well as in the gaols of their own country, or
in a state of so-called liberty in which they were
constantly under the eye of the police, and, even in the
midst of society, more isolated than those confined to
their solitary cells, the intelligent class of Naples have
mostly given to the world an example of dignity,
perseverance, and self-sacrifice that may be paralleled,
but certainly cannot be surpassed. Under a succession of bad kings, without the benefit of public
schools, deprived of the stimulus of emulation, with
no means whatever of association, they bravely fought
and conquered their way to intellectual and moral
eminence. Separated from the rest of Europe, they
did not lag behind while in other countries the

cause of justice and freedom, to which they had devoted themselves, was advancing to new triumphs.
The contingent of soldiers and captains which they
gave to the cause of civilisation did their fair share
of work, for most of them, I may say almost all, were
heroes or martyrs—men who not only laboured, but
who also suffered, in the cause of their country and
of humanity.

In thus speaking, I am only rendering justice to a
class whose merits have not been always fairly appreciated; and, having done so, I shall now speak
more freely of the people. As it was not from the
intelligent and educated class that the brigands
sprung, as the bandits who ravished the fairest provinces of Italy were neither followed nor applauded by
them, I shall no more have occasion to speak of
them in the present work, unless it may be in the
way of casual allusion.

As it was in the lower class that the system of
brigandage mainly had its origin, I must confine
my attention to it almost exclusively. My object,
therefore, will be to describe the position of that class,
to point out the state of degradation in which it
has long been sunk, and to explain the causes by
which it has been brought down to a condition so
debased.

By the classes whom, in this work, I designate as

low, I mean particularly the small landed proprietors
and the petty tradesmen of Naples—in a word, such
as are commonly called, in Italy, *i mezzi galantuomini*, a class which includes all those who, though
they can scarcely read, wear, as a common saying has
it, tails to their coats. This vicious, or, more properly, vitiated class, for, doubtless, the individuals composing it originally possessed certain good qualities,
the traces of which were occasionally exhibited in
their character and conduct, have, since the fall of the
Bourbons, as I will show later, considerably improved. But at the moment I am speaking of they
were dominated by a fatal feeling, imperious, over-
whelming, absorbing every other, and that was fear,
or superstition—on the one hand, what we may term
religious fear, the terror with which they were filled
by those representations of a future state in which
an avenging demon—the devil—played the principal
part, with which their priests had rendered them only
too familiar; and, on the other, political fear—that
mysterious awe which is inspired by the divinity
that doth hedge a king.

The abject terror with which the masses regarded
all forms of authority—a disposition which, during
long years of oppression, had almost become natural—
neither the government nor the clergy did anything
to remove. The unreasoning submission with which

their dictates were received by a slavish population, was preferred by them to the conscientious submission rendered by patriotic men to laws which they knew to be just and necessary. Eager only for their own aggrandizement, their object was to check every generous and patriotic feeling. The misery which prevailed among the people, the ignorance by which they were debased, being favourable to their selfish views, they made no exertions to promote national industry, or to establish schools for the instruction of youth. Force, violence, terror, were the means by which they insured their dominion. The agents of authority maintained their power by the menace of a scaffold—the representatives of religion by the threat of hell. A nation enslaved by fear, not inspired by the consciousness of right and wrong, was what they desired to see at their feet. Laws enforced by fear of the means of punishment which they possessed, and not obeyed merely because they were conducive to the general welfare, formed their ideal of legislation. Order was maintained by degrading every man's character to the same low level—the same abject uniformity. No attempt was made to improve a people naturally of quick and lively talents, of ready apprehension, capable of being ardently inspired by all that is good, beautiful, and generous. In a country which, from the open and trustful character

of its population, seems naturally made for equality,
there were, so to speak, two camps : those of the
rulers and the ruled—the privileged and those to
whom all privileges were denied. And even in the
hierarchy of authority, the various grades were kept
rigidly distinct by the same influence, that of fear.
The soldier was frightened by the uniform of his
corporal, as a Neapolitan cabman may occasionally be
awed by the superfine quality of your coat. Hence,
the same man who would have fought a duel to death
with his equal for a farthing, cowered before him who,
by the exhibition of some higher badge, by the possession of some superior title, showed that he not
only had a tyrant's power, but could use it as a
tyrant.*

Such a system could only be destructive of all that

* I desire to insist upon this distinction, very important in my
opinion, because many a misinterpretation regarding the Neapolitans arises from its not being properly understood. The people
were not cowards, far from it, but made so by the Government,
who had endeavoured to destroy in them every feeling of morality.
Those who think them cowards are greatly mistaken. For
the defence of their homes and their families they have often
displayed the most wonderful bravery; the French under
Championnet knew it well enough. All the Neapolitan
revolutions, at least those which were successful, have been
plebeian, from Masaniello to Garibaldi. Antonio Ranieri, the
Neapolitan patriot *par excellence*, is of opinion that if the Inquisi-
tion never could be established in his country, it was only owing
to the *lazzaroni*, who had always opposed it.

was just. Law was sacrificed to violence—might everywhere prevailed over right; and if the people of those unhappy provinces had dared to give utterance to their complaints, they could have proclaimed, far more eloquently and efficiently than M. Proudhon, how law and justice had been trampled on in their persons by rulers who, triumphing in their strength, had been deaf to every dictate of humanity, in their determination, *per fas et nefas*, to gain their own ambitious and selfish aims.

There is one point, however, upon which misinterpretation sometimes arises, and regarding which I particularly desire not to be misunderstood, namely, the conduct of the authorities, which produced in time its natural effect on the people. Brigandage had its origin in misgovernment. It was founded on that system of fear which the authorities so freely employed. In a country suffering from the worst effects of misrule, men, reckless and unprincipled, but bold and energetic, associated in bands to carry out in town and country a system of terrorism similar to that which the Government exercised over them. The strong united to strike terror into the weaker and more timorous part of the population. Such really was the origin of the Camorra. We are not acquainted with the mysterious freemasonry of that infamous association, but we know that it had its ramifications in the remotest parts of the country, and that it inspired with terror a Government which was never able to crush it. It was the pride of every man who could draw a knife to become an adept of this frightful association. But before anyone could be admitted to the full rights and privileges of the order, he had to pass through a noviciate of two stages, after which, if considered worthy, he was received into the terrible brotherhood They had chiefs in the twelve districts of Naples, in every town of the kingdom, and in every battalion of the army. They reigned unopposed wherever they considered it worth while to exercise their secret and irresponsible authority. They levied a tax on the fare of your cab-driver, they watched the markets and had their part of the profits, and in every gambling-house they gathered a contribution from the winner.

Even in the prisons their power was acknowledged, and, what is scarcely credible, the police not only never dared to oppose this illegal organisation in the exercise of the authority it had assumed, but they sometimes found it convenient to employ it in the accomplishment of their own work. These ruffians, either to gratify private vengeance, or for the sake of a reward, were occasionally employed to track and arrest criminals in the name of the king. In the performance of this task they were by no means scrupu-

lous.   Not very long ago a murder was committed,
the perpetrator of which they were incited to discover.
It was not long before they laid their hands on the
criminal, for he was one of their own guilty brotherhood.   The maxim that there is honour even among
thieves had no force with them.   They tracked
and pursued him, and when, wounded and covered
with blood, he fell into their hands, they delivered
him up to the police, by whom he was thrown into
prison.

Sometimes the police, in order to make an example,
would arrest and send some of them to the galleys.
But even in the hands of their jailers they could
exercise their illegal power.   The threats that issued
from the depths of a dungeon were still formidable
enough to alarm their trembling victims.   So great,
indeed, was the awe they inspired, that, while loaded
with chains, they would be visited by some poor
wretch, who, to assure his safety, would humbly pay
the monthly contribution his persecutor had been in
the habit of levying.*

The association was in the habit of holding regular
meetings.   They had an exchequer, a strong organisa-

---

* This is no exaggeration, for miserable indeed would have
been the condition of the man who attempted to rebel against
so unjust an imposition.   The dread of assassination would
have accompanied him wherever he went, and the dagger of a
mysterious and pitiless hand would soon have reached him.

tion, and inflexible laws. The authority of the chief
was absolute. The adepts owed him unquestioning
obedience, however repulsive might be the duty he
ordered them to execute. And frightful was the test
that sometimes, in obedience to their oath, they were
obliged to submit to. If he commanded them to
commit a murder, their life would have been the
price of disobedience, or even of hesitation. There
were many willing hands to punish him who was slow
in the execution of their chief's orders. Every
camorrista wore two clasp-knives, and when he used
them he always struck *nella cassa*—more plainly, deep
into the heart.

In such a state of society, and with such habits, is
it to be wondered at that brigandage has so long been
the reproach of Italy? Consult history, and you will
find the same evil under every reign, every dynasty,
from the time of the Lorraines and Normans up to the
present day.

Communication has never been very safe between
Rome and Naples; and the more interior and less
frequented parts of the country have been so overrun by brigands, that they could be compared only
to an immense *coupe-gorge*. In some provinces it has
never been safe to travel even in uniform. The
letters that Paul Courrier has written on this subject
will never be forgotten.

Italy is naturally a country favourable to the development of brigandage. The very configuration of its surface, intersected as it is everywhere with mountains, affords safe hiding-places for those fearless spirits that defy the law. The Government, slow to initiate improvements of any sort, has taken little interest in the development of the mountainous districts.

In consequence of the want of roads, travelling, even if it were safe, is in most places impracticable; and the various princes among whom Italy was so recently divided, did little to remove this disgraceful state of things. There are entire districts across which it is impossible to go in a carriage; and there are roads where it is even dangerous to adventure with mules. The Apulian system of agriculture, moreover, is scarcely calculated to develope the resources of the country; and the nomad habits of the shepherds, who spend their lives in a wild solitude, is not one likely to foster the social virtues.

Travellers without an escort never ventured with safety into those passes. Such as were compelled to undertake a journey, strange to say, used, as the best guarantee of safety, to obtain an escort from the brigands themselves. A few years ago, before the Revolution, a traveller, wishing to ascend the mountains of Matese, took with him a guide, in whom he

necessarily placed unlimited trust. The route they
pursued over a very difficult country was one which
could not be accomplished under several hours.
When they had advanced about two-thirds of the way,
they stopped to admire the sublime scenery displayed
before them.   At the bottom of a wild valley, a lake
extended far into the woods, whilst groups of ancient
firs covered the majestic surrounding rocks, and from
the top of the mountain the eye could discover the
two seas.   As the traveller and his guide were making
their way alone in that imposingly grand and somewhat awful solitude, they were suddenly stopped by
a cross.   After they had contemplated it for a few
moments, the silence they had hitherto maintained
was broken by the guide, who said musingly—

   " This was placed here by me."

   " By you !—and for what reason ?"

   " It's a vow, Eccellenza."

   " A vow !   May I ask its cause ?"

   " Why, it was for a certain misfortune which befell
me on this very spot."

   " What do you mean ?"

   " I killed a man !"

   " You ?"

   " Yes, your honour, there !" and the man pointed
out the place with his hand.

   The information thus coolly communicated was by

no means calculated to reassure the mind of the traveller; but when, before they left the mountain, his worthy guide had shown him no fewer than nine-and-twenty crosses which he candidly confessed had all been planted by himself for similar vows, we must leave it to our reader to imagine what must have been the state of his mind. I need not say how freely the tourist breathed when he reached the end of his journey.

All the European tribunals sitting together would contrive in vain to judge the dark mysteries of those solitary mountains. Within their remote fastnesses has been committed many a deed of blood which has been expiated by the only atonement that human justice can demand; but how many unknown crimes have been perpetrated there in silence is a mystery which only the great Last Day will reveal.

The Bourbon Government never offered any serious opposition to these relentless brigands. Such was the inertness of the authorities, that they had almost practical impunity for their crimes. They were allowed to assemble in small bands. They found safe refuge in some impregnable wood, whence they issued on their adventurous expeditions at every favourable opportunity. Read again the novel of Lesage, change the names of the places, and you will find in Gil Blas a faithful narrative of their romantic campaigns.

Although solitary travellers were always more exposed than any other class to their depredations and
violence, yet gentlemen of property who lived in
those dangerous neighbourhoods were perpetually
kept on the alert by the presence of a peril to which
they were every moment exposed. If their servants
had not been always on the watch, armed to the
teeth, they would have run the risk of being carried
away far into the mountains, to those almost inaccessible dens where the banditti felt secure from all
pursuit. Then a ransom, proportioned to the rank
and wealth of their prisoner, would have been fixed
upon. He would have been obliged to write to his
family, praying them to forward the sum demanded
for his freedom and safety. One of the brigands would
have been the bearer of the message. The family
would have had no alternative but to pay, for, had they
hesitated, the prisoner's life would have been forfeited.
Such captures were of common occurrence—stories,
we may say, of every day.

Not many years ago, a man was thus carried away
by the brigands. His family, who resided at Naples,
received the usual message from them. A ransom
of a thousand ducats was demanded for the release
of the captive. His relations, unable instantly to
raise such an amount of money, offered a third of
that sum. The same messenger came back with one

of the ears of the unfortunate man, threatening to
bring the other in the same way if a third demand
was necessary; after which, if the whole ransom was
not paid, his life would, without further delay, be
taken. The family paid the sum demanded, but were
utterly ruined. This fact was, at the time, related
by all the papers, which published the name of the
unfortunate victim, and all the particulars of the sad
story.

Such things would have been impossible in any other
country. In Italy they were encouraged by the inertness of the Government, and by the fear with which the
brigands were regarded by the peaceable inhabitants
of the land. Nobody ever dared to denounce the
bearers of such messages; on the contrary, they were
well received, and people shook hands with them in a
familiar and friendly manner. A single man sometimes frightened a whole population.

The system of crime was so widely diffused among
the people, that a man feared to excite the vengeance
of his neighbour by any overt act of hostility. Even
in the neighbourhood of the largest cities, one man
suspected another. Strange as this statement may
appear, it is corroborated by a circumstance which
took place at an hour's distance from Naples, and of
which I myself was a witness.

A workman, who had just stabbed his employer,

was seen, after the commission of this deed, which
anywhere else would have set not only the ministers
of justice but every honest man on his track, walking quietly about the village as if nothing had occurred. No man was bold enough to accuse one who
might be allied with some formidable band of assassins.
Even the syndic, whose duty it was to repress crime
of every sort, was so much of a coward, that, from
fear of vengeance, he did not dare to issue a warrant
against the criminal. Power trembled before the
man who so daringly defied it.

Some time ago a sort of rural guard was ordered
for the protection of the country districts; but this
armed peasantry, in many instances, were but the
accomplices of the brigands. Government has thus
often put arms into the hands of the very men whom
it wished to destroy. That secret organization which
was the source of the brigands' strength, baffled such at-
tempts as the authorities made—not very energetic—to
repress them; and Government, being unable to exercise its power to any effective purpose, generally
remained supine. It was not till the bands of the brigands had grown too strong, and they threatened
to hoist a regular flag as a belligerent power, that
the Government shook off its lethargy, and the
officers of justice made up their minds to prosecute
these enemies of the public peace and safety.

A campaign into the mountains was then undertaken, but with little prospect of success. The task before them was one of almost insuperable difficulties. The brigands in a country every step of which was known to them, and where the peasantry generally were friendly to their cause, could easily baffle the regular troops sent against them, who found it no easy task to track an enemy always disappearing like a dissolving view. When they were searching the mountains for them, the brigands would be concealed in the woods. When, as they imagined, they were hard upon their track in the broad plain, the robbers would be securely entrenched among inaccessible rocks. Wherever they might be, hidden in the bushes, or creeping away along the waving corn-fields, they were always impregnable, invisible—everywhere, and yet nowhere. This went on until the king, tired out by a pursuit which seemed interminable, granted an amnesty to all who would surrender; and the monarch, in such cases, frequently found it politic to keep his royal word.*

* Not always, though. "The Bourbons, at the period of their restoration, when they found themselves powerless against that brigandage they had *themselves* fomented for their own political views, used other means of repression. When the band of Vardarelli, who was the terror of Puglia, capitulated to General Amato, he pledged his word that not only pardon and forgiveness of the past should be granted to them, but also

One day, for instance, even Ferdinand II. had to
treat with Talarico, who for a long time, among the
mountains of La Sila in Calabria—those wild
passes which have at all times been haunted by
bandits—had braved his lieutenants. It was agreed
that Talarico and his followers should not only have
their safety assured, but also that a subvention should
be granted them by the king. The only restraint
imposed upon them was that they should be sent in
perpetual exile to Ischia, the loveliest and richest
among the fairy islands of the bay—a place where
anyone might be happy to live, and where, in the
enjoyment of peace and liberty, they long received
their pension from the king.

Such was brigandage in the time of peace, and such
it has never ceased to be. The system never lost anything of its perfect organization during the last days
of Ferdinand II. A regular service for the transport
of stolen horses had been established at the frontiers
of the kingdom. Stages were appointed from place
to place, as far as the Roman States, where the horses
were sold. A well-known Bourbonist, now famous

that the band should be transformed into an armed privileged
legion, for the service of the king, to whom they were ready
to take oath of fealty. These stipulations once settled, the
bandits gave up their arms, and were taken to Foggia, where,
by order of the general, they were all shot."—*Circular of Baron
Ricasoli.*

for his attachment to Francis II., was the soul of that profitable commercial operation; and it must be added, for the edification of my readers, that his name was not Chiavone.

In periods of political trouble, brigandage invariably increased, for then outcasts of every kind, crowds of vagabonds, the dregs of the infuriated mob, and the scum of the galleys, which at such times are generally thrown open, and their miserable captives released, fatally swelled its ranks—facts well worth noticing, inasmuch as they throw a great light upon the iniquitous system pursued by the Bourbons.

In times of revolution, when the populace, roused by indignation, endeavoured to shake off an iniquitous yoke, the king and Government looked for support not to the intelligent and honourable of their subjects, but to the brigands, men stained with every crime. Need I here call to mind the sanguinary expeditions of Cardinal Ruffo, in 1799? There were then chiefs who acquired a sad celebrity in the annals of crime—Fra Diavolo, Mammone, Proni, Sciarpa, De Cesari—"of whom I would not say anything," writes Carlo Botta, "except that I pity the cause which had them for supporters!"

CHAPTER II.

CHAPTER II.

I AM not going to harrow the feelings of my readers by again reminding them of the atrocities of that infamous army which the Bourbons retained in their service—they are well enough known to all who have watched the progress of events in Italy; but I shall stop to examine the brigandage of the times of Joseph Bonaparte and Murat. Here I am guided by recent publications, which will enable us to consider facts under their proper point of view; and I shall have to refer to many a singular coincidence between the events of that time and those of the present day.

The following is a curious and almost unknown passage from a MS. of Pietro Colletta,* written about

* The generals Mariano d'Ayala and Errico Cosenza, the Duke of Cirella, the Baron G. Marsico, and Messrs. Del Giudice, Filippo Agresti, and Giuseppe del Re, have collected the unpublished works of this popular historian, which will be published under the following title:—" Opere inedite e rare di Pietro Colletta." It is from them that I have extracted the above passage.

thirty years ago, on a subject already half a century
old:

"What was brigandage?" asks Pietro Colletta.
"Let us examine it under the aspect of fact and
right—or, in other words, let us consider by whom it
was carried out, and what was their purpose. During
1806 and 1807, it was chiefly kept up by the heroes
of 1799—Fra Diavolo, the Pizzas, the Gueriglias,
the Furias, the Stodutis, and others equally ill-famed.
But during those two years they were all either killed
or taken prisoners, and such as escaped death or
captivity were so terrified that their daring spirit
was subdued, for the easy plots of 1799 were no
longer practicable in 1806. Other means as well as
other men were required. It was a hard and fatal
work, into which many were thrown by despair.
Such was the reason why, in Sicily, prisons and gaols
were emptied, and Neapolitan convicts, who had
escaped from their country, were recruited.

"Swarms of them were vomited into the kingdom
during the two first years, in order to protract the
siege of Gaëta (exactly as it happened in more recent
days), as well as to help the expeditions of Maida
and Mileto. But after this period the feats of the
brigands grew more limited. A few men were disembarked on an uninhabited shore, and almost always
in the depth and mystery of night. They then

advanced into the interior of the country. If their
expedition was successful, they murdered, robbed,
burned down houses, devastated farms, destroyed the
crops, and killed the cattle. If, on the contrary,
laden with spoils and stained with blood, they were
discovered and pursued, they re-embarked, and seeking a refuge in Sicily, or at Ponza (then occupied
by the Prince of Canosa), they found there the reward they most coveted—gold in return for the lives
they had taken. Isolated French soldiers treacherously surprised and killed, a small detachment pursued and butchered, the murder of a courier, the
plunder of a mail-coach—such were the only exploits
of which they had to boast, for with them crime was
heroism.

"The whole kingdom could not, as a matter of
course, escape from the evil. Criminals of every description, vagabonds, thieves, and assassins, flocked
around the brigands, increasing the Sicilian bands,
or creating new ones. They all had but one aim
and one trophy, plunder and murder."

And now, who were the chiefs of these brigands?—
the leaders of these assassins? I speak of days which
are gone by, and of interests which are now of the
past. We can, therefore, without partiality, examine
and criticise the reigns of Joseph Bonaparte and of
Murat. I shall not thus, I trust, incur the blame of

altering facts, or of misrepresenting men, in the interest of any party whatever. The undisputed truth of the past will explain the mystery of the present.

During the reigns of Joseph Bonaparte and Murat, brigandage flourished nearly throughout the whole kingdom.* In Basilicata, Taccone and Quagliarella; in the two principalities, Lorenziello; in the district of Castrovillari, Campotanese; on the heights of Polino, Carmine, Antonio, and Mascia; and in the mountains of Calabria, Parafante, Benincasa, Nierello, Il Giurato, and Il Boja. Brigands also occupied the forest of Sant' Eufemia, the woods and mountains of Mongiana, in the neighbourhood of Aspromonte, and the thickets along the Rosarno; Paonese, Maggiotti, and Il Bizzarro. In the Abruzzi we find Antonelli, Fulvio, Quici, Basso Tomeo, who had assumed the name of the King of the Forest.

And who were those chieftains whose names were

* On the brigandage of those days, besides the books of Botta and Colletta, we have two very interesting works concerning the campaigns of General Manhès, one of them very curious and rare: " Notizia Storica del Generale Manhès, &c. Scritto da un antico ufficiale dello stato maggiore del suddetto Generale Manhès nelle Calabrie. Napoli pei torchi di Giovanni Ranucci," 1846. The other, a very cleverly written work, was published only two or three years ago under this title: " Memorie autografe del Generale Manhès intorno ai briganti, compilate da Francesco Montefredine. Napoli, stamperia dei fratelli Morano, 1861."

household words in Southern Italy? Antonelli (an
illustrious name), a native of Fossaceca, not very far
from Lanciano, occupied the whole territory of Chieti.
Joseph Bonaparte was compelled to treat him with all
the honours due to a belligerent power, sending him
two plenipotentiaries, the French general Merlin, and
the Baron Nolli, a Neapolitan, who became later Minister of Finance. Antonelli insisted upon being acknowledged as a colonel, and they had to comply with
his demand, providing him also with the uniform and
insignia of that rank. The two plenipotentiaries, on
going to meet him a few miles from Chieti, were actually
compelled to enter the town with him in a sort of triumphal procession, the astonished population looking on
bewildered at so extraordinary a sight. At the accession
of Murat, our colonel once more took the field, perhaps
in the hope of being appointed general. Far, however,
from arriving at such an honour, he was taken and
sent a second time to Chieti, where, a melancholy example of the instability of human things, he made an
entrance thoroughly different from the first—mounted
on a donkey, with his back to the ears of the animal,
and its tail in his hands instead of a bridle. A pla-
card attached to the back of the gallant colonel bore
the inscription: "This is Autonelli the assassin!"

Taccone, who was the terror of the Basilicata, appeared one day within the gates of Potenza, the

capital of that province. The authorities, at the head of a procession, receiving him with the honours due to the king himself, our hero was graciously pleased to step with them into the cathedral, where he ordered a *Te Deum* to be sung in thanksgiving for the success of his arms. After this pious ceremony, it was the misfortune of a young lady, belonging to one of the first families of the place, to excite his brutal lust by her unrivalled beauty. That he might possess her, he broke into the house where she lived with her family, and, turning a deaf ear to her prayers and entreaties, carried her off with him to his retreat in the mountains.

On leaving Potenza he hastened to besiege the castle of Baron Labriola Federici. After a blockade of several days, he compelled the Baron to surrender with his family, pledging his word that no harm should be done to any of them. No sooner, however, had the brigands been admitted than they perpetrated the last of outrages on his wife and daughters. After having thus gratified the brutal impulses of their nature, they set the castle on fire. So dead, indeed, were these barbarians to all the gentler feelings of human nature, that they even threw a helpless infant into the burning ruins. By an extraordinary miracle the innocent creature was saved, and about twenty years ago was still alive. The merciless brutality of these men is almost beyond

credibility. A chief, surnamed Il Bizzarro, is said to
have trained large mastiffs to hunt men. When he
was attacked by the troops sent against him, he would
unloose these savage animals, making them the instru-
ments of his vengeance against his enemies. Many an
unfortunate wretch has died in their fangs.

It was in this horrid way that an unfortunate officer
belonging to the staff of General Partouneaux met with
his death. After the arrival of Manhès, Bizzarro, deserted by his followers, having only two or three men
of his band left, was reduced to so savage a despair,
that, in order that his retreat might not be betrayed
by the cries of his own newly-born child, a son, he
killed him by dashing his head against a tree. The
woman who had followed him, the mother of the child,
swore to revenge the cruel fate of her offspring, and
take the task of justice into her own hands. Waiting,
therefore, for the moment when the brigand was asleep,
she drew out his dagger and cut his throat; and then,
with the consciousness of having done a meritorious
deed, presented herself to the authorities of Mileto,
claiming the money which had been promised for the
death of Bizzarro. The sum was duly paid to her,
and with this handsome dowry she married and became
a respectable woman.

I will not say anything of Basso Tomeo, the "King of
the Forests," who burnt a barrack belonging to the gen-

darmes, throwing into the fire the wives and children of the absent soldiers. It is not desirable to have a surfeit of such horrors. But I am anxious to say a few words regarding Parafante, a man of great power and audacity. This brigand seized one day, in the wood of Sant' Eufemia, a Frenchman named Astruc, belonging to the Administration of the Royal Domains. Knowing who he was, Parafante concluded that a handsome sum might be obtained in return for his liberty. Among the conditions which he imposed upon him was one to the following effect :—All the families of the brigands still held in prison not only to be released, but provided with clothes and goods. And yet when this brigand made such a demand the Government had an army of sixty thousand soldiers at its disposal, and more than five and twenty thousand troops in the entrenchments of Piale and Aspromonte; the whole of which force, concentrated on that point against an expedition that was being organized in Sicily, was personally commanded by the King. Nevertheless, so formidable was Parafante, that the Government found it convenient to agree to the conditions imposed by him.

Another episode in the life of Parafante is no less remarkable. A battalion on the point of leaving Cosenza was commanded by a superior officer particularly hated by the brigands, to whom their chief had the

insolence to send a challenge, informing him that
he would attack him on the highway between Cosenza
and Rogliano, at a place called Lago. The officer,
despising the warning, departed with his battalion
from Cosenza. Precisely at the point indicated
by Parafante, the brigands fell upon the troops, and,
with the exception of two lieutenants, Filangieri and
Guarasci, who were taken alive with five and twenty
soldiers, the whole battalion was cut to pieces. After
their victory, the brigands held a court-martial upon the
two officers and the soldiers who had escaped death, their
proceedings being conducted with all the formidable
display of those terrible tribunals. After what we must
consider the mockery of a trial had been gone through,
it was decided that the two officers should be shot by their
own men—upon compliance with which condition the
lives of the latter were to be spared. Animated with
the true spirit of soldiers, the latter unanimously refused to sacrifice their officers, whatever might be the
consequence to themselves. The officers, however,
anxious to save the lives of these five-and-twenty
brave men, generously ordered them to obey the
command of the banditti. After a long and painful
hesitation, and with feelings which it would be vain to
attempt to describe, the soldiers determined to obey
the order of their officers. A firing party was
selected. Filangieri and Guarasci placed themselves

in position, gave the word, and fell by the fire of
their own men. But were the lives of these poor
soldiers spared ? No! As soon as their officers had
suffered death at their hands, they were every one
massacred in cold blood.

The next exploit, selected from a multitude before
me, is one with which Parafante has nothing to do.
A company of light infantry had left Cosenza to
join its regiment (the 29th), which was quartered at
Monteleone.   When they arrived at a short distance
from Rogliano, they halted under the beautiful chestnut
trees which adorn both sides of the road.   Looking
around them, they perceived a number of persons advancing towards them, with every appearance of the most
friendly anxiety.   It was the mayor, with the " nota-
bili" of Parenti, a little village not very far
on the mountains of La Sila.   The whole party
wore tri-coloured favours in their hats, and the
Mayor had put on his official belt, the insignia of
his dignity.   When in the presence of the commander, the deputation, as they professed to be, said
that they had come to invite the troops to visit their
village, in order to repose themselves after the fatigues
of their march under a scorching sun.   The soldiers,
harassed and weary, gladly accepted a hospitality so
heartily offered, and without hesitation followed the
deputation.

Arrived at Parenti, they found that all the little population was out of doors to welcome them with cries of " Long live the French !" The soldiers, then, to use the term now generally adopted, hastened to fraternize with the villagers, every man of whom professed himself anxious to make one at least of the gallant Frenchmen the recipient of his hospitality. The officers were received at the municipal hall, and comfortably lodged by the authorities of the village, while their company was dispersed among the inhabitants. Long ere midnight all were drowned in the deep sleep of fatigue, little dreaming of danger from so kind and hospitable a people. Alas! their trust could not have been more entirely misplaced, for in the middle of the night the inhabitants of Parenti rose suddenly and murdered the defenceless troops, thus perpetrating an act of treason which they had long prepared, and by which they hoped to gratify the malevolent feeling with which they regarded the French.

Their merciless task, however, had not been fully accomplished, for one of the French soldiers, escaping from the daggers raised to dispatch him, carried the horrid tidings of the massacre to General Manhès. That officer, without loss of time, resolved to revenge the slaughter of his men. Collecting a number of troops, he advanced against the village, set it on fire, and, with

all its inhabitants, burnt it to the ground. Manhès knew
by experience the nature of savage war, and that it was
not to be carried on à l'eau de rose. The instrument of
an inexorable justice, he did not shrink before any
severity that he considered necessary. The measures
which, with the unflinching determination of a French
officer, he carried out, resulted in a short time in the
pacification not only of a small district, but of the
entire kingdom. By the execution of one man he
saved ten lives; by the destruction of a village he
gave security to numerous small communities; he took,
in a word, the terrible responsibility of the severe
measures which saved the country.

"I should not have liked to be General Manhès,"
says Colletta, one of his most bitter enemies, "but I
should not have liked either that he had been absent
from the kingdom in the years 1809 and 1810. It
was by him only that the evil was destroyed."

I shall have occasion afterwards, at greater length,
to speak of the repressive measures of General Manhès.
I will, however, mention here a single fact illustrative
of his character, an incident lighted up by a flash of
his peculiar genius.

In the wild passes of Aspromonte are the two
parishes of Serra and Mongiana, which are surrounded
by immense impracticable woods. In their depths, as
was well known to the inhabitants of the surrounding

country, the most dangerous brigands were concealed,
fierce Calabrians, who used to defy the choice battalions which formed the escort of the generals
on their way to inspect the iron-works of Mongiana.
One day these brigands announced to the authorities
of Serra that they were ready to make their submission,
the subordinates immediately, but their chiefs not till
night, when at a certain hour they would surrender, in
a house they had designated for the purpose. At the
appointed hour the mayor, the commander of the
National Guard, and the French Lieutenant Gérard, of
the Royal Gendarmerie, repaired to the place named by
the brigands. The four or five chiefs kept their
appointment with punctuality, and, when they were
all assembled, began at once to discuss the conditions
on which they might be allowed to surrender. All of
a sudden, while the attention of the mayor and the
officers was engaged in the consideration of this question, the house was surrounded by the brigands, who
broke in upon them with the utmost violence. Totally
unprepared for such an encounter, the mayor, the commander of the National Guard, and the French officer
were at once seized and brutally murdered on the spot.

No act of atrocity, indeed, was too cowardly or
bloody for these ruffians. A few months before, the
wife of Lieutenant Gérard had been shot on the
mountains of Galdo, between Laurin and Castelluccio,

after an engagement in which the brigands had taken by surprise and overcome the guard of a number of waggons carrying uniforms for the 20th French regiment. The victorious brigands, after having dispersed the little escort, invested themselves with the uniforms they had taken, covered with all the insignia that distinguish the French *militaire*, and retired again to their caverns.

But let us return to the affair at Serra. This treacherous and savage deed was left unpunished by the authorities of the place. The consternation that prevailed had paralyzed not only all the private inhabitants of the town, but also the officials whose duty it was to see justice administered.

As soon as he was informed of what had occurred, Manhès ordered the destruction of the house which had been the scene of a crime so remorseless; but his order not having been executed, he demanded an audience of the king, and asked him what punishment he thought ought to be inflicted on the town for its blameable remissness. Murat, in reply, said—

"Do what you like; but whatever it be, see it done yourself. Go to Serra—proceed there immediately—judge, and strike!"

Manhès obeyed, and arrived at Serra without a moment's delay, having proceeded straight across

country, in order to reach it with greater celerity.
When his unexpected presence was announced by
the bugles of his escort on their appearance at the
gates of the town, the population was struck with
terror. Manhès entered Serra at the head of his
troops, and, on arriving in the principal square, beheld an appalling sight, namely, some human
heads, still red with coagulated blood, hanging from
the trees under which the inhabitants promenaded.
On asking the meaning of such a horrid spectacle,
he was informed that it was the revenge accomplished by the mourning families upon the
proprietors of the house where the foul crime had
been committed. The brave general, who had never
trembled at the sight of blood on the field of battle,
turned his head away from these bloody objects, and,
without any further remark at the moment, retired
alone to a room, where he spent the night in meditating on the course he ought to adopt, for it was
impossible that deeds marked by such atrocity could
be passed unpunished.

The case was a difficult one. He could not think
of putting to the sword all that industrious population occupied at the iron-works which supplied
nearly all the fire-arms of the country; an act of
severity which was unnecessary, as the main body
of the army was encamped at no great distance

to protect the threatened shore.   At the same time,
while it was impossible to reach all who were guilty,
it was important to make a terrible example.

The people of Serra, expecting that the whole town
would be destroyed, spent the night in transporting
to the woods their most precious property. The
following morning, Manhès ordered the whole population to assemble in the principal square.   The
order was so promptly and thoroughly obeyed, that
at the appointed time not one was absent. Manhès
forced his way into the midst of the crowd, and addressed them with incredible vehemence.   While they
all trembled at his words, he told them that they
had behaved like men without courage or honour,
that not one among them was innocent, and that not
one of their lives was to be spared. The terror
excited by this address among the population of the
village was excessive. They saw that Manhès was
meditating some measure of unusual severity, as
indeed they found, when, as it were by a flash of
genius, he determined to subject the place to a punishment which the Pope himself no longer dared to
inflict   He laid Serra and its inhabitants under an
interdict.

"I order," he cried, "all the churches of Terra
to be shut, and all the priests, not one excepted, to
be transported to Maïda. Your children shall be

born without christening, and you shall die without
sacraments. Like reprobates, you shall be shut in
your deserted town, and you shall not be able to
escape my punishment by emigrating to another
place. You are now for ever separated from the rest
of the country. A severe watch shall be kept upon
you, and if anyone dares to go out, he shall be hunted
up like a wolf!"

None but those who are intimately acquainted with
the country, who understand the character and faith
of the people, can imagine the terror and the desolation which struck the wretched population as they
listened to words of such fearful omen. When Manhès
left Serra the same day with the sixty lancers who
formed his usual escort, the town was like a desert.
Before, however, he had proceeded far on his return,
he was overtaken by a long procession of spectral appearance, consisting of the whole population, everyone
covered with a sort of white garment, the heads of
all bound with hair-cloth, and their feet bare. The
moment they beheld the general they all fell on their
knees before him, beating their breasts with stones,
and imploring for mercy.

"Let us sooner be executed!" they cried, "for
this is worse than death!"

Manhès, determined to pay no heed to the
entreaties of this wretched and guilty race, with

incredible energy dashed through their midst at the
full speed of his horse, and, leaving their prayer
unanswered, disappeared from their sight. He had
resolved that his words should be more than a mere
threat, and, strange to say, notwithstanding the
strong opposition of the high clergy, the sentence
was carried into execution. The inhabitants were
for the time deprived of the consolations of religion,
all the priests, without exception, even an old
crippled octogenarian, being transported to Maïda.

The effect of the interdict was wonderful. "Where
human laws have no power," says Vico," religion
only can be efficient."

The inhabitants of Serra now rose unanimously a-
gainst the brigands. A pitiless, savage, incessant chase
began, which did not end till the last of the assassins
had died of hunger in the woods. Not one escaped.
When, after the lapse of only a few days, the brigands
had been thoroughly rooted out, General Manhès
ordered the interdict to be withdrawn.

In honour of this joyous event, the whole population
went in a triumphal procession to fetch their priests
at Maïda; and from that moment, so deep and lasting
was the impression produced, that district no longer
required the presence of troops, either for its defence
or for the maintenance of order. The National
Guard continued to occupy a little stronghold, half

hidden in one of the wildest passes of the mountains, and bravely kept it against all who attempted to drive them out.

One of the most curious examples of the lasting effect of the interdict was the fact that for their common exclamation of "Santo Diavolo!" the mountaineers of that province substituted that of "Santo Manhès!"

From October to December twelve hundred brigands were taken, and those who could not be reached died of hunger and want in the woods; and from the first days of 1811 order was established in that part of Calabria.

CHAPTER III.

CHAPTER III.

It is now known what brigandage was in the reigns of Joseph Bonaparte and of Murat; and it is still the same, only on a greater scale, and with more terrible proportions, in the history of the present days. The old system of Government had been abolished, and the new one had not been firmly established. The royal family had fled to Sicily, as now Francis II. has gone to Rome; and the brigands, supported, as they are now, by the partisans of the fallen dynasty, were ready for any act of violence.

There is a wonderful resemblance between the revolutionary movements of 1799 and those of 1848. The false reports spread in those days, just as they are now, encouraged the fatal belief that the banished Bourbons would ere long come back.

The agitation repressed at the end of last century by General Manhès may thus be said to be repeated in the present. The only difference is, that the theatre of events is changed. It was in Calabria

when Ferdinand I. was conspiring in Sicily. Now
that Francis II. is scheming at Rome, the most disturbed places are the bordering districts of the
Abruzzi and of Terra di Lavoro.

In the Abruzzi the counter-revolution began after
the arrival of Garibaldi. Those provinces on the
frontiers of the Papal States and of Terra di Lavoro,
then still occupied by the Bourbons, situated as they
are beyond that strong line of the Volturno which
stopped Garibaldi in his triumphant march, had,
under the command of the Prefect of Teramo, M.
Pasquale de Virgilii,* risen on behalf of Victor Emmanuel. Elected pro-dictator, M. de Virgilii put himself at the head of the national movement, and soon
after the Italian flag was hoisted over all the surrounding country. But the mountains were still
under the heel of the Bourbons.

The fortress of Civitella del Tronto, boldly built
upon a pile of almost inaccessible rocks, being in the

* Pasquale de Virgilii, first a poet, had been one of the
leaders of the romantic school at Naples. Like everybody
in 1848, he took an interest in politics; and after twelve years
of persecution, gave himself entirely up to them in 1860. Prefect of Teramo, then pro-dictator, and afterwards governor, of
his province, M. P. de Virgilii had the honour of receiving
Victor Emmanuel when the chivalrous king trod for the first
time the Neapolitan soil. It is from his authority, which is on
every point reliable, that I have drawn all these particulars regarding the insurrection in the Abruzzi.

hands of the Royalists, it was in their power to offer
a long resistance ; for that celebrated stronghold had
the reputation of being nearly impregnable, as it was
found to be more than two hundred years ago when
attacked by the Duc de Guise, who, with all his exertions, was unable to make himself master of it; and
more recently, in 1805, when a very small number
of artillerymen defended it for many months against
a regular siege of the Franco-Italian army, and
only surrendered the fortress when they could muster
no more than seven men for its defence.

If Civitella, in a strategic point .of view, was
perfectly useless for the defence of the kingdom,
which it was easy to invade from every side, its position was highly advantageous as a centre from which
a number of active and daring men could keep the
whole province of Teramo in a state of continual
agitation. At that time several hundred gendarmes
were garrisoned in the fortress; and although the only
relation between them and the surrounding population
was that of undisguised hostility, yet within its solid
walls they found themselves in a state of perfect
safety from the fury of all who were opposed to them.
From that secure fortress, when the revolution which
gave liberty to the people had triumphed, they were
able to prepare those counterplots by which the
progress of Southern Italy was so long arrested.

Civitella was a centre from which the adherents of the Bourbons could spread on all sides the seeds of reaction, a task to which they applied themselves with all the energy in their power. Their efforts, it is true, were momentarily interrupted when Victor Emmanuel entered the kingdom, and by his presence baffled the efforts of those who were opposed to Italian unity and independence. But the work of reaction began again when the king proceeded with his victorious army to besiege Capua.

The reactionary movement burst out on the 19th of October, two days before the Plebiscite, when universal suffrage was to consecrate the annexation of the Two Sicilies to the future kingdom of Italy. The gendarmes who had been garrisoned in Civitella then issued from the fortress with the Bourbonist flag, and, at a given signal, all the mountaineers of the chain of the Apennines, which separates the province of Teramo from that of Aquila, made an irruption into the plain, where, for a time, they committed great havoc. The authorities in many places were overpowered, several villages were plundered, the private houses of peaceable citizens were broken into, and many patriots were murdered in cold blood. Although it might perhaps be considered unfair to assimilate this movement of the adherents of the house of Bourbon to such invasions of brigands as we have recently seen, yet such were the cruelties committed by them, that even the most ferocious bandits could not have exceeded them in ferocity.

In the Abruzzi at least, in October, 1860, insurrection had a political reason. The royal dynasty, only partially fallen, was still struggling at Capua for the maintenance of its throne and dominion; while the king, not having yet left the country, was actually reigning at Gaëta. The outbreak in this part of the country took place before the will of the people had been declared by universal suffrage. The object of the reactionist party was to oppose this important act, which had not yet sanctioned either the revolution or the annexation; and, so far as they acted by legal means to maintain what they considered the cause of justice endangered by the revolution, the mountaineers of the Abruzzi did no more than they had a perfect right to do.

Their measures had been concerted with so much foresight, that, for a moment, they were successful. They nearly reached Teramo, driving before them the National Guard sent by the governor to check them in their victorious advance; and it was only through the bravery of the legion of volunteers, under the command of Curci, and the steadiness of a detachment of regular troops, that they were arrested in their progress, and the cause of order was re-established.

When the reactionist band was at last cut off
from the gendarmes of Civitella del Tronto, they
were driven from valley to valley as far as Valle
Castellano, upon a culminating point of the Apennines.   From this natural stronghold, the key of
three provinces, they resisted still for a long time
the forces engaged in hunting them down.   Every
now and then they would make a descent to renew
their provisions, for which they paid with discharges
of musketry.   Their numbers, however, gradually
dwindled down.   Many of the honest mountaineers,
who were disposed to recognize the new order of
things, made their submission to the authorities.
Several of the peasantry, fearing that their ignorance
had been taken advantage of to mislead them, forsook
their ranks, and, in a short time, the band was reduced to a mere troop of brigands—a host of assassins, men polluted with atrocious crimes, who,
knowing they were beyond the pale of mercy, fought
only to escape the scaffold and the galleys.

These malefactors resisted to the last, and, when
brought face to face with their enemies, fought with
the courage of despair.   So resolute, indeed, was the
opposition which they persevered in offering, that
Government was at last compelled to send against
them General Pinelli, a stern and energetic Piedmontese soldier. The General commenced his operations by

endeavouring to make himself master of the fortress
of Civitella; but finding his efforts against its ram-
parts unsuccessful, he, with the practical experience of an old soldier, ordered the brigands—for
such were now the defenders of Valle Castellana—dispersed in their hiding-places over the country, to be
pitilessly hunted up.

It was while engaged in this expedition that he
struck terror into the souls of even the boldest and
most hardened among them, by that terrible proclamation which made so great an impression all over
Europe, in which he publicly announced his determination, considering that leniency was always misinter-
preted by the brigands, instantly to shoot every one
of them taken with arms in his hands.

Owing to the cries of indignation raised by the
philanthropists of London and Paris, who, comfortably
seated in their houses, fortunately for themselves, did
not know what it was to live with their families at
the mercy of men dead to every sentiment of pity,
and obeying only the impulse of the worst passions
of our nature, General Pinelli was recalled, and deprived of his commandment. Before he left it,
he had already destroyed all traces of brigandage in that district, to which, by the vigour of his
measures, he brought security. Only such a man
was fitted, by his determined nature, to deal

with the inhabitants of Valle Castellana, who, not satisfied with plunder, wantonly slaughtered all who had the misfortune to fall into their hands. The instant execution of a number of these reckless brigands was necessary, in order to strike terror into their companions.

Civitella del Tronto may at any rate justly lay claim to the merit of having fought bravely for the cause which it supported. Even after Gaëta and Messina had fallen, it refused to the last to surrender. Let honour be paid to whom honour is due; and let us make a distinction between the gallant resistance of that little garrison and the unyielding obstinacy of the felons, who were brave only because there was no other means by which they could save their necks from the hands of the public executioner.

With these events ended the Bourbonist movement in that part of the Abruzzi which is on the borders of those Roman provinces now annexed to Italy. But that portion of the Abruzzi and of Terra di Lavoro, touching on the Papal States, still continued to be infested by strong bands of partisans, to whose movements, however, little attention was paid; the eyes of everybody being at that period turned towards Gaëta. The proceedings of the Bourbonists, nevertheless, in these districts were really far more important than those events which have since been much more generally talked about, for they involved more than the partial uprisings of a discontented peasantry —they were real strategical movements.

A German of the name of Kleischt, who had assumed the name of De Lagrange, had, with General Scotti, concerted a plan of invasion, according to which the former marching by Isernia, and the latter by Aquila, they were to have gone through the entire length of the Abruzzi, subduing the whole territory, and afterwards effecting their junction at Popoli. Kleischt had even spread among the populations the report that an Austrian army had just entered the kingdom by Teramo. It is impossible to say whether he really believed his own assertion. People belonging to that political creed are very credulous, and often the victims of strange illusions. Unluckily for the Reactionists, it so happened that those supposed Austrians turned out in the end to be a strong body of Piedmontese, into whose hands Scotti, with eight thousand Neapolitans, fell, two days before Kleischt had resolved to leave Avezzano, in order to carry out his wonderful strategical movement upon Aquila.

When the sad event of the capture of Scotti was announced to Kleischt, the German general went back again as fast as he could, riding, without the interruption of a single halt, sixty miles on horseback. Kleischt had under his orders a very curious diminu-

tive being called Giorgi, who, strange as it may
appear, became afterwards known as the chief of a
gang of brigands. He was, however, in reality, the
most inoffensive creature that one could meet with,
as honest as Gil Blas, and, like him, fond of adventures.

This wonderful little man was, I believe, a native
of Civitella, and, if my memory does not betray me,
by profession a lawyer. He possessed the most versa-
tile genius, and was ready to attempt, even to execute, anything. Arrested for his sad misdoings in the
month of September, 1860, he was brought before the
prefect of Avezzana by two officers of the National
Guard, whom, with that strange humour which was
peculiar to him, before they were able to state their
charge against him, he gravely introduced to the
minister of justice as his most intimate bosom friends;
a joke, however, which did not save him from finding,
for some time, a home in prison. The amnesty granted
by Garibaldi restored Giorgi once more to liberty.
He immediately hastened, as a matter of course, to
Gaëta, to offer his services to Francis II. As it was
one of the many faults of this youthful monarch to
accept the services of everybody who tendered them,
Giorgi's offers were favourably received, and he was
placed under the orders of Kleischt.

He distinguished himself, I believe, in that cele-

brated engagement of La Marsica where the National
Volunteers of Paterns, and the Bourbonist Crusaders,
commanded by Lagrange, turned their backs on each
other, and fled with such speed that it was doubtful
to which of the two little armies the honour of defeat
was most justly due. Both sides, it is certain, claimed
the victory ; each pretending, hurried as was the flight
of both, to have carried away all the enemies' artillery.
A strange assertion, seeing that, for the sake of
historical exactitude, we are compelled to add that
neither Bourbonist nor Nationalist was provided with
a single piece of artillery of the smallest calibre.
After this doubtful affair, Giorgi, tired of military
life, performed the functions of under-prefect of
Arezzano, an appointment in which, by the exercise
of his native wit and shrewdness, he managed to earn
a very decent livelihood.

On the arrival of the Piedmontese in the south, an
event occurred which added greatly to the fame of this
remarkable character. When it was announced to
him that these northern barbarians were approaching,
he got on the back of a horse (the best and the fastest
of the district), which, by the way, did not belong to
him, and, making the greatest possible speed, did not
stop till he had reached Rome. The owner of the
horse, doubtful of ever seeing it again, and sorry for
the loss of an animal which he greatly valued, offered a

handsome reward to any one who should succeed in
restoring it to him.   An enterprising speculator in a
small way, thinking he might honestly make a trifle by
the recovery of the horse, started without delay for
Rome, where he arrived in time to find Giorgi offering
it for sale to the highest bidder.

"It's a pity," said the new comer, after a careful
examination, "that the brute walks lame."

"What!" cried Giorgi, "lame!   Why, he is the
best horse of both the Abruzzi!"

"I tell you again that he is lame!"

"I flatly deny it!"

Assertion and denial thus followed each other in
rapid succession; the discussion grew very hot; and
although the ostler made the horse walk, trot, and
canter, the obstinate fellow persisted in his assertion
that he was lame.

"And would be lamer still," said he, "with a man
on his back."

"Try it, then," cried Giorgi, fairly losing his temper,
"and you'll see!"

This was all that the man wanted.   Mounting in a
moment, he started off at full gallop, to the great
delight of Giorgi, who, clapping his hands with satisfaction, shouted after the rider:

"Is he lame?—is he lame?"

The rider, paying no heed to him, continued his

onward course, and Giorgi, we need hardly add, never
had the satisfaction of beholding either him or the
horse again.

In the second fortnight of the same year, whilst
Gaëta was still in the hands of the Bourbons, and
Pinelli was endeavouring in vain, by a bold attack, to
take Civitella del Tronto, Lagrange and his faithful
Giorgi attempted a new expedition, the particulars of
which were collected expressly for me at the time and
on the very spot.*

Giorgi, who, with his acolytes, was at that time
under the command of General Luvara, a very old
man, had collected as many adherents of the Pope and
disbanded Bourbonist soldiers as could be got, adding
to the little army some regular Papal Zouaves, graciously granted by His Holiness for the occasion, a
few peasants of Cecolano, and a small band of monks
—the whole numbering, perhaps, about fifteen thousand men. Their equipment was, of course, rather fan-
tastical, and so far from uniform that probably no two
wore similar costumes ; while their arms ranged from
the double-barrelled gun and the classical blunderbuss
down to the daggers and clasp-knives of the brigand.

* These particulars I give here without altering a word, in
order that their original character may be preserved. The same
may be said of many other documents, never published before,
and therefore thoroughly unknown, which will appear in this
work.

Some of them, and they were, perhaps, the most dangerous, carried, like the Polish insurgents, long poles with
scythes fastened to them.

This band, with Giorgi at their head, decorated
with the order of San Gennaro,* fell upon the
Abruzzi. Having occupied and plundered Togliacozzo,
Petrella, Curcomello, and other places, they levied
everywhere impositions and taxes upon the defenceless inhabitants. But when they attempted to raise
the country in behalf of the dethroned prince, they
totally failed. Even before they were crushed and
swept away by the Piedmontese under General de
Sonnaz, their enterprise was checked by the indiffer-
ence with which it was everywhere regarded by the
people, notwithstanding the fact that the band of
royalists included in their number some staunch and
enthusiastic supporters. Among these was a Neapolitan corporal named Biaz, who, although he had formerly
been a Garibaldian at Arezzano, was now a devoted
Bourbonist, taking long journeys in the mountains, in
order to obtain recruits, which he did by preaching to
the ignorant peasantry the holy cause of legitimacy,
and especially by promising them money, plunder, freedom to indulge their vilest passions, and plenary indul-
gences from the Pope. As in all wars of partisans, the

* The order of San Gennaro was the highest order of the
Neapolitan Bourbons, like the Garter in England.

device of this band seems to have been "Kill or die!"

On the 19th of January, about three o'clock in the afternoon, the heights of La Scurgola were suddenly attacked by the men of Giorgi. A single company of the 6th Piedmontese regiment of Foot, commanded by Captain Foldi, was then occupying that position. The attack was so unexpected, that the troops, greatly inferior in numbers, were compelled to retire. In the meantime, however, the alarm had been given to two other companies stationed at Magliano with a detachment of cavalry. This reinforcement at once set out for La Scurgola, where they arrived with the least possible delay. The place was immediately invested on all sides, and everyone of the insurgents who had entered it was taken prisoner. The remainder were attacked without delay, and, after a short contest, entirely routed, most, if not all, being killed.

Captain Foldi displayed the greatest bravery that day. By the most providential chance, Colonel Quintini, of the 40th Foot, arrived at Sora the same night. Ascending the Salviano, he heard in the distance the first discharges of musketry. At once divining what was taking place, he hastened back to Avezzano, sending onwards without delay such reinforcements as he thought necessary. Quintini was alone as useful as two battalions. The fire lasted interruptedly for two hours, and the insurgents lost about three hundred

men, including in that number those taken prisoners
and those who lost their lives in the battle. The Italian
troops had only two killed and four wounded. A victory so complete, and with so little loss on the part of
the conquerors, one might almost imagine exaggerated;
but, as I have already stated, the particulars are taken
from the official report.

Luvara, the commander-in-chief, who signed the
proclamation, and the staff, had prudently kept aloof
from the engagement, remaining concealed at the convent
of Sant' Antonio, a mile distant from La Scurgola, on the
side of Tagliacozzo. It is needless to say, they took to
their heels on beholding the rout of their band. One of
their colours, or standards, was taken in the engagement.
It was a shabby wooden crucifix, to which was tied
with a string a dirty old red cloth stolen from some
church; the staff of this strange oriflamme being no
less than the stick of one of the tents left by the
Piedmontese at Tagliacozzo. This ludicrous rag,
however, which showed by the manner in which it was
torn by the bullets that it had been borne as bravely in the fight as the most orthodox standard, was
not the principal banner of the royalists, which,
that it might not be exposed to the dangers and
vicissitudes of war, had been left at Tagliacozzo.
"It was a magnificent piece of white silk," says
an eye-witness—"quite adapted to be carried at a

procession. On one side was the portrait of Maria Cristina (the mother of Francis II., who, it will be remembered, was a princess of the house of Savoy), kneeling before the Virgin, and treading under her feet the white cross of Savoy. On the other side was represented the Immaculate Conception."

This flag, so venerated by the royalists, had been blessed by His Holiness, and great were the expectations entertained by them of the victories to which it was to wave them onward. Their first unlucky expedition, however, by no means presaged success in any future campaigns on which it might still be their destiny to enter.

Together with Giorgi and Luvara (I am still quoting the letter of an eye-witness), also marched at the head of the army, dressed like Giorgi as a colonel, that celebrated Venetian who, although mistaken at the beginning for a cardinal, was simply a Monsignore di Corte.

Among the prisoners were found a great many old soldiers, to whom pardon was granted. No mercy, however, was shown to those who were known to be the active partisans of the cause of reaction. One of their chiefs, Doctor Mauti of Luco, was shot, and died bravely. His life, however, would not have been taken, had he consented to make some revelations which there was no doubt he could have made. But

he would not say a word; to everyone who pressed
him on the subject he gave the same reply, that it
was only by chance he had become involved in the reactionary movement, and had taken an active part in
it. Although they continued to urge him with questions,
he resolutely persevered in his determination to make no
avowal that might endanger the cause to which he had
devoted himself, or place in peril the lives of any of
its adherents. Such a brave man would have been
worthy of mercy, but unfortunately too many aggra-
vating evidences of the active part he had taken
against the revolution were found upon him. He
was accordingly shot, on the esplanade of the
castle.

Three other prisoners, the men who had taken to the
Piedmontese commander a somewhat insolent summons from the Bourbonists, were then directed to
Sora. Two of them were Neapolitans, one a major
and the other a corporal of the old Neapolitan Rifles,
and the third was a Papal Zouave, a Spaniard, who
had once served among the Carlists. These wretches
told a long story, which they had evidently concocted,
for it consisted of a series of falsehoods. At Rome, according to their account, they had been assured there
really was a royalist army, which was expected with the
greatest anxiety by the enthusiastic populations, who
were ready to welcome its arrival in their midst as the

signal for a general insurrection. They had been made to believe that they were strong enough to bear down all opposition, and that in a fortnight they would be at Naples, sweeping before them the miserable supporters of Victor Emmanuel. How great, they added, was their discouragement when, instead of a numerous, well-equipped, and enthusiastic army, they found only some five or six hundred disbanded soldiers, about two thousand peasants badly armed, and a stupid mob, either indifferent to the cause or afraid to adventure boldly in it. They expected, also, to have found arms and ammunition for their adherents at Carsoli, but the French had stopped them.

Among the prisoners who were shot were two priests, a Monsignore, and the curate of Monte Sabinese. At Poggio Filippo, a neighbouring village, one of the wounded died, and, on burying him, it was found that he wore purple stockings, from which it was assumed that he was a Cardinal.

I have discovered since some very curious details among the depositions made at the time by the peasants themselves. Some of them, impelled by a sort of rage, had sided with the Bourbonists. It was reported that a woman had killed a Garibaldian with a monstrous refinement of cruelty, the mere description of which would be sufficient to make the strongest man shudder with horror. I therefore hesitate to inflict on my

readers the pain of reading an account of sufferings so
harrowing.

An incident, illustrating how little confidence could
be placed in the word, or even in the oath, of the
adherents of the Bourbon cause, may be here related.
After Giorgi's defeat—who, by-the-bye, never returned
to the South—there were left at Avezzano about fifty
prisoners, whom the conquerors were rather at a loss
how to dispose of. It would have been useless cruelty
to shoot them, and dangerous to allow them to go free.
After some consideration, it was determined, with the
co-operation of the curé, who was in the confidence of
this humanitarian plot, to assemble them in the church,
where they were informed that they were all condemned to be shot.   In the anticipation of the speedy
execution of this sentence, they were exhorted to prepare themselves for eternity.   The minister of religion,
in a most eloquent and faithful address, reminded them
of the guilt of their past lives, and conjured them to
make all the atonement in their power, now that the
fatal moment was arrived.

Easily impressed as the Italians generally are, the unhappy men were almost frightened out of their wits, and,
throwing themselves on their knees, began to beat
their breasts and beg for mercy.   The curé, as if
yielding to a sudden movement of generosity, told
them that perhaps human justice might be clement

towards them, but only on the condition that everyone of them should take an oath on the holy cross
that he would never again enter any band of insurgents. They all agreed to take the oath proposed,
and were accordingly restored to liberty. Incredible
as it may appear, a week had scarcely elapsed when
they were all taken again at Corsoli, in a new band
formed by Giorgi.

It was about the same time that the somewhat cos-
mopolitan band of M. de Christen, after it had
been beaten on the field of battle, was pursued
into the Papal States by General de Sonnaz.
M. de Christen was a legitimist adventurer, fighting for Francis II., as well as for the Popish cause.
Surrounded at Bauco by the Piedmontese, whose first
attack he had repelled, he was defeated and taken
prisoner. After some negotiations, it was determined
to spare his life; in acknowledgment of which boon,
he gave his word of honour no longer to bear arms
against Italy. He was no more faithful to his word,
however, than Giorgi's brigands, for he once more
organised a band of followers, with whom he engaged
in many expeditions, showing himself a determined op-
ponent to the cause of Victor Emmanuel. After some
time he came to Naples, under a false name, with a
British passport, to scheme and plot against those to
whom he owed his life. In the midst of his conspiracies

against the cause of Italian liberty, he was again apprehended, and placed in the hands of justice, before whose tribunal he answered for his deeds.*

The purely legitimist expeditions being finally brought to an end by the fall of Gaëta (Feb. 13th, 1861), Francis II. dismissed his supporters, particularly M. de Christen ; any outbreak in his behalf, as it was said in the Bourbonist memorandum at that time published in the papers, being henceforth purposeless. The country, after the victory of the Italian cause had been crowned by this conquest, breathed more freely. The people everywhere rejoiced, and looked forward with hope to the entire regeneration of the Italian kingdom. The towns, brilliantly illuminated in spite of the high clergy, resounded with the echoes of thanksgivings sung to the Almighty.

It is not to be imagined, however, that brigandage had disappeared from the country. There were numerous bands of ruffians at that time infesting various parts of Italy, who were in no way identified with the partisans of the fallen king. They were generally convicts, who had escaped from the galleys when the prisons were thrown open on the arrival of Garibaldi. The dictator, in his victorious march from

* M. de Christen has been condemned to several years' imprisonment, but has since been comprised in one of the King's amnesties.

Reggio to Naples, had had but little time to reorganize
the army and police in the provinces he had so
rapidly crossed in his triumphant career. Prisons
and bagnios had been thrown open on his passage.
Felons had assumed the red shirt, and proclaimed the
popular hero, from whom all expected the great
Italian redemption.

According to the cruel Bourbonist system, political
prisoners and criminals had been thrown indiscriminately into the bagnios; and as the latter had been
condemned to the same captivity, they hoped to be
included in the same amnesty as that accorded to
their fellow-sufferers. Many of them had followed
Garibaldi till under the fire of the guns of Capua,
where they had fought with great bravery. But
when the regular authorities were once more re-established, and an organized administration was substituted for the somewhat fantastic government of the
dictator, the hopes with which these criminals
had so long deluded themselves received a decisive
blow. For reasons that will be easily understood, and
above all, in faithful subservience to the cause of
morality and justice, the Italian Government declined
any offer of service from men to whom the name of
felon could be applied. One of them, Cipriano la
Gala, who has since acquired so sad a celebrity, offered
to aid the Government in putting down brigandage;

but his services were declined, and he was given up to the magistrate.

Those bands of criminals, whose destiny it was to fight for a time in behalf of the cause of liberty, then took the alarm. Discovering that they had been deluding themselves with hopes which the authorities were determined should not be realized, they, as a measure of prudence, placed themselves beyond the reach of government, and began to form those bands of banditti who assaulted helpless travellers on the highways. Such was the real origin of brigandage in the aspect which, in recent times, it has worn. These bands, at first, not being strong, only made their appearance now and then in some of the less densely populated districts. The number assembled under each chief not exceeding, on the average, twenty men, they used to keep to the woods, or those wild passes of the mountains—such as La Sila, for instance, in Calabria, the traditional resorts of brigands.

Their measures at first were rather timid, for success had not inspired them with courage. They levied a few taxes in some distant districts, and were satisfied with moderate results. Without any political object, their sole desire was plunder. They had no ambition to come in contact with the regular troops, for they well knew that a few battalions of bersaglieri would have soon put an end to their career.

But at that early period the Piedmontese Government had committed many errors, and particularly in the department of its military affairs, a circumstance so excusable in that time of transition, that it need not excite any wonder, considering that, at the period we speak of, they had three armies to organize, provide for, and direct—their own, Garibaldi's, and the Neapolitan, the last of which particularly embarrassed the Government.

All the Bourbonist soldiers, according to the capitulation of Gaëta, had been prisoners of war as long as Messina and Civitella del Tronto refused to surrender. But when these two places fell, the last on March 20th, it became a serious and embarrassing question, what was to be done with the army ? After some deliberation, it was determined that two months' leave should be granted to all who had surrendered at Gaëta ; after which time those belonging to the conscriptions of the last three years were to be called immediately to resume their military service. The others were allowed to make a new engagement if they chose.

These concessions, prompted by the liberal spirit of the new Government, turned out to be the greatest mistake they could have committed. The two months' leave, in particular, granted to the Bourbonist soldiers (a condition which, indeed, had been stipulated

at Gaëta), seriously endangered the cause of Italian
unity in the Southern provinces. These men, having
soon spent the indemnity which, also according to the
stipulations of Gaëta, they had received, began to feel
embarrassed as to the means by which they might
obtain a livelihood for the future. Unfortunately
the Neapolitan kingdom was, at that time, in a
totally different position from that in which England
was when, as Macaulay tells us, at the restoration of
the Royal dynasty, the army that had served Cromwell was disbanded. "Fifty thousand men," according to that historian, "accustomed to the profession of arms, were at once thrown on the world; and
experience seemed to warrant the belief that this
event would produce much misery and crime—that
the discharged veterans would be seen begging in
every street, or that they would be driven by hunger
to pillage. But no such result followed. In a few
months there remained not a trace indicating that the
most formidable army in the world had just been
absorbed into the mass of the community. The
Royalists themselves confessed that in every department of honest industry, the discarded warriors
prospered beyond other men—that none were charged
with any theft or robbery—that none were heard to
ask an alms—and that if a baker, a mason, or a
waggoner attracted notice by his diligence and

sobriety, he was, in all probablity, one of Oliver's old soldiers."

We must not assume, however, from this description of the eloquent historian who has so vividly depicted the state of England, that, at the period of which he speaks, there were no brigands in it. Macaulay himself informs us that it had its highwaymen as dashing and as bold as any of those brigands that threw a certain lurid halo over crime in Italy. There was, for example, at that time, as he tells us a little further on, the celebrated William Nevison, that free-handed and generous Yorkshire thief, who, though he levied a regular trimestrial tax upon all the cattle-dealers of the North, and freely appropriated the purses of those whom he attacked on the public road, liberally shared with the poor the money thus forcibly extorted from the rich; and also that other renowned chief, an old page of the Duke of Richmond, Claude Duval, so distinguished for his gallantry to the fair sex, of whom he was a devoted admirer, that one day, on stopping the coach of a very handsome lady of rank who carried with her four hundred pounds, the gallant Frenchman was pleased to take only one hundred, upon condition of her dancing a "courante" with him.

We thus see that though England, as well as other
countries, had its dangerous class, the veterans of
Cromwell, who were kept in the path of rectitude
and honour by their own conscience of right, combined with the sentiment of their personal dignity,
were not to be found among them. Such feelings, alas!
had no existence among the Neapolitan soldiers. In
that country the privileges of a corrupt aristocracy,
and the state of abject subjection in which the army
was held, had demoralised the soldiers of Francis II.
They had none of that spirit which constitutes the
citizen, and they were incapable of that continued
labour which makes the humblest independent. They
could not, therefore, amalgamate with the peaceful
working-classes.

Accustomed to the idle existence of the Neapolitan
barracks, the disbanded soldiers had no inclination either for an agricultural life, or for any other
kind of daily labour that would have secured to them
an honest livelihood. Still less did they care to
enlist under the cross of Savoy, partly on account of
their natural aversion for the brave, straightforward
Piedmontese, an antipathy the cause of which I shall
afterwards explain. The Piedmontese service also was
harder, and the soldiers under the White Cross were
not paid so liberally as those under the Lilies of the Bourbons. In fine, it was no recommendation to the degraded

and indisciplined Neapolitans that Victor Emmanuel
was a fighting monarch, for they had no desire to be
brought face to face with the tried legions of Austria.*

The above are the only causes that can account for
the defection of the Bourbon troops. Some poetical
minds would now hint that fidelity to a holy but
ill-fated cause, devoted attachment to an unfortunate
prince, and pious veneration for the heroine of Gaëta,
were the chief reasons by which they were influenced.
If there are many people credulous enough to believe
that there is any foundation for these amiable excuses
for the conduct of the old Neapolitan troops, I do not
consider it necessary to argue against a delusion so
pleasing. It is only to be deplored that, under the
influence of such reasons, an army which we are
invited to credit with bravery, should have betaken
itself to the highway, to rob and murder the defenceless. Those Neapolitan soldiers, who might have
honourably devoted themselves to a good and worthy
service, chose rather to live by crime and violence
on the highway; for on this point I must insist that
in the beginning they were nothing else but common
burglars and assassins. Hidden at dusk in the depths
of a thicket, or by a lonely roadside, like the debased

* I may state that this severe judgment is applicable only
to the old Bourbonist soldiers; for, from all accounts, the young
Neapolitan recruits proved to be excellent troops.

Burgraves of Victor Hugo, knife in hand, they watched the steps of the imprudent traveller or the distant bell of a mule. Sometimes a hundred of them would seize a poor man, and when they had murdered and despoiled their victim, fly back to their dark caves and thickets, to await, like heartless cravens, a new victim.[*]

It was at a later period, when the disbanded soldiers had joined the regular bandits spread all over the mountains, that the Bourbonist committees existing at Rome and Naples, and in almost every part of the country, desiring to concoct a plot of unusual magnitude, for which they required conspirators who would hesitate at no crime, cast their eyes upon these lawless ruffians. Then, but only then, brigandage began to assume a political character. Let us see now what that conspiracy was.

[*] " Le pas d'un voyageur, le grelot d'un mulet ;
Ils étaient cent pour prendre un pauvre homme au collet.
Le coup fait, ils fuyaient en hâte à leurs repaires "
VICTOR HUGO—Les Burgraves.

CHAPTER IV.

CHAPTER IV.

THE heroic adventures of Garibaldi, during his victorious progress in Sicily and Naples, took everyone by surprise. His victories had been so rapid, that they were hardly believed, even when they were known to many as accomplished facts. In every part of the country one heard but a single question, Has he really landed? when, in fact, he had made himself master of town after town, no one daring to oppose his unparalleled advance. Regarded almost as a mythical hero, fascinating the vivid imaginations of those southern populations, he was in their eyes the realisation of the heroes of the most cherished legends of Ariosto. His wonderful adventures, both on land and sea, in the four parts of the world—the wrecks, the combats, the victories, in which he had been engaged—all tended to awake that delight with which, in all Italy, but more particularly in the south, everything which is strange, romantic, supernatural, and out of the ordinary way, is regarded. The *mise en scène*, the scarlet tunic, the recollection of Velletri, spread and exaggerated eleven years before by the routed soldiers of Ferdinand II. (Bomba), the terror of his name, and, to crown all, the superstition which so magnified his exploits, as to make him, in the bewildered eyes of the Neapolitans, appear like a demigod, completed his success. They believed that, when in the thick of battle he was struck by the enemies' bullets, he had but to shake the folds of his tunic to make them fall harmless at his feet.* All these things had rendered Garibaldi almost the equal of San Gennaro.

A race of bold and independent freemen cannot understand the influence which, in such a country as Southern Italy, was exercised by the sentiment of fear, of terror, of superstition. "Fear rules the world!" is one of the favourite mottoes of Garibaldi. Fear made the Italian cause triumph; and that mysterious awe inspired by the plebeian hero, who, within the short period of ten years, drove from Rome and Naples, into the stronghold of Gaëta, the army of the father and of the son, kept the unsettled population of the Southern capital entirely submissive under his sway.

In such a country as England it is almost impossible to realise how a population like that of Naples

* I can positively testify to the truth of this absurd belief.

could be kept in subjection by terror. Before Garibaldi drove them away, even the infamous mercenaries of the Bourbons inspired it. Their recent iniquities in Sicily, the destruction of Carini, the bombardment of Palermo, the enormities committed in the very streets of Naples, the recollections of the 15th of May, 1848, and the brutal aggressions of the 15th of July, 1860, all tended to keep the peaceful citizens in a state of trembling subjection.

The details of the last-named event afford a striking example of the manner in which that disorderly soldiery tyrannized over the city. The grenadiers of the king's own household brigade fell, one Sunday evening, not upon a riotous assemblage, but upon peaceful citizens, on noblemen and officials driving in their carriages, and even on the British consul, to all of whom they acted with great violence, seizing them by the throat, menacing them with their daggers, and even killing many, amid shouts of "Long live the king!"

From that day the whole town continued in a constant state of alarm, the eyes of all turned with awe towards the batteries of the fortifications, ready to transform, in the twinkling of an eye, the opulent city into a heap of ruins. The wealthiest merchants had already hired steamers and other vessels to save their goods and valuables. The greater part of the aristocracy

attached to the Bourbons had already fled from
the country. The foreign squadrons anchored in the
bay were crowded with people who, loaded with
articles of value, prayed for refuge and protection.
All the foreigners in the city had deposited their
money at their respective consulates. Panic was the
order of the day in Naples. At every moment the
town was alarmed by some new rumour, causing the
shopkeepers hastily to put up their shutters, the
streets to be suddenly deserted, and carriages, horses,
pedestrians, and street-venders, &c., to fly in a con-
fused, stormy mass before an imaginary danger. Of
such scenes I was myself almost daily a witness.

Under these circumstances, Garibaldi's entrance was
regarded as the supreme delivery. Every one experienced a certain relief as soon as he appeared. The
town from one end to another, calm and reassured
once more, breathed freely. But, in fact, the real
danger had just begun; for when Garibaldi, followed
only by his staff, consisting of twenty persons at the
utmost, made his entrance into Naples, there were
still in the barracks six thousand troops. A thought-
lessly-fired shot might have been enough to kindle
the flame of civil war, and to lead to the effusion of
much precious blood. If the army had been disposed
to fight, the leaders of the national movement could
have done little at this time to resist it.

Of the main body of the army, which was only two hours distant, the rifles, a brigade composed entirely of Bavarian mercenaries, were anxious to fight the Garibaldians, whom at many points they vigorously resisted. In some places Garibaldi met with serious opposition. He was detained almost for two months before Capua, without taking it.

On the 1st of October the royalists, who had approached Naples, were almost on the point of re-entering it again. On the following day there were still many thousand of the king's troops at Caserta, which they had taken, and might, perhaps, have retained, had they not lost much precious time in plundering private houses.

Notwithstanding these real dangers, however, so universal was the faith in Garibaldi, that the inhabitants, with their southern hopefulness, instead of being harassed into fears and doubts, never for a moment lost their confidence in the leader of the national cause, but gave themselves up entirely to the happiness of the moment. The citizens were everywhere to be seen walking arm-in-arm with their brethren in red shirts, the streets being gloriously illuminated and decorated with the bright colours of that Italian flag which was as the star of hope to a country looking forward with exultation to the future. With all the warmth of their meridional nature, the crowds of southern Italians laughed, wept, and sang in the intoxication of joy with which they greeted the prospect of recovered liberty.

During all that explosion of enthusiasm the representatives of many of the parties into which Italian politicians were divided, had been attracted to the city, but not a single partisan of the Bourbons was to be seen, not a trace of the party was anywhere to be found.

At the approach of the great popular leader, Mazzini, Cattaneo, Saffi, and many others appeared in Naples, drawn thither by the revolution ; men representing all varieties of opinion into which the great liberal majority is divided—Mazzinians, independent republicans, monarchical democrats, pure Garibaldians, temperate Garibaldians, anti-Garibaldians, moderate unitarians and confederates, partisans of a united Italy and partisans of a confederate Italy, annexionists with and without conditions, Piedmontese swearing only by Turin, and Neapolitans swearing only by Naples.   But in this infinite variety of opinion not a single voice was raised for the fugitive king.   Not a club, not a private or public circle, dared to speak one word in favour of Francis II.

In the general excitement caused by a revolution so remarkable, it is not wonderful that some difficulty should have been experienced at first in re-establishing

a settled form of government. Garibaldi himself was no
politician, and he was perplexed by opposing counsels.
It was not till the arrival of Victor Emmanuel, and
the appointment of a regular administration, that the
Neapolitan enthusiasm, as if by enchantment, cooled
down. In endeavouring to restore a system of
order in the administration of affairs, the Government found itself face to face with two strong
parties of opponents, who raised their heads almost
simultaneously at that moment; one among the intelligent class, and the other among the people, both
of them growing more and more prominent, and acquiring additional influence from day to day. I am
aware that it must be a very delicate task, and one both
difficult and full of danger, to analyse, as it were, the
elements of which these two parties were composed,
and to explain the principles by which they were
guided. The opposition of that very intelligent
class which I have tried to describe in the first
chapter (I do not use the word *bourgeoisie*, for at
Naples it has a meaning different from that usually
affixed to it), derived its origin from a thousand different
causes, but chiefly from municipal passions, and, alas!
I must add, in many cases, from deceived or disappointed
ambition. A powerful coterie had taken the reins of
government into their own hands. Political refugees
were the principal members of this party, consisting in

general of those glorious victims of the reaction of
1848, who, with reason considered as the best and
most enlightened patriots of the kingdom of the Two
Sicilies, were disseminated all over Europe, but in
greater numbers in the hospitable land of Piedmont,
where they had met everywhere with the warmest and
most generous reception, for Piedmont was the Hol-
land of our Neapolitan Whigs.

Considering the state of things in which these men
had been driven from their native land, it is not wonderful that they should occasionally have conspired
against the tyrants by whom the fairest parts of Italy
were kept in darkness, poverty, and chains. Our
refugees therefore did conspire, but with moderation.
Led in the beginning by Manin, who directed them
from Paris, they protested against the tyranny of their
monarch by a sort of legal or justifiable resistance. They
wrote pamphlets and memorandums, in which they addressed the question to civilized Europe, whether it was
possible to make Ferdinand II. follow a liberal policy.
Manin died, and Ferdinand did not change. Then the
refugees turned their hopes to the youthful Francis II.,
some of them, very few, looking forward to Prince
Murat as a leader whom they might fashion according to their principles. This pretender, however,
was narrowly watched by the representatives of England in the Two Sicilies. Francis II., on taking

possession of that throne so long polluted by his
ancestors, announced to his anxious subjects that
he could not hope to be able even to approach the
sublime virtues of the beloved Ferdinand, a declaration from which little hope of improvement was to be
gathered. In the meanwhile, the emigration had acquired
additional strength. Before his tragic death, the father
of the last king of Naples had partially opened his
gaols. Baron Poerio, with his unfortunate fellow-sufferers, managed with difficulty to effect his escape.
The fact must be fresh in the remembrance of my
readers. On his way to America, whither he was
to be transported, he managed to land in Ireland,
whence he made his way to Turin.

It is to be remarked that, though in prison, Poerio
had always been corresponding with the leading members of the Italian emigration, and with the most influential liberals in Europe. Under his rough convict jacket he had never lost the consciousness of
his personal dignity, or ceased to entertain the hope
that he might be of service to his country. It was
he who led the patriots of Naples—who, from the
depth of his dungeon, inspired them with the hope
that animated himself, directed them by his counsel,
and ruled them by the power of his mind.

With Poerio and his companions at Turin, the emigration found themselves complete, united in a strong and

compact body, already known and admired all over
the world for their intelligence and boldness, and,
above all, formidable on account of their misfortunes.
After having despaired in turn of Ferdinand, of Francis,
and of Murat, they had found protection under the
constitutional flag of Piedmont. So strongly did they
feel the beneficial influence exercised by a free
Government, that they had become in spirit Piedmontese. The campaign of 1859, the annexation of
the Duchies, the Papal Legations, and Tuscany, gave,
for the first time, something like consistency to the
long caressed dream of a united Italy, which, by many
men not unfriendly to the country, had been so long
regarded as a fatal illusion. Now, however, the
aspect of things was so thoroughly changed, that
the realization of this dream appeared the only
solution for the difficulties of Italy. A principle
had at length been discovered, to rally around it
all Italians, not only the calm thinker, but the
warm, heedless, audacious child of the people, in
one united band.

When Francis II. proclaimed the constitution and
granted an amnesty, the whole body of emigrants returned to their native land. About this time certain forced
reforms, dictated to the young monarch by a supreme
necessity, were proposed, with the hope of inducing
the people to ask for no more. The returned

emigrants, however, aware of the insidious nature of these half measures, incited the Neapolitans to treat them with contempt. Going still further, they tried, without the aid of Garibaldi, who was still in Sicily, to rouse the country against the young monarch, from whom they saw that no amelioration in the state of the country could be expected. But the guns of Sant' Elmo were too menacing, and they had not yet the courage to act. The secret committee, however, the influence of which was so great that it might have been called an occult Government, still continued to watch the progress of events. It was owing to them that, on the 7th of September, 1860, Garibaldi found not only the population ready to receive him, but a provisional Government completely prepared.

As a matter of justice, I have insisted upon the measures of the "consorti," as they were called in Italy. It has been my desire to show the eminent services they rendered to the national cause, before attacking the errors into which they subsequently fell. I may go still further, and assert that it was through them that the country was saved during the dictatorship. They had not only the ability, but also the power, to face the revolution; and I may even venture to say that, without them, the party of action would have offered no opposition to the French in

the Pontifical States. Moreover, they did all they
could to hasten the arrival of Victor Emmanuel;
but, on the appearance of that monarch, my belief is
that they exceeded their power. In making this
statement, I am not merely echoing all the calumnies
of the petty press, for I repudiate the idea malig-
nantly insinuated regarding the venality of these men.
I only think they submitted too blindly to the
Cabinet of Turin, which was not the best judge as to
the manner in which Neapolitan affairs should have
been conducted.

In a few words, this was the situation. The
Neapolitans had declared, by popular suffrage, their
desire to be associated with the rest of Italy under
the constitutional sceptre of Victor Emmanuel. Turin
understood that they wished to be annexed and assimi-
lated as soon as possible. Thence the mistake and
the discontent that followed. The "consorti"
scrupled at no scheme by which, at any cost, they
might bring about the absorption of Naples by the
new Italian kingdom. The excise rates were increased at once; a proceeding from which the local
industry received a severe blow. Laws were modi-
fied in a Piedmontese point of view—a sad disappointment for the lawyers of the country, who, under the
Bourbons, having had good reasons for being
satisfied with them, had no other complaint to

make except that they were not always carried into execution. In almost every branch of the administration, the consorti changed the names without altering the existing state of things; whilst, on the contrary, the secret of governing a new country, in such a manner as to obtain the confidence of all classes, is to change the old system without altering the names. In effecting these changes, too, instead of making them gradually, and in such a manner as not to rouse the jealousy of the people, they were determined on and executed at once: without the slightest deference to the feelings of the Neapolitans, the central jurisdiction of Turin was increased, while Naples was deprived of much of that official authority which it once exercised. In a word, instead of skilfully concealing the governmental action of the new capital, they showed it with ostentation; and this was an enormous blunder, for such a capital, distant, unknown, and comparatively poor among the glorious old Italian cities, was, in its way, almost an intruder, and had nothing to boast of but its king, who happened to be an honest man.

These were really and truly the grievances complained of by the intelligent class. An immense mass of men, indifferent to all political principles, but who were yet strongly attached to their own local interests, sided with these malcontents, making

the Government responsible for the stagnation of affairs
that was the inevitable result under such circumstances.

Then there was that large class of impatient waiters
on Providence who were disappointed because they did
not immediately reap all the benefits they had anticipated from the revolution—a result for which they blamed
those who were at the head of affairs, not considering
that the recovery and future progress of a state so
ill-governed as Naples had been, must have necessarily
been a matter of time. Naples required schools, asylums,
prisons worthy of a Christian government, streets,
roads, railways, harbours, light-houses—in short,
everything; and with the exception of some ill-timed
and unpopular theoretical changes, nothing was
given to the Neapolitans. Discontent being thus excited, opposition spread beyond the city, and became
general throughout the kingdom. Through the representations of zealous optimists, who could not be pacified,
because nothing less than the impossible would satisfy
them, the partisans of the Government grew rarer
and rarer every day. Yet this opposition—the fact
is to be noticed—preserved its conservative character.
They had no desire for reaction, nor did they wish
to hasten the revolution. They called neither for
Francis II. nor Mazzini. They complained of Piedmont, indeed, but none of them dreamed of separation
from the great Italian body.

It is thus explained how the country in its discontent almost unanimously returned to Parliament ministerial members. In spite of ill-feeling and calumny, those men, enlightened and moderate, whose names were known from one end of the Italian Peninsula to the other, were still those who most faithfully represented public opinion. People feared Radicals of advanced opinions, and almost instinctively shrunk from contact with a party most of whom—men whose names were utterly unknown to them—were violent and passionate Utopists, often wild and unpolished to excess. In the absence of any marked and distinctive principles, the opposition had one peculiarity, that it was purely a Neapolitan one, nothing more.

We have ample evidence of this in the debates that took place in the Italian Parliament. Neapolitans who moved interpellations to the ministry about the state of their native country, belonged to all sides of the house, rising from the left and the right, and even from the ministerial benches of the centre. All their speeches were essentially municipalist in character, municipalism being the chief cause of the opposition of Naples.*

* It ought not to be forgotten that this was written two years ago, since which time a wonderful transformation has already taken place among the Neapolitans. It would be doing them injustice still to attribute to them the same prejudices.

The member who most distinguished himself by
his zeal in the cause of municipalism was Mr.
Ricciardi. He, more than anyone else, occupied
the time of the house with complaints as to the mis-
management of the affairs and institutions of his
country. Mr. Ricciardi, who is a perfect gentleman,
is firmly convinced that he is a pure republican, in
entertaining which conviction he is certainly labour-
ing under an error, seeing that he is but a Neapolitan.

Having thus sketched the nature of the opposition
by which, in the early period of the revolution, the
intelligent class in Naples hampered the action of
Government, we must now describe the opposition of
a lower order—that of the people, which, naturally,
was stronger, more decided, and more unequivocally
expressed.

The people of Naples plainly declared that they
liked neither the Piedmontese nor Victor Emmanuel.
Against the Piedmontese the plebeians of Naples had
the natural aversion of the Southerners for the inhabitants of the North. The contrast between the
red shirts of the Garibaldians and the grey uniform of
the Piedmontese soldiers, and the characteristic peculiarities of the two bodies, also excited in them an
impression unfavourable to the latter. When, after
those glorious, buoyant volunteers, gay, noisy, and ro-

mantic, who recklessly threw away their money, and endeavoured to live merrily before going to meet death
with a patriotic song on their lips, arrived, without
transition, the stern, disciplined, quiet, sober, poor, cold
soldiers of the north, the veterans of twenty battles,
who neither drank nor smoked, who lavished no money,
their arms being all they possessed, the difference in
their appearance made a greater impression on the Neapolitans than it would have made on any other people.
The Piedmontese troops had neither glittering helmets
nor waving plumes to strike those Southern imaginations with the idea of power and glory; and even on
the Sunday, that universal holiday, they appeared dressed
in the same garb as on any other day of the week, their
simple, modest uniform, the well-known rough grey
tunic of the days of battle.   Their voices were rarely
heard in animated debate; they had little of that
life and action peculiar to the Southern Italian; and
they spoke a strange, uncouth dialect, singularly
contrasting with the expressive idioms of the
Lazzaroni.   The people, therefore, kept aloof from
those severe-looking, taciturn grey-coats, and looked
upon them as, in former days, they used to look upon
the Swiss.   Nor was the feeling with which they regarded Victor Emmanuel more favourable.   Indeed,
the popular opposition was still more unjust to him.
When he came to Naples he made a great mistake,

one in perfect conformity with his own character, but
which showed that he had given little consideration
to that of the people whose good-will it was important for him to gain.   He entered the city on foot,
with no glowing plumes waving over his hat, with no
golden epaulettes on his shoulders, and with no glittering sword in his hand.   The masses of the people
everywhere like show ; but in that country even more
than anywhere else.   The Neapoitans, then, were
deeply disappointed when they beheld the " Re Galantuomo " entering the city without that brilliant reti-
nue by which King Murat had delighted and dazzled
them.   Victor Emmanuel, indeed, was doubtless as
brave as Murat.   Yet here, and perhaps elsewhere
too, bravery, without display, does not strike the mass,
who, however, had some stronger motives for opposition.   The Lazzaroni never thoroughly understood for
what reason Victor Emmanuel had then come to Naples.
The Italian question seemed to them too far off to
excite their interest, and they never understood it
thoroughly.

At this time, in the early period of the great Italian
movement, the population were particularly struck by
one thing which did not make a favourable impression upon them ; and that was, that the arrival of the
King was followed by the departure of Garibaldi,
their favourite hero, who, after he had been the

master of Naples, and had given to his sovereign
a kingdom of nine million inhabitants, departed,
solitary and mournful, from the kingdom and city his
valour had won. The people saw in this an act of notorious injustice, of cruel ingratitude; an opinion which
was fostered in them by the complaints of the discontented Garibaldians. In their sorrow and indignation
they forgot what was the end of the great Italian
revolution; they forgot the universal suffrage by which
Victor Emmanuel had been elected, and they imagined
that he was a third potentate, who had come to Naples
to turn out Garibaldi, in the same way as that popular
hero had turned out Francis II.

Foolish and absurd as these ideas were, they were
soon spread widely among all classes of the population,
and, especially among the ignorant lower classes, produced a great amount of indignation. Such, indeed,
was the main cause of the plebeian discontent; and
those who seek to explain it by any other reason
are greatly mistaken. To believe that a Lazzarone
was more for King Francis than for Mazzini, or *vice
versa*, is to betray the fact that he who makes such
an assertion has never been in that country, or, at
any rate, knows very little of its institutions and
inhabitants. This is not a question of principles or
convictions, but simply a matter of sympathy or of
antipathy. I may now also add that in this case four

(I shall always come back to it) was by no means
the ally of power; and neither the learned nor the
illiterate classes were compelled to allegiance by that
sentiment.

The extreme mildness of the new Government
allowed the press to discuss every political topic whatever, not restraining it even when the most violent
language was used.   Public demonstrations also were
tolerated.   The Piedmontese army, too, displayed the
most admirable forbearance.   No more the plunderers
of the 15th of May, nor the ferocious mercenaries of
the 15th of July, the new soldiers were of proved
bravery, well-disciplined and honest.   I remember,
one day, a vile mob, in the hope of getting up a serious
riot, made a demonstration against one of the public
functionaries, with cries of "Death to Spaventa!" *
They threatened to invade the building occupied as
Government offices.   A detachment of soldiers was sent
to defend the entrance of the palace, with strict orders,
however, to do all they could to avoid an encounter
with the people, which might lead to the useless
effusion of blood.   These soldiers I saw shamefully
insulted and disgracefully outraged.   Although earth
and rubbish were thrown at them, these brave fellows,
who had been in the Crimea, at Solferino, and at Gaëta,

* This able statesman was then director of the police department.

stood calmly erect, with loaded muskets and fixed
bayonets, not moving a muscle, nor making the
slightest attempt to punish the insolent rioters. Knowing perfectly well that, had they made a movement,
the mob would have been dispersed in a second,
one could see by the contracted muscles of their
manly features how fearful was the struggle that was
raging within them. Anywhere else than at Naples,
conduct so noble would have disarmed the hostility
of the malcontents, but there it only incited them to
acts of insult more provoking and unbearable.

These riots, after all, were very harmless affairs.
The one I have just mentioned was the most important,
but, as it led to no result, it might have been charac-
terised as a new version of "Much Ado About Nothing." Spaventa remained at the head of the police;
and barricades were not set up in the streets. The
opposition of the people, it should be specially remarked, never assumed a political character. They
contented themselves by giving vent to their regret
for the departure of Garibaldi, whom they esteemed
for his fame and valour rather than for his principles,
which probably few of them understood; and, of
course, the ex-dictator was everywhere greeted with
enthusiastic ovations on all occasions. Wherever
he appeared he was received with hearty cheering;
the enthusiasm on each successive occasion rather in-

creasing than diminishing. Each time the town was
illuminated.   Crowds of people, with torches and
banners, walked in procession along the streets, carrying the statue of Gáribaldi, with a red shirt, framed
into the golden shrine of a saint, borrowed from some
church, and shouting with frantic cries, " Viva Garibaldi !"   This was the cry of every day ; when Cialdini took Gaëta ; when Cavour proclaimed the
Kingdom of Italy ; when Naples celebrated the birth-
day of Victor Emmanuel—on all these occasions
" Viva Garibaldi !" was the cry of the people.   If
Francis II. ever makes his re-appearance at Naples—
which God forbid !—nothing is more probable than
that the crowd, with that animation which is habitual
to them, will again raise their favourite old cry,
" Viva Garibaldi ! " •

I have thus shown how general was the prevalence
of discontent among the enlightened class, owing
chiefly to the spirit of contradiction and municipalism,

• . I speak of the populations as they were in March, 1861.
They now understand the great national idea of Italy under
Victor Emmanuel.   On the second entrance of the king (April,
1862) not a single cry of " Viva Garibaldi !" was heard in the
crowded streets of the town during the passage of the royal
procession.   This cry would not have had in itself any seditious
character, but it might have been mistaken for an allusion to
the past disagreements, then so happily buried.   The population
felt this by instinct, a circumstance which shows how much they
had improved.

and, among the people, on account of the compassion
felt for a leader—the hero of Caprera—and his followers, whom they regarded as having been shamefully wronged. The Bourbonist party, when they saw
how widely prevalent was this hostile disposition,
raised their heads once more, and resolved to turn it to
their own purposes. Reaction began among the
clergy. Priests were naturally opposed to a power so
greatly disapproved of by the Pope, though this
hostility was not nearly so universal as it is generally
believed to have been.

At Palermo, on the 4th of April, 1860, the signal
for the national revolution was given by the monks of
La Gancia, in Basilicata, a province strongly in
favour of the Italian cause, and which had not waited
for the arrival of Garibaldi to rise. A legion of
priests, who had been spontaneously formed, marched
at the head of the people. Even at Naples many
sacred orators—among others the eminent Father
Guiseppe da Foria—had raised from the pulpit their
voices on behalf of the national cause; and, what is
more significant, revolution numbered in its ranks
many a dignitary of the Church, especially the Bishop
of Ariano, a very useful monsignore, for the performance of *Te Deums* in particular. The Government
ought to have encouraged these favourable dispositions among a class who by their influence might have

rendered the cause to which they adhered more generally popular.

Garibaldi, with his exceptional good common sense, used to respect not only the priests, whom the people revered, but even popular superstitions. The day after his entrance into Naples he accomplished the Pilgrimage of Piedigrotta, of Bourbonist recollection. At his desire the miracle of San Gennaro was performed, and, if anything, the wonderful result followed more quickly than usual. Garibaldi, a very religious man himself, was always followed by a chaplain ; and this reverend gentleman used to preach with great devotion, although on the field of battle he occasionally transformed himself into a soldier.

The new Government followed at first the same example, and even went still further, recalling the Cardinal of Naples, Riario Sforza, who had left his seat.   All of a sudden, however, no doubt badly advised by impatient minds, or by some stern bureaucrats, always demanding logical deductions (forgetting all the while that logic is the worst adviser in politics), the ministry, doubtless with the idea that they were giving proof of strength in taking a step that even Garibaldi had never dared to attempt, issued three decrees against the clergy, one of them, the most severe, abolishing the majority of the convents.

Had things been in a settled state, and the Govern-

ment firmly established, this would have been but
justice; but at that time, for the reasons 1 have
already mentioned, it would have been a wiser
policy to have held on good terms with the clergy.
Although they exhibited a certain amount of courage in issuing such a decree and carrying it into
execution, yet it was undoubtedly a great fault, for
they irritated the priests to the utmost, without diminishing their power.   The Government, in taking
such a step, not only displayed their hostility, but
also, as many could not fail to discover, betrayed their
weakness. The measure was a badly advised one, and,
as a priest never forgives, even to this day the fatal
consequences of these premature decrees are still felt.

The clergy openly declared war against the newly-
established kingdom; but, however hostile might be
their feeling to the power that had dared so openly
to resist them, they acted with caution at first, organ-
izing measures of resistance not only at Naples but all
over the country.   After timidly surrounding themselves with mystery and plotting in the dark, they
at last ventured boldly and insolently out into the
broad daylight, hurling, in violent discourses from the
pulpit, outrageous insults at the king.   Victor Emmanuel, whom they excommunicated, was designated
by the name of Herod, and King Francis was sacri-
legiously alluded to as the Holy Lamb.

In the country curates and monks carried out the impious crusade against the excommunicated Italian king, pointing him out to the superstitious and stupid populations as the Antichrist. Convents put themselves in communication with Rome. Those of Naples, in order that they might be able to disguise the low mercenaries in their service, whom they intended to send, knife in hand, all over the town, wherever they thought it possible to make a disturbance, concealed in their recesses the uniforms of the national guards. Wherever they could possibly manage it they had depots of arms and ammunition, and in every town they disseminated their reactionary proclamations.

At Aquila, in the house of a certain Cocco, a very suspicious individual, a list was found containing the names of a great many notorious liberals. When he was asked by an official whose names were those written on the paper, he had the impudence to say it was the list of his debtors.

"I owe you, then, some money," said the official, who had come to arrest him, "as I see my name is here."

At these words Master Cocco, struck with alarm, remained silent.

The focus of the conspiracy was naturally at Rome, the last refuge of the fallen king, who, in the opinion of many was already the soul of these intrigues. Although I do not see any reason to induce me to think so, I know that pathetic and fatidical words were attributed to him when he departed from Gaëta.   Before he got on board the ship that was to carry him away for ever, he bade his soldiers farewell, and, kissing the last of them, said to him,

"Go and give this embrace to all who love me, and tell them that before a year is elapsed we shall meet again."

But, on the other hand, it is well known that Francis II., in a proclamation read throughout Europe, entered into a solemn engagement not to make the slightest attempt to disturb the country; and if one cannot but hope that, perhaps, in the beginning, he kept his royal word, there is no doubt that at Rome, among the persons around him, and among his own family, they were already conspiring.

I am not aware whether the committees, of which I shall have to speak by-and-by, were already in existence. But I know that arms were actively collected, and that coins were struck in the name of Francis II. This money was thrown into his ex-dominions; and, in order not to excite any suspicion, those coins which bore for their date the year 1859, had been artistically blackened with some skilful preparation that made them look genuine.   Some of them, which I had in

my possession, were so adulterated, that their intrinsic
value was no more than ten centimes, when it ought
to have been twenty. That money was used to enlist soldiers, the enlistments taking place at Naples,
either in convents or in priests' houses.

A domiciliary visit held at "San Giovanni a
Carbonara," led to the discovery of a young woman
hidden under a bed. What could have been the object
of her concealment? In order to avoid being thrown
into prison, this wretch was obliged to confess the truth.
The police then took possession of the room, and held
themselves the enlisting board. I need scarcely say
that those who came for such a purpose were immediately handcuffed and sent to the isles. At the same
time, the Duke of Cajaniello, who was suspected to be
corresponding with Rome, was arrested, and kept for
many months in prison. It must be remembered he
had been ambassador of Francis II. in Paris. I will
not repeat here all that has been said against him, and
it is possible he may have been calumniated. The
truth is that, as sufficient proofs of his guilt could
not be obtained, he was acquitted, and it is therefore impossible to say what part he had taken in the
conspiracy. But that such a conspiracy had existed,
is a fact beyond contestation. Not only were all its
particulars discovered, but it was known that the movement was to burst forth at Naples in the month of April,

1861 ; that all the prisoners detected at the "Vicaria"
were to have been let loose and provided with arms; that
the gaolers were in the plot ; that rebellion was to have
been instigated both in town and in the country ; and
that bands of brigands were being raised and paid by
the Bourbonist committees. Thus, for the first time,
brigandage assumed a political character. Reaction
found these men in a state of military organisation,
compelled for their own sake to fight against authority,
and thus ready for its service. As may be easily
conceived, it made use of them without hesitation.
On the other hand, all those gaol-birds were but too
glad to receive six carlini (about two shillings) a day,
and to have a sort of legitimate excuse for robbing
and plundering. Thus taken into the service of the
State, they were no longer highway assassins. In the
eyes of reactionist Europe they appeared as political
partisans.

Rosaries, blessed by the Holy Father, were distributed to them, together with no end of sentimental
talismans. They received, moreover, symbolic rings
and metal buttons, on which a royal crown, and a
hand armed with the traditional poniard of the banditti, were engraved with the motto : "*Fac et spera.*"
The Bourbonist agents also gave their military banditti full permission to continue their usual occupation, regardless of any consideration human or divine

—substantially giving them to understand that they might commit as many depredations, rapes, and murders as they chose, provided they did so for the sake of Francis II.   As a matter of course, they were strictly cautioned to be very careful in directing their assaults only against the persons and properties of the liberals.   They were at liberty to disarm as many of the National Guards as they could.   No restriction was put on the number of patriots they might ·slay. They were directed to substitute everywhere for the cross of Savoy the Bourbon lilies, and when they laid waste peaceful districts, or sacked hamlets and villages, they were to do so to the cry of "Viva Francesco II.!"

And such, as everyone knows, was the conduct of these men, who exhibited to the world on the one hand the strange spectacle of a king allied with assassins ; and on the other that of assassins, who, without changing their character, suddenly became royalists, the professed adherents of a legitimate monarch blessed by the Church !   Shameful connection !

The state of Italy now became alarming.   Disorders were simultaneously fomented all over the country.   Disbanded soldiers, wearing the mystic ring, flocked in from the different points of the kingdom.   The band of Somma (a mountain behind Vesuvius) was formed at that time ; and likewise those of Nola, Gargano, and Calabria.

At Castiglione, on Easter day, serious disorders, followed by many atrocious murders, took place, and at last the movements of Basilicata broke out. This was the only district where, during that long year of civil strife, counter-revolution held out for a few days. The events of which that unlucky province was the theatre, brought it so prominently before the public eye, that I consider it desirable to give a detailed account of proceedings which were regarded with so much interest and anxiety by the whole country. We shall thus be enabled to form the best criterion by which to judge of what happened in the other parts of the kingdom; and there will be nothing afterwards to prevent us proceeding more rapidly in our further examination.

My task will be so much the easier, and I hope, at the same time, that the picture of events I shall be able to draw will be so much the more vivid, from the circumstance that I shall follow the excellent indications I have collected from the lips of an eye-witness, M. Camillo Battista, who wrote a genuine narrative of those events in Basilicata* of which he had personally been an eye-witness.

* Reazione e Brigantaggio in Basilicata nella Primavera del 1861, per Camillo Battista (Potenza, Stabilimento tipografico di V. Santanello, 1861). With the following motto from Botta: " La moltitudine commette il male volentieri e si ficca anche spesso il coltello nel petto da sè, tanto i moti suoi sono incom-

In thus collecting the evidence of facts from all available quarters, an example is set which ought to be imitated by all writers when they are about to relate the history of stormy revolutionary periods. Instead of allowing their preconceived ideas to lead them astray in useless discussions or premature decisions, they can only gain by consulting such modest and conscientious chroniclers as M. Battista, whose record of his own personal experience must necessarily be a more useful and more durable guide than the thousands of pamphlets hastily issued from the press by many a rash and passionate politician.

History, above all, demands witnesses. Afterwards, when events have been faithfully related, when facts in their proper sequence have been established on the groundwork of truth, criticism may appear and pronounce its judgments.

posti, i voleri discordi, le fantasie accendibili, e tanto ancora sopra di lei possono più sempre gli ambiziosi che i modesti cittadini."

CHAPTER V.

CHAPTER V.

LET us now, therefore, make our entrance into Busilicata, and instead of a "Murray's Hand-Book," take with us as our guide the interesting volume of M. Camillo Battista.

Roads and thoroughfares in that province had, at all periods, been proverbially unsafe. As thieves were almost acclimatised in every part of the country, the new Government paid little attention to them. It is true they ordered now and then search to be made by the National Guard; but no important discovery having been made, they did not consider it necessary to make any further investigation. The consequence was that the bands of robbers, availing themselves of the impunity which was offered to them, grew in audacity and number; increasing to such an extent that they used to tax the proprietors, steal horses, and capture men and children, whom they only released on payment of heavy ransoms. Soon masters of the surrounding

country, which they had struck with terror, they
occupied the heights and woods of Melfi, where they
established themselves in positions of great strength.
The Government at Naples having no spare troops to
send to the rescue of that province, the brigands
became more powerful every day, and at last put
themselves in communication with the chiefs of the
re-actionist movement. Marching under the colours
of King Francis II, they entered, on the 7th of April,
into the vast properties of Prince Doria, at Lagopesole, the peasantry settled on which they forced to
unite in the cry, " Viva Francesco II.!" promising to
all, if they would join them in the service of
the king, six carlini per day, besides all that they
might realise by their ransacking and plundering expeditions. In the meanwhile they announced to them
that the legitimate monarch had just landed on the
shore of Italy, at the head of forty thousand
Austrians; a report which had been spread elsewhere, and which were strengthened by the solemn
affirmation of the priests. At their instigation, a
few hundreds of these frightened boors assembled
under the Bourbon colours, and, armed anyhow, ran
riot all over the neighbouring country, shouting
whatever they were commanded by the ringleaders to
shout.

One of their adventures was the following. Dur-

ing the night of the 7th of April they invested
the post of the National Guard at Ripacandida. The
captain, Michele Anastasia, who tried to give the
alarm, was killed, his death being an act of private
vengeance committed by a man of Melfi, called Ciccio.
The next day they were reinforced by the arrival of
about four hundred men, partly peasants and partly
disbanded soldiers, with their chiefs. Carmine Donatelli of Rionero, surnamed Crocco, assumed the position
of general and chief of this formidable band. This
man had made his escape from the galleys, where he
was confined after having already been convicted of
thirty crimes, including fifteen cases of robbery, four
captures of individuals whom he had afterwards set at
liberty on payment of a ransom, three manslaughters, two
attempted murders, many cases of public blasphemy,
armed resistance to the authorities, and other minor
offences. Vincenzo Nardi of Ferrandina, another formidable member of the band, had already been accused of fifteen cases of burglary, and had committed
four assassinations. I do not say anything of other
offences, the list would be too long. He took the
surname of Amati, and the rank of colonel. It was
he who said ironically, when he entered the little town
of Rapolla, "They say Francis II. is a thief. Well, I,
a professed thief, come to replace the royal thief on his
throne." Michele La Rotonda of Ripacandida, accused

of four thefts, two attempted murders, &c., was appointed
lieutenant-colonel. Finally, Giuseppe Nicola Summa,
who could only boast of three robberies and two at-
tempts to murder, had to content himself with the
grade of major.

This band, under leaders so notable for their unre-
lenting character, and for the blackness of the crimes
with which they were stained, when they took possession of Ripacandida, gave orders that the bells should
ring a peal of triumph, and commanded a thanksgiving
to be sung in the church. Having hoisted the white
flag of the Bourbons, they appointed a provisional
government.

In the meanwhile, they had already forced and
ransacked the house of a rich farmer named Giuseppe
Lorusso, whom, by a diabolical refinement of cruelty, they
fastened to his own door, in order that the poor
man might witness the spectacle of his ruin. The
house of the unfortunate Captain Anastasia, whom
they had treacherously murdered, was also destroyed.
His family, being naturally anxious to recover his body,
with the pious intention of giving it Christian burial,
obtained possession of it only by paying a very heavy
ransom. For two days Ripacandida was the prey
of a maudlin joy. Crackers, bonfires, and illuminations,
evinced the supreme satisfaction of a brutal popu-

lace. Taxes were levied *ad libitum*, and every
ruffian amassed plunder to his heart's content.
Lawlessness was enjoying its triumph without restraint.

At the same time signs of reaction made their
appearance at Ginestra, and the next day at Venosa.
Venosa is regarded as an important town, not so
much for its population, which does not exceed a
few thousands, as on account of its recollections. It
possesses a cathedral and a bishop. It was the
ancient Venusia, the birth-place of Horace. It was
one of the only two towns—for, notwithstanding its
small population, as such it was regarded—which
during these times of trouble were occupied by the
brigands.

The intendant of the province, M. Raccioppi, had
done his best to oppose the reactionary movement.
Having sent to Naples for help, he had in the meanwhile gathered around him the National Guards of the
neighbouring villages. Many of them had answered
the appeal—those of Venosa, in particular, being prepared to resist the invasion of such a band of malefactors. Barricades were got up for the defence of
the town, and many suspicious individuals were arrested—among others, Crocco's brother.

On the morning of the 10th, a detachment of about

sixty National Guards, going out of Venosa to recon-
noitre, were met by flying crowds of peasants, who,
pale with terror, exclaimed, when they saw the small
party of National Guards, "Thousands and thousands
of brigands are behind us!—go back, if you care for
your lives!" The detachment, on hearing this, thought it
prudent to retire. When they returned to the town the
inhabitants were struck with a dreadful panic. Another
reinforcement of National Guards, however, having been obtained from the villages in the neighbourhood, they came to the resolution of resisting the
bandits to the last extremity. More barricades
were accordingly erected in the streets, while the
steeple of the cathedral and the old castle were
hurriedly put in a state of defence.

The brigands soon made their appearance, six hundred in number, of whom a few were armed with
muskets, the rest being provided only with axes and
scythes. Kept at a respectful distance from the side
of the town occupied by the National Guard, they
directed their attack on a weaker point, where they
had noticed the friendly waving of a white flag, displayed, as it afterwards appeared, by the mob, with
whom they had secret intelligence, and who held out
ladders to facilitate their entrance. The National
Guards were desirous of availing themselves of the
castle and the steeple, in order to oppose the assail-

ants ; but the timid burghers, whose momentary
valour had already evaporated, prayed them to make
no further resistance, hoping to obtain more favourable terms by a ready submission. Recoiling at the
very idea of a scene of carnage, they earnestly en-
treated the civic troops not to fire, fearing that
such an act might lead to the destruction of their
town and the massacre of its inhabitants. In the
presence of the whole population of women and
children kneeling imploringly before them, and en-
treating them to consider the sufferings to which they
would be exposed from the bandits, what could
these National Guards do? Their services, therefore, being rejected they ceased to offer any resistance, and the brigands were allowed to enter.
The commander-in-chief, Crocco Donatelli, at once
ordered the town to be plundered, a command which, as
we may suppose, was willingly obeyed. The bandits,
after they had seized the treasury of the community,
impelled by the spirit of destruction, burnt and reduced to ashes all the property they could not carry
away. In that scene of devastation not even the
glass of the windows and the doors was
spared !

These heartless ruffians disgraced themselves
further by acts of the most sanguinary cruelty. When
the houses of the two canons, Almano and La Conca,

were attacked, they laid hold of the niece, a young
lady of prepossessing appearance, whose handsome
face they entirely disfigured with their knives. Another
young lady, assaulted by one of the bandits, discharged a loaded pistol at him; but unfortunately
missing the villain, the brave girl threw herself out of
the window, and perished in the street. Alas! they
had not all the same courage, and the weakest
as well as the strongest obtained no mercy from
men who were strangers to every touch of
pity.

The Abbot of the Monastery of San Benedetto was
compelled to pay a very heavy ransom. The doors
of the prisons having been thrown open, the convicts,
rushing wildly into the streets, broke into the house
of a watchmaker, M. Montrone, in the hope of finding
a rich prey, but discovering they had been deceived,
they killed, before the eyes of the distracted father,
his only son, a boy twelve years old. . . . They
then invested the house of a doctor, M. Francesco
Nitti, a venerable old man, respected by all his fellow-
citizens. As he was stepping forth to address these
ruffians, they laid him dead on the pavement with
the blow of an axe; and, more merciless than tigers,
trampled upon his dead body with a savage fury.

Such were some—only some—of the deeds of this
cruel band. Shame, eternal shame, be upon the

Government which, in the nineteenth century, and in the presence of civilized Europe, could employ and let loose upon peaceful country places men whose cold-blooded atrocities would have made even savages shudder.

When the National Guard, yielding to the importunities of the citizens, ceased to offer any resistance to the entrance of the brigands, they retired to the castle, where they resolved to defend themselves. As they were still resisting, a parliamentary was sent to them, containing an assurance that the plunder of the town should immediately cease on their surrender. They did surrender; but the work of plunder, instead of being discontinued, was carried on with increasing activity and fury, this scene of lawless violence being further disgraced by many acts of wanton cruelty.

After the awful tragedy had been completed, it was succeeded by a ludicrous comedy. The day after the invasion of the brigands, some two hundred disbanded soldiers, drawn up in line before the house inhabited by the commander-in-chief of the former, with drums beating and colours flying, marched out of the town, to meet, as they said, General Bosco,* who was expected to arrive at the head of his army. The people of Venosa

* General Bosco was the only one who had, deservedly or not, some reputation in the Neapolitan army. He was, however, in Sicily at the time of Garibaldi's invasion, and followed the king to Gaëta. He has been since one of the staunchest supporters of the Bourbonist party.

believed this assertion, for in that country they are
so credulous that they believe anything, even the
many absurd reports that were spread regarding the
restoration of Francis II. to the throne of his fathers
having been received with implicit credit.

The plunder of Venosa lasted for three days. All
the *galantuomini* were taxed, fined, and ransomed,
except those who had favoured the invasion. Those
who refused to pay were shot. A man called Giuseppe
Antonio Ghiura, who seemed to hesitate a few moments before he would consent to cry " Viva Francesco
II. !" was slain on the spot. After this triumphant
exploit, General Crocco reviewed his gallant soldiers.
One of them, named Romaniello, having asked leave
to go home, the chief, in reply, sent a bullet through
his heart, fired from the man's own pistol.

On the 14th, early in the morning, the brigands
left Venosa, having previously sent to Ripacandida
nine mules loaded with no less than twenty thousand
ducats. But even when the town was thus delivered
from its chief enemy, there was still danger from the
mob, who were eager to carry on and complete the
work of plunder, for while the place was in its present
defenceless state they would never be satisfied until
all that they coveted was in their hands. The poor
plundered inhabitants, in these circumstances, did not
feel themselves in perfect safety till the 16th, when a

column of the National Guard, numbering more than
four hundred men, of whom one hundred and thirty
took up their quarters in the town, commanded
by Major d'Errico, arrived for their protection.
They had been assembled in two days, and were received with acclamations of joy; the bells of the
churches ringing, and even those who had cried
" Viva Francesco II. !" raising their voices still louder
with shouts of " Viva Vittorio Emanuele !"

Among the leaders of the national party was the
celebrated Gabriele Bocchicchio, of Forenza, who,
with only ten men, had prevented the invasion of
Maschito. Waiting in ambush near the road for the
brigands, he had attacked and dispersed their vanguard, consisting of about twenty men, who had preceded the main body in order to explore the ground.
Bocchicchio, to judge from the following letter, must
have been one of Crocco's old acquaintances :—

"Melfi, April 16th, 1861.

" MY DEAR GABRIELE,

" To-day the Provisional Government of
Melfi has been re-established by a court-martial.
Things are going on satisfactorily. I have acted in
consequence of superior orders, and the decree of
authorisation was signed the 28th of February,
at Rome, by our beloved King, his Majesty, Francis
II.—may God aid and protect him ! If you want

R 2

to enter the service of the Holy cause, the authorities here will give you arms and instructions, and you will be raised to the same dignified position which I hold in His Majesty's army. Collect, then, as many volunteers as you possibly can, and contrive to do what I did ; that is, disarm the country, and destroy the usurper's standards ; and be sure that you will see the populations rise in enthusiasm at the cry of 'Viva Francesco II., King of the Two Sicilies !'

"If you accept, announce it to me by some splendid deed ; but if your sentiments be different, then come out into the open field, with your followers, and give me an appointment anywhere you like, for I am ready to meet you rifle in hand, and make you pay dearly for your imprudence. I am sure you will listen to my voice, and not force me to be your enemy.

"CARMINE DONATELLI, *Commander-in-Chief.*"

* This letter, if it had been written by Crocco, would have been his masterpiece ; but he only signed it. Hence there is only one fault in its orthography, and that is in the signature—Donatella instead of Donatelli. There are many autograph letters of this general of King Francis, one of which, the shortest of them, I cannot resist the temptation of giving here—it will be amusing to number its faults. It is only a receipt, delivered by Crocco to M. Luigi del Bene, Prince Doria's agent, from whom he had just extorted a sum of 360 ducats.

"*Il generalo si ha preso dalla gento D. Luigi del Bene, del prigipi dorio Docati trecento tessanta, perchè servono per i miei soldati.*

(Signed) "IL GENERALO CARMINE CROCCO DONATELLA."

Bocchicchio, who fought bravely for the Italian cause, of course did not answer such a letter. A brigand (as he has sometimes been accused of having been) would not have resisted so great a temptation.

The letter I have quoted was dated from Melfi, where Crocco had taken up his quarters after the exploits of Venosa. He had passed by Lavello, which was likewise in insurrection, and many other neighbouring villages—Arigliano, which had been roused by its octogenarian Vicar, Francesco Clapo, of whom I shall have to speak by-and-by; Ruoti, where not a single gentleman nor a single priest (a fact well worth noticing) helped the reactionist party; Caraguso and Calciano, perhaps the two only hamlets where there has been insurrection without the aid of the brigands; Rapolla, whose inhabitants savagely cried, "The mice have eaten the cats!" meaning by the mice the Bourbonists; Atella, Barile, Rionero, Grassano, Santo Chirico, where a touching episode took place, which I must stop to relate.

The National Guard of Tolve, on their way to Grassano, being obliged to spend the night at Santo Chirico, were badly received, the inhabitants refusing to give them shelter. After a few angry words on both sides, they came to blows, the result of which was that several were wounded, and two killed. Among the latter was a man of Santo Chirico, of the name of Lacava. The captain of the National Guard of Tolve thought it prudent to retire, in order to avoid a greater effusion of blood, leaving behind seven of his men in the hands of the inhabitants, still excited by the recent engagement. One of these poor fellows, flying the fury of his persecutors, found himself by chance under the roof of Lacava's wife, mother of seven children, whose father the people of Tolve had just killed. The poor widow offered the hospitality of her home to the fugitive whose life was so eagerly sought for, and, as a good Christian, gave him a safe shelter for the night. A similar act of humanity would have been but natural in England. In that country, where vengeance is almost imperative, and murder is readily absolved by a false sentiment of religion, it seems almost divine.

At Lavello, since the 10th of April, the inhabitants had taken every precaution to resist the inroad of their enemies. In order to avoid the horrors of Venosa, the patriots did all they could to direct the disposition of the mob, in order to prevent them from associating with the brigands. To that effect, general distributions of bread and money were made among the lowest classes; but, alas! with no avail, for once more fear paralysed everybody, and made the task of the brigands a very easy one.

Having left Venosa, Crocco occupied Lavello without striking a blow. One of his vanguard, on entering the town on horseback, sword in hand, shot, by way of announcing their arrival, the first burgher he met on his passage, a certain Pietro Bagnoli, who fell lifeless at his feet. For a whole day the little town was plunged into all the horrors of a place given up to plunder. The assassins took everything worth stealing, even ear-rings being brutally torn from the ears of the women. When the work of plunder had been completed, the Commander-in-chief ordered a trumpeter to announce that theft would be punished with death; and, in fact, a transgressor who was taken in the act was at once sentenced to be shot; but though a pistol was fired at him, and he fell apparently lifeless, the inhabitants of Lavello have since discovered that this scene was a mere theatrical performance, the pistol having been only loaded with powder! The men of the town having been ordered to give up their arms, three hundred muskets were surrendered to the commander of the bandits. Crocco, however, being informed that there were still in the village seven-and-twenty double-barrelled old muskets, demanded them also, and, though reluctantly, these too were handed over to him.

On the 15th of April, Crocco paid a visit, with a detachment of his bandits, to M. Palmieri, the com-

munal treasurer, requesting him to give him immediately the seven thousand ducats which were still left.
On Mr Palmieri's humbly remonstrating that the
sum had been grossly exaggerated, Crocco made a
sign, and the house was forced. Palmieri then begged
the general to allow him to retain something for
the poor, and, to the great astonishment of everyone,
the bandit took for himself only 500 ducats. More
than this, he signed a declaration, still in existence,
giving all the particulars of the capture of this money,
and under what circumstances it had taken place.

Lavello was fortunately spared the melancholy scene
that was to have been enacted in it on the following
day. Seven and twenty patriots had been set apart
for execution on the 16th of April, when, by good
fortune, several messages from Melfi having turned
the eyes of the brigand in the direction of that important prey, he suddenly departed with his men, leaving
the unhappy place exhausted by his short but terrible
apparition. The next day, when Lavello was delivered from the terror inspired by his presence, the
white Bourbonist flags were once more folded up, and
the Italian colours were everywhere restored.

The insurrection in Melfi is the most important
episode among the events attending the reaction in Basilicata, and perhaps among all the other circumstances
by which Southern Italy has been agitated. Almost
everywhere, in fact, what do we see but partial dis-

orders, occasioned by sudden invasions, for the purpose of disarming posts of National Guards, and plundering whenever there was an opportunity? And invariably it was the lowest class of the population, the hungry mob, who gave assistance to the invaders. As a general rule, these armed bands only directed their attacks upon the smallest and most unimportant hamlets, the name even of which is not often to be found on the maps. Such, however, was not the case as far as Melfi was concerned. The name of this town is an historical one, and the earthquake, which nearly laid all the more ancient part of it a heap of ruins, came quite seasonably to revive its celebrity. It is defended by a citadel, and possesses a cathedral and a bishopric. Statistics make its population amount to seven thousand inhabitants. Melfi is the *only* country town of some little importance which rose on behalf of the fallen dynasty. Insurrection in it had not so exclusively a plebeian and communist character as in other parts of Italy; for the movement, excited at first by persons of rank, assumed, as we know, in its development, quite a different character, and was supported mainly by the masses. The reaction in Melfi was the result of a conspiracy, and excesses were restrained by the chiefs themselves. It was a well-directed movement, the only one that the present reaction ever produced.

Among the old influential families of the town who
were still faithful to Francis II. were the Aquilecchia, a very powerful race.   They had always
dreamt of a restoration, but he who desires an end
does not always study the best means of attaining it.   In Italy this was almost a law in politics.
Since the first appearance of the brigands at
Venosa, the Bourbonist party at Melfi had put
themselves in communication with them.   In the
meanwhile, they stirred up the people by publicly
announcing the entrance of Francis II. into the
Abruzzi at the head of the Austrians.   They informed them of the sudden appearance in the Bay
of Naples of a French fleet, having on board the
Neapolitan army, a part of which had already landed
on the coast of Puglia.   Finally, the approaching
arrival of General Bosco, with twelve thousand men,
was bruited about.   The Syndic for some time denied
these falsehoods, opposing, when necessary, lie to lie.
He had announced in his turn the approach of the Italian
troops, and had even appointed a committee entrusted
with the special care of preparing lodgings for them ;
but with no avail, for an official dispatch had arrived
from Foggia, which, treacherously opened and read before it reached the Syndic, brought the sad news
that unfortunately the Government could not spare a
single soldier at that moment.

The insurrection broke out on the 12th of April. The people assembled in crowds in the market-place, crying, " Viva Francesco II. !" "Death to the patriots !" As usual, the prisons were thrown open, and many disorders were committed. A soldier of the disbanded army of Francis II., Ambrogio Patino, assumed the title of general, and obliged all who passed before him to salute him with respect. Another, a certain Michele Projetto, took the portraits of Garibaldi and Victor Emmanuel into the middle of the market-place, and there beheaded them with an axe, after having outrageously insulted in the pictures those whom they represented. The National Guard, involved in the general movement, joined the insurrection, and the people, guided by the priests, went in a mass to the house of Cavaliere Colabella, a notorious Bourbonist, who appeared on the balcony, and, after delivering a speech remarkable for its violence, threw to the assembly an immense white cloth, as the emblem of the Bour-bonist colours. This cloth, cut into a hundred little flags, waved over the multitude, and Colabella, with his friend Aquilecchia, was carried about in triumph. From this moment, newspapers being no more admitted into the town, reactionists could spread any absurd report they might think useful to their purpose, without the slightest fear of its being contradicted.

During four days Melfi was literally in the hands

of the mob; and it was really a frightful spectacle to
behold that infuriated multitude, armed, at random,
with any weapons they might happen to possess or be
able to lay hold of—some with muskets and pistols,
and others with swords, axes, and large carving
knives, which they brandished in a threatening
manner as they rushed through the streets, disarming
citizens, plundering houses, and appropriating everything on which they could lay their hands. The women
were even more savage than the men. A horrid old
woman of sixty, ludicrously attired with a soldier's
coat, was seen everywhere, fiercely threatening
massacre and destruction. A spirit of fury seemed
to have seized upon the masses; and yet, strange to
say, comparatively few excesses were committed.
Beyond the plunder of some houses, there were not
many of those deeds of violence and crime by which
such scenes are generally disgraced.

Aquilecchia was elected prodictator, and he succeeded in stopping depredations. In the cathedral,
after a *Te Deum* had been sung, the priest spoke
words of peace, recommending his hearers to respect
the life and the property of the peaceful citizens.
The humour of the mob having been soothed by a
large distribution of money, they began decorating
the town with the Bourbonist colours, and with a
profusion of images representing King Francis and

his queen, Mary Sophia. All these preparations were got up to welcome the expected arrival of the Bourbonist army. Their worthy general, the gallant Crocco, was to appear in a gorgeous green velvet uniform, which, as a token of their admiration, the people had hastily ordered to be got ready for him.

On the 15th, in the evening, Crocco entered the town which had made such preparations for his reception. Two carriages had gone out to meet him, conveying guards of honour and many priests, carrying, in addition to the Bourbonist emblems, four splendid white Oriflammes embroidered with gold. A great crowd with torches met the hero of the night, and paid homage to him by strewing his path with flowers. In the midst of an ovation so triumphant, the brigand must have asked himself whether he was not a king receiving the submission of his admiring and obedient subjects.

Acquilecchia and Colabella received him at the gates of the town, amidst the frantic acclamations of the enthusiastic people. His entrance within its walls was, so to speak, solemnized by an act which we can regard only as a scandalous parody of religion. The general knelt down before a sort of altar, which had been erected for the occasion at the entrance of the Municipal Hall, and with his sacrilegious lips dared to address a thanksgiving to the Holy

Virgin, acknowledging it was she who had protected
his victorious arms, and to whom he owed his present
triumphant position. After this ceremony, Crocco,
in his progress through the streets, was everywhere
greeted with unbounded enthusiasm.

· The general's next step must have been of a nature
to cool the enthusiasm of his ardent admirers.
Crocco, who was not one to remain satisfied with the
empty breath of popular applause, imposed heavy
taxes on the inhabitants of the town, representing to
them that it was necessary to maintain the holy cause
by substantial support. He thus replenished his
empty pockets. People were somewhat astonished
at this sudden change; but what could they do in
the presence of the unscrupulous Dictator who had
already ordered certain persons to be shot for their
apparent hesitation in submitting to his decrees? We
may easily imagine that the command of one whose
word was so soon followed by a blow, was thenceforth
obeyed with unfailing promptitude.

This state of things lasted for three days, till the
18th of April. Learning then that the Piedmontese
were really advancing, Crocco packed up bag and
baggage, and quickly retired, leaving Melfi to its
well-deserved punishment. He carried away with
him more than thirty thousand ducats. On the approach of the Piedmontese army, the town which had

manifested so much noisy enthusiasm in favour of the
Bourbon prince, considered it prudent, in evidence of
its Italian sympathies, to display the national tri-
coloured flag, and, instead of the portraits, statues,
and busts of Francis II., to restore everywhere, on
all the public buildings and in all the public places,
those of Victor Emmanuel and of Garibaldi. The
people even went out to meet the Intendant, who, as
a measure of prudence, had left the town a few days
before, declaring, in the most solemn way, that in their
hearts they had never wavered in their attachment to
the national cause, of which they had ever been the
zealous supporters. Colubella and Aquilecchia were
seized by the same mob who had carried them in
triumph, and, accompanied by the insults and hisses
of that base multitude, were thrown into a prison
among thieves and murderers. Such is the instability
of human things!

A few days before the insurrection in behalf of
Francis II., the borough of Melfi had returned to
Parliament one of the most advanced members of the
Radical party, the well-known writer, Guerrazzi. At
that time, as I have already stated, the Piedmontese
were approaching, though, unfortunately, a little too
late. The Government, however, had scarcely any
troops to dispose of, and it was with difficulty that
they had at last been able to send against the brigands

a few companies of infantry. The Piedmontese were
received with outbursts of joy; for, though in an absolute minority, the representatives of Italian order
and progress were influential enough, under favourable circumstances, to guide and protect public feeling. The National Guard were up at once, ready
to fight; nor had they long to wait for an opportunity
of signalising themselves by their zeal. Having come
in contact with the insurgents between Barile and
Rionero, an engagement ensued, which lasted more
than six hours, and resulted in the capture of a
hundred and fifty brigands. It would only weary
the reader to dwell on all the minor incidents of the
campaign, and to detain him by a minute description
of every skirmish that took place. Nor, unless he
had under his eyes one of those large maps con-
structed by the labours of the Staff, would it be
possible to follow with the slightest interest the
chase of the brigands from one unknown village or
hamlet to another. An account of one adventure
will be sufficient to give an idea of this partisan war.

Captain Davide Mennunni, of Ginzano, was one
of those zealous adherents of the revolution, who,
eager to distinguish himself in the cause of his re-
generated country, was dying to have a good fight
with the Bourbons and their brigand adherents.
Leaving, therefore, the main body of the volunteers

commanded by Major d'Errico, he was entrusted with
the command of about a hundred horsemen, with
whom he proceeded to scour the country. In the
course of their movements, they drew near Lagopesole, at a place on the verge of a wood near the
estates of Prince Doria, where some huts are built for
sheltering cattle during the winter season. The place
had such a lonely and solitary look, that it appeared
in every way adapted for the concealment of brigands.
Approaching it therefore with caution, they discovered a sentry walking outside the huts, within
which, by taking proper measures, they succeeded
in discovering more than twenty brigands. When
the sentry perceived Mennunni and his companions,
who wore no uniforms, and were dressed like
peasants, he imagined that they must be connected
with some other Bourbonist band, and shouted,
" Hurrah! Welcome to our friends!" One of his
comrades, however, within the huts, who had a more
experienced eye, saw the error, and lowering his
rifle, aimed at the captain of the patriots. Fortunately enough, the charge being damp, his musket
did not go off, and the brigand himself almost at
the same moment fell dead; for Mennunni, having marked him, had taken aim, and immediately
after he discharged his piece, had shot him through
the heart.

"Cheer up, my lads! straight forward, and Viva Garibaldi!" cried the captain.

At this cry, which had so often struck terror to their hearts, the brigands fled at full speed for their den, some on foot, and some on horseback, closely, pitilessly, pressed upon by the patriots, into whose hands all who were not slain in fight fell. A pistol was raised by one of the volunteers to shoot down a man clad with a sort of grey cloak, and with a Piedmontese cap on his head, when the latter cried out: "Stop! for heaven's sake do not fire! I am a Piedmontese, one of yours!" And so, on inquiry, he turned out to be.

This man, as the following story will show, had a few days before made a very narrow escape with his life. The troops stationed at Carbonara, having set out on an expedition, had only left behind eleven men to protect their stores. These poor fellows were soon after attacked, and, overwhelmed by superior force, had been obliged to retire, leaving two of their party prisoners in the hands of their assailants, by whom they were literally cut to pieces. A third, who was carried away as a hostage, was the one who had just had so narrow an escape.

On one of the men killed in this affair of Lagopesole was found a letter addressed to " His Excellency Don Carmine Crocco, by a certain Luigi Caputo, of

Rionero. Among other matter it contained the following passage: "You ought to grant me, on my oath of allegiance, to enter the Sacred Legion of our beloved father, Ferdinand II., by the grace of God, of your Excellency, and of all our troops."

Some of the brigands, after their dispersion and flight, effected their retreat, plundering on their way Monteverde, Carbonaro, and Calitri. The Archbishop of Conza, an adherent of the Bourbons, not only gave them a splendid reception, but profaned his sacred office by blessing, in the name of the God of justice and mercy, the sacrilegious host who were stained with so many unpardonable crimes. The bands of Crocco, now decimated and discouraged, roved about in the neighbourhood of the river Ofanto, robbing and assaulting the defenceless passengers on the road and in the diligences. One day some priests belonging to the Italian party, of whom the number was very few, were on their way back to Melfi, which they had left during the period when the scenes consequent on the reaction were transacting in that town. At a few miles from their journey's end they heard behind them cries for help. Supposing naturally that the life of some human being was in danger, they immediately hurried back; but their humanity unfortunately led them into a great peril, the cry being part of a snare prepared by the brigands in order that they might be able to entrap and seize the poor priests, one of whom fell into the hands of the ruffians.   The others, who were well mounted, becoming aware in good time of the danger into which they were about to fall, succeeded in effecting their escape, although they were pursued with musket-shot as far as the gates of the town.

The National Guard of those districts performed their duty faithfully during that terrible campaign. The names of many of these men became almost household words, on account of the bravery with which they had acted in their various campaigns against the brigands.   A short time after the suppression of brigandage in the province of Basilicata, on the motion of Terenzio Mamiani,* the National Parliament at Turin, in acknowledgment of the effective manner in which the National Guard had performed its duty, declared in a solemn form that—"The National Guard of the Southern provinces had well deserved of their country during the last eventful months of troubles!"

If any document were required to throw some light upon the feelings by which the reactionist districts were animated, it would be found in the letter of a woman of Ripacandida, addressed to

* Formerly Minister of Public Instruction, and lately Italian representative in Greece.

her husband, who was in one of the Bourbonist bands. The style in the original Italian, which is very peculiar, would be almost unintelligible to those who understand only the pure Tuscan idiom. In giving no punctuation with my translation, which is as literal as possible, I follow the letter itself:

" MY DEAR HUSBAND

" My heart rejoiced when I heard you were well and that God had protected you from misfortunes I am continually addressing prayers for you but they say at Ripacandida you have all fought well for the sake of our country and that Heaven helped you to the last moment and ensuring you an easy victory for one only thing I feel very sorry all the men of Ripacandida have sent no end of valuable things to their families from the last plunders while my poor weeping self said why does my husband forget his wife considering besides how I never had luck at any time poor sorrowful woman that I am and was asking myself why does my husband who was once so kind and generous show now such a heartstone cruelty I earnestly beg you to put an end to my miseries my brothers want to be remembered to you and they ask you also to send a double-barrelled gun to each of them which they will keep as a token of your good feelings and the gun you have sent I have never yet received. I kiss you dearly.

"Written by me Michele Guglielmucci professed letter-writer and to me also do send a little gun.

"Your very affectionate wife

"TERESA SAIENA."

"To the hands of Donata Rega Venosa."

If it were not that we might be accused of exaggeration, we might give such an account of the atrocities committed by the Bourbonists as would almost transcend belief; some of them even carrying their ferocity to such an extent as to wear on their persons portions of the bodies of their murdered victims. In the sentence pronounced on a Calabrian of Feroleto Vecchio, of the name of Ferdinando Pietropaolo, we are informed that he was ascertained always to have carried with him, on his person, a *human chin-bone, with beard "à la Napoleon,"* cut from the face of some poor patriot.

Although perhaps the majority of these bandits engaged in the Bourbon cause only from their innate propensity to crime, and their desire for plunder, there were doubtless among them some sincerely attached to the cause of the exiled family. Such, for instance, was the curate of Avigliano, Don Ferdinando Clapo. This learned octogenarian, a strong supporter of the temporal government of the Pope, and of Francis II., once, when a *Te Deum* was sung in the church of Avigliano, for

the victory of the Italians on the 21st of April, had
the daring to announce, after the ceremony was over,
in the very face of the Italian National Guard,
and of the Piedmontese officers, that Francis II. would
certainly soon appear again among his beloved subjects; on which ground he earnestly exhorted them,
even in the midst of the most discouraging circumstances, to remain faithful to him. When the curate
was reminded that he was in the presence of the
officers of the King of Italy, and was invited to change
his language, he not only refused to do so, but increased the vehemence of his attacks against the Revolution and its authors. Of course he was arrested,
and taken to Potenza, chief town of the district,
where, whenever he had an opportunity, he still continued to insult king and country, making it evident
that, in the excess of his zeal, his ambition was to be
invested with the honours of martyrdom, a triumph,
however, which his captors did not consider it necessary to grant him the enjoyment of.

Basilicata, as we have seen, was thus gradually
restored to order. The inhabitants of the country, re-
covering from the state of alarm in which they had so
long existed, were beginning to be re-assured. Unfortunately they were again thrown into a state of
alarm and anxiety by a report suddenly spread among
them that on the third of May, at two o'clock in the

morning, about two hundred brigands had fallen upon
Monticelli, a little place in the province of Terra di
Lavoro, near the Roman frontier, where, after signal-
izing themselves by their usual acts of violence and
cruelty, they had established themselves in the
houses of the villagers. The fact that a company of
soldiers, who had been sent from Fondi when the
report of the attack reached that place, had been repulsed by them, tended still more to increase the
alarm of the people. The banditti, meanwhile, had
possessed ample time to load themselves with the
property of the poor people, and to secure their retreat; so that when, next day, some new troops, with
a few pieces of artillery, arrived on the spot, they
found that the aggressors had already made good
their retreat, carrying along with them an immense
amount of plunder. During their flight they invaded
many other districts, carrying with them destruction
and desolation wherever they passed, defying the
authorities, and issuing decrees and proclamations, as
if they had been the conquerors of the country.

The Bourbonist bravo who was thus making such a
ludicrous mimicry of Garibaldi, the noble popular
chieftain, was the celebrated Chiavone, a man about
whom there has been no end of talk, the reports in
circulation grossly exaggerating his importance. Chiavone was, in reality, neither a partisan nor a brigand,

but only a commonplace rogue. Formerly a game-
keeper at Sora, he had acquired a certain influence
over the poachers and vagabonds of the district.
During the last revolution, while there was that perpetual movement of patriots and Bourbonists passing
through Sora, each in turn remaining for a short time,
and then departing from it, he offered his services to
maintain public order with a handful of coal-men
whom he had under his orders. I use the word in
its literal sense, meaning real coal-men, and not the
old political "Carbonari," who had so great an influence under the Bourbons as well as under Murat.

Chiavone's proposal was agreed to; and it is possible that, thus employed, he might have been useful,
but unfortunately, when the patriots came back, his
services being no longer considered necessary, he was
discharged. Disgusted by such ungrateful behaviour
on the part of his fellow-citizens, he almost immediately disappeared with his coal-men, from whom
the band of banditti, which he afterwards commanded,
derived its origin. Armed with such weapons as
they could at the moment lay hands on, they infested
the country with the already mentioned German rob-
ber who had assumed the name of Lagrange. The
authority exercised by this Teutonic bandit fell, ere
long, into the hands of Chiavone, who, with his
followers, continued to devastate every province into

which they entered. He occupied the mountains which command the whole district around Sora, and kept the town itself in check. The terror inspired in it by his name was not without reason, for such was his temerity, that he even made a descent into it on the 3rd of December, and remained there the whole day, till the troops who had been sent for were almost on the spot.

Since that time the predatory operations of his band have been almost exclusively confined within the wild passes of the Roman frontiers. Making it a point that he should never be personally seen, he has always remained hidden behind his men until they had loaded themselves with plunder, when, still preserving his position in the rear, he would protect . their retreat. Very tenacious of his authority, and of the honour due to a bandit chief, he gave himself the airs of a viceroy, constantly issuing proclamations, which he dated from many different places. One of his decrees, professing to be issued from the general headquarters of Sora, I once had my curiosity gratified by the sight of.

When such proclamations were read, many believed that he was really concealed in the town to which they were addressed, but in all probability he was hidden some ten miles off, in the dominions of the Pope. On the 29th of May he sent from the mountain where he had his stronghold, a parliamentary to the Piedmontese garrison, summoning them to surrender, with the promise that life should be granted to all, and that they should be allowed to depart with a safe conduct for Turin. The only answer vouchsafed by the Piedmontese was the exhibition of the muzzle of a cannon, at the sight of which Chiavone had the prudence to fall back immediately upon the "Holy Land," for, when he could avoid it, he did not like fighting, and was always fond of consulting his safety by keeping to the extreme edge of the Neapolitan frontier. With such a refuge at hand, as soon as he was attacked he had but to make a rapid march backward, and he was out of reach of the Piedmontese, who were then at a dead lock, for they were forbidden to go beyond these fatal limits. France was there protecting St. Peter's estate. The brigands, emboldened by the protection given to them by the Pontifical authorities, sneered at the French sentinels as they passed over, and the Piedmontese, foaming with rage, stood on the other side of the line, powerless against them.

This prudent conduct of their leader explains how a band of robbers, formed from the very scum of the felon race, continued together so long, formidable in their unity. Watching the departure of the soldiers from any village, they would then fall upon the

defenceless inhabitants of such places as Luco, Monticelli, Castelluccio, Roccaviva; and when they had
ravaged, plundered, and destroyed to their hearts'
content, they would retire in safety to their dens.
Chiavone himself used to go to Rome for the purpose
of obtaining money and instructions. On these
journeys he adopted a military title, assuming on
each occasion, · as his ideas of his own importance
increased, a higher rank. First calling himself captain, he then took the title of colonel, subsequently
that of general, and finally lieutenant-general. Although this ridiculous bravado was no doubt partly
the result of mere vanity, yet there is also reason to
believe that it formed part of an artful plan. The
summons which he sent to the Italian authorities,
he vauntingly displayed to the members of the
Bourbonist committees, thus inspiring with a certain
awe and respect the very people who supplied him
with money; for the only exploit in which he distinguished himself was that of amassing plunder
by ransoming the small proprietors whom he had
made captives. At heart a thorough coward, without that spirit and dash by which many of those
brigands who had made their names terrible to the
country were distinguished, he was unquestionably
the greatest scoundrel of the race, his only object being
to speculate on the credulity of his king.

In the following anecdote we have a faithful revelation of Chiavone's character. One day, when two Piedmontese gendarmes were brought before him, instead of ordering them to be hanged, as most of the other bandit chiefs would have done, he overwhelmed them with civilities, even inviting them to partake of some coffee with him, which he had stolen for the purpose from a neighbouring house. After they had enjoyed this unexpected treat, he tried to persuade his two prisoners to take service under King Francis or the Pope; and, on their refusal, allowed them to go, contenting himself with the appropriation of their uniforms. The next day the two gendarmes made their appearance at Sora, clad in the garments of mountaineers, and presented to the authorities the following precious autograph, which had been put into their hands by Chiavone himself :—

"*To the civilian and military authorities of the country:*

"These two peasants shall not be molested on their way.

(Signed)   "CHIAVONE, General."

There is no reason for believing that Chiavone, lawless as he was, had any pleasure in acts of cruelty. The merciless deeds committed by his band are not to be attributed to him. So far as I have been able to ascertain, only one execution was directly ordered

by himself, in which he displayed a sort of grim
humour. He had stolen a considerable number
of mules belonging to a proprietor, which he offered
to restore on payment of a certain sum of money.
As the owner, however, did not approve of the bar-
gain, Chiavone assembled a court-martial to discuss,
not the fate of the man, but that of the animals.
The result of their deliberations was that the poor
mules were condemned to capital punishment, and
executed on the spot. The brigands fired no fewer
than seventeen volleys at them, shouting at every
discharge, " Viva Francesco II.! Viva Chiavone!"
According to an account received from a prisoner who
had been a witness of the deed, the mules stood fire
with all the steadiness that in the circumstances
could have been expected of them.

Chiavone's mania was to imitate Garibaldi. But
his efforts in that direction were utter failures ; for the
ape, with its most successful mimicry, cannot assume
the semblance of man. With some appreciation of
the picturesque in personal appearance, he had preserved the showy costume of Fra Diavolo—the sandals,
the felt hat, the velvet suit, the gorgeous silk scarf,
and the rich belt stuffed with poniards and pistols.
But he had neither the bravery of Fra Diavolo, nor
the courage and disinterestedness of Garibaldi. His
orthography was peculiar to himself. I have in my

possession a letter written by his own hand, so full of
barbarisms that the perusal of it is sufficient to make
one shudder. That document, however, is marked
with the seal of King Francis. I do not give the
bandit's letter here, because, although it is possible
to obtain some glimmering insight of its meaning,
it is, on the whole, almost entirely unintelligible.
I venture, however, to present the reader with a
proclamation issued by Chiavone, which, although
the meaning is intelligible enough, I have had great
difficulty in translating :—

"June 30th, 1861.

" Commandant of the Brigade of the Neapolitan Army.

    " Mr. Major,

        " On the presentation of this order, proclaim
without delay our lawful king, and have his flag
displayed everywhere, instead of the Cross of Savoy.
If this shall not be done, the whole district shall be
put to fire and sword. Get me, also, two thousand
rations of bread and cheese, to supply the wants of my
brigade when I arrive at Dalsorano.

                    " Chiavone,
            " The Lieutenant-General in Chief."

Chiavone, taking him all in all, was not one of the
most dangerous adherents of Francis II. The impor-

tance attributed to him by foreign Liberals has
always roused the hilarity of the Neapolitans. It
would be a great mistake to believe that he ever was
the commander-in-chief of the insurgents in the
Southern Provinces. The brigands had never yet
acted in concert; and the chiefs of their disunited
bands were never able to do more than harass the
forces of the Government, even when it was only
with great difficulty that troops could be dispatched
to act against them. Ulloa, the only man of political
ability who at Rome followed Francis II., complained
bitterly, in a confidential letter which was seized, of
the utter want of union and concert in those undisci-
plined bands that had arrayed themselves around the
king. All these outcasts had been collected at random,
and consisted of separate bodies, acting independently
of each other, under different chiefs, who followed the
impulse of their own will.

Chiavone was much talked about simply because
he never ceased one moment to be in communication
with Rome, where he published his proclamations.
The others, confined to the mountains of the interior,
were scarcely known anywhere but at Naples,
which was too well acquainted with the character of
these bands to exaggerate the importance of their
deeds; and yet there were few of the chiefs in any
part of the kingdom who were not by far more daring

and more dangerous than Chiavone. In their
utter isolation, however, they were all of little avail
to the deposed king of Naples—everyone acting for
his own peculiar advantage. Brigandage, so far as
it had assumed a political character, was by no means
very threatening in its aspect.

In the last days of May, the Chevalier Nigra* took his
departure. Beaten in every direction, whenever it

* The Chevalier Nigra, as everyone knows, was the private
secretary of the late Count Cavour, in those busy years during
which the great Piedmontese statesman was preparing the events
to which Italy owes its independence. The young secretary, by
his brilliant talents and captivating manners, soon acquired an
important position. Possessing the unbounded confidence of his
master, he was employed by him in the most important transac-
tions which preceded and followed the war of 1859. After the
Treaty of Zurich, when it was most required to have in Paris
an able diplomatist, Count Cavour sent his secretary to the
Court of the Tuileries, as the only one who could well fill that
difficult place, and soon afterwards appointed him resident
minister, in recompense for his successful services. But when
the Cabinet of Turin was obliged, by the threatening attitude
of the Papal Government, to invade the Roman Legations, the
Emperor, disapproving of that step, expressed his dissatisfaction by
the recall of his representative at Turin, obliging the Chevalier
Nigra, in his turn, to ask for his passports. It was then that
Count Cavour sent him to Naples, with Prince Carignano, who
was the King's Lieutenant in the Southern Italian provinces.
There, again, notwithstanding the great difficulties by which he
was surrounded, he gave proofs of singular ability. He was at
Turin when Count Cavour died, and was sent again to Paris by
Baron Ricasoli, when the Emperor Napoleon, after this great
national calamity, recognised the new Kingdom of Italy, as if

ventured to show itself, political brigandage did not
inspire the chiefs of the National cause with the
slightest uneasiness. The internal disorders of the
Administration were the source of much greater dissatisfaction to the Neapolitans than the agitated state
of the provinces.

In this state of things, as it was desirable to con-
ciliate the Neapolitans, Count Ponza di San' Martino,
one of the ablest administrators in the kingdom,
was sent to them. The new King's Lieutenant, with
the best intentions in the world, inaugurated his administration with a system of conciliation which,
though good as a general rule, proved in that instance
a complete failure. Opening the Government house
to everyone without distinction, he gave great receptions, to which even the Bourbonists themselves
were invited. Naturally enough the supporters of the
dethroned king appeared on these occasions in great
number, affecting to be animated by the best intentions. Pretending to be fully sensible of the benefits
of the mild policy that was followed, they gained
access to many of the higher employés of the Government, to whom they hinted at the possibility of their

thereby expressing his sympathy with the country in the Irre-
parable loss it had suffered.

being gained over entirely to the National cause.
Thus acquiring the confidence of men too ready to
trust them, they obtained much information as to the
designs of the Government, which they communicated
to the reactionist committees. Encouraged by the
manner in which they were received, they increased
in audacity and activity, and were enabled to contrive a
plot against the National Government, which they hoped
they should be able to bring to a successful issue.
The conspiracy soon spread its ramifications all over
the country, Rome being the focus from which the
movements of the plotters were directed. When King
Francis was informed of what was going on, he hesitated
for a long time to give the plot his approval, seeing the
perils and difficulties by which he would be beset;
but at last he made up his mind, and though he openly
disavowed it in his proclamations, put himself at the
head of the party of reaction. M. Del Re, his
ostensible minister, daily declared that the insurrection of the Neapolitan populations was entirely
spontaneous, neither instigated nor approved of by
Francis II.

An important discovery proved how little re-
liance was to be placed on these assertions. A
prince of royal blood, the Count of Trapani, the
king's uncle, with several others who assumed the

M 2

position of royal ministers, was at the head of this
vast Bourbonist conspiracy.   Owing to the seizure of
a great quantity of their correspondence, all the
details in reference to it came to the knowledge of
the Italian Government.   Under the name of a
religious association, a general committee, it was
discovered, held its sittings in Rome, presided over
by the Count of Trapani.   By his side stood, as
minister of war, one of the king's brothers, the Count
of Trani, who is often mistaken for his uncle, on account of the similitude of their names; and beneath
them sat General Clary, as secretary.   A central
committee was established at Naples, with branches in
all the provinces.   These sub-committees consisted each
of a deputy and a private secretary ; a president,
provided with full powers, duly specified in a printed
diploma despatched from Rome ; a secretary, entrusted with the care of maintaining, and, if possible,
rendering more frequent, the communications with
the other committees ; a sort of chancellor, to
countersign the proceedings ; eight decurions,
chosen among the most influential men of their
party, giving the preference to those who were
known to be of a religious character ; a
cashier, who was generally, if possible, a priest ;
four censors, invariably priests, to keep an eye
upon the cashier, and to control the acts of the

adepts; and, finally, eight delegates, for the relief of the poor.

These committees, chiefly by bribery, attached as many people as they possibly could to their cause, whose active participation, when they obtained admission to the committees, was only asked for one thing, that they should be ready to go out and rouse the neighbouring districts. These agents were under the direction of a commander-in-chief, and certain officers, whose number was regulated by the committees. They all had a diploma, the production of which was recognised by the other bands as a proof of membership, and which, if the former government had been re-established, would have entitled them to rewards for the services they had rendered. The oath which everyone who became a member of one of these committees was obliged to take, was rather a curious one, to the following effect :—

" We swear before God and before the whole world to be faithful to our most august and most religious monarch, Francis II. (may God always bless him !) ; and we faithfully promise, upon our souls, to do all that is in our power to help to restore him to the throne of his fathers, to obey blindly all his orders, and to attend to all his wishes communicated to us, either directly, or by the deputies of the

central committee in Rome. We swear to keep the
secret, in order to secure the triumph of our holy
cause, which is under the protection of the Almighty
God, Sovereign of all sovereigns, through the return
of Francis II., king, by the grace of God, defender of
religion, and son of predilection of our beloved father,
Pius IX., who carries him in his arms, in order that
he may not fall into the hands of the incredulous, the
perverse, the pretended Liberals, and the heretic
Protestants, who all have one object, the destruction
of our holy religion, after having robbed our most
blessed king of his own legitimate throne. We also
pledge ourselves, with the help of God and our Mother
Church, to avenge all the rights of the Holy See, and
to crush for ever *the Lucifer of Hell, Victor Emmanuel,
and his accomplices !* We promise and swear it, in
the name of God !"

After the perusal of such a document, little doubt
will be left, I suppose, as to the complicity of
the king, or, at least, of the royal family, in the
sanguinary deeds of re-action by which the cause
was rendered detestable to all right-thinking
men. It is beyond doubt that, from the great
focus of conspiracy in Rome, the government
of Monseigneur de Mérode tolerated, and even
encouraged, the secret enlistments ; a point upon

which all the revelations made by prisoners perfectly agree.

A certain Pietro Cimaglio, of the Province of
Campobasso, who had fallen into the hands of the
Italians, has related all the particulars of his enlistment. Established for many years, with his family,
in Rome, where he followed the trade of a shoemaker,
he received one day (the 25th of June) the unexpected and somewhat strange visit of an ex-Neapoli-
tan gendarme, accompanied by two or three *sbirri* of
the Roman police, who summoned him to enter without delay the band of Chiavone, saying that, in laying this injunction upon him, they were acting in
pursuance of superior orders. The unhappy shoemaker spent a very uncomfortable night in the stables
of the Palazzo Farnese (the property of the King of
Naples), in the society of many other poor fellows, who
had all shared the same fate. The next day he and
his companions in misfortune, still under the escort
of the Pontifical *sbirri*, were marched out of Rome,
and conducted across the Campagna, until they
reached the Neapolitan frontier, where they were
handed over to the different bands for which they had
been so summarily enlisted. During their long and
tiresome journey through the Papal dominions, the
unfortunate men composing this mournful procession
were frequently met by detachments of His Holiness's

gendarmes, who, although they stopped them at first,
allowed them to continue their journey on the simple
declaration of Corporal Pezzino, who was at the head
of the convoy: "*E roba del Re di Napoli!*"   (They
are the King of Naples's goods!)

These facts are taken from the answers made to
the official interrogatories which were addressed to
all the prisoners.   Without entirely relying on the
truth of their statements regarding the involuntary
nature of their enlistment, by insisting on which
they were evidently anxious to lessen their own responsibility, there is no doubt that they were encouraged by the Papal authorities, who not only did
not make the slightest attempt to stop them in their
passage through the Pontifical territory, at any place
between Rome and Alatri, but, on the contrary, even
helped them in every possible way.   It further appeared that the recruiting sergeants, as an incitement
to induce them to enlist, assured them that, besides
four carlini a day, they would have abundance
to eat and drink.   When they were introduced
to Chiavone's presence, this illusion was soon dis-
sipated by the frank avowal of the chief, who said
to them:

"You will have no other ordinary but ours, and
you will be paid when Francis II. comes back to
Naples."

These men, while in the service of the ex-King of
Naples, suffered great privations.   Such of them as
fell into the hands of the Piedmontese soldiers appeared to have suffered much from cold and want of
food, and, according to their own statement, rarely
had anything like a sufficiency of even the poorest
viands, sometimes   passing   whole   days,   after
their departure from Rome, in which they did not
taste food of any kind.   Even in Rome itself their
position was by no means the most desirable, their
relation to the French garrison of occupation being
such that it was requisite for them to act with the
utmost caution.   At that time, the French being at
Rome, as they still are, only for the protection of the
Holy See, the Bourbonist recruits were more than
once under the necessity of disguising themselves as
Pontifical gendarmes, in order to deceive the vigilance of the French.*   Having passed in this garb
unmolested before the French posts, they assumed
their Fra Diavolo garments only when they arrived
at the frontier.

The connivance of the Roman Government in the

* A letter, dated from Rome the 5th of September, and
addressed by a soldier of the old Bourbonist army, of the name
of Annibale Samcino, to a friend of his, Michole Jammazino,
a carpenter of Larino, province of Campobasso, contained
the following passage: "I am apparently in the gendarmerie
of the Pope, but in reality we are still paid by Francis II."

enlistment of troops for Francis II. being a matter on which no doubt can be entertained, the question has been much discussed to what extent the Roman Pontiff afforded them his countenance and protection. It was maintained by many that the brigands were not only paid with Peter's pence, but also that they were armed with Neapolitan muskets, handed over to the Pontifical Government by General de Goyon.* Whatever may be the truth of this assertion, it is a fact that .by the side of almost every dead brigand a musket bearing the Pontifical arms was found!

What the courts of Rome and Naples expected from an invasion conducted in such a manner, it is almost impossible to say.   If they anticipated a restoration, one can hardly credit the existence of such blindness not only to the signs of the times, but

---

* This took place in November, 1860. Capua had been taken, the Piedmontese had beaten the Bourbonists on the Garigliano, Gaëta was on the point of being besieged, when a Neapolitan division, mostly composed of cavalry, in order not to fall into the hands of the conquerors, crossed the frontier, and found refuge in the Papal States. The Piedmontese general, De Sonnaz, was in pursuit, but he was requested by the Commander-in-Chief of the French army, General de Goyon, not to go beyond the Pontifical lines. The Neapolitan division was then disbanded by the French, and the arms given up to the Papal Government.

also to the most recent facts of their own history.
If the Bourbonist dynasty, supported by eighty
thousand men, had been overthrown by a handful of
volunteers, how could they hope, in the presence of a
powerful and well-disciplined army like the Piedmontese, to reconquer the lost kingdom with a handful of
turbulent and ill-disciplined brigands? Strange as
it may seem, there were undoubtedly at Rome men
possessing great influence over the weak mind of
Francis II., who did believe in the possibility of such
a miracle. Ulloa, for example, was certain of the
final success of the cause to which he had devoted
himself.

There is no doubt that, in the prosecution of the
plan their leaders had conceived, they had it in their
power, weak as they were, to do a great deal of mischief.
In keeping the country in a state of agitation, in
throwing the population into constant anarchy and
disorder, they may have hoped to show either that
Victor Emmanuel could reign over the kingdom of
Naples no better than Francis II., or that the un-
interrupted state of disturbance prevalent throughout
South Italy was a proof of the attachment of the
people to the fallen dynasty. In obliging the Italian
Government to keep a large force in the southern
provinces, they may also perhaps have hoped to

compel the Government, perplexed by such difficulties, to leave the lines of the Mincio and the Po
undefended. And even supposing that any or all of these
objects were unattainable by them, they still had it in
their power, if there is any truth in the last word
addressed by a powerful ally to the Italian Government, to delay indefinitely the pacification of the
South, and thus adjourn *sine die* the evacuation of
Rome by the French. Be this, however, as it may,
conspiracy was in active existence, and spreading in
every direction. While the committee at Naples
were acting in an underhand manner in the dark,
conventicles of adepts were held openly in the
country, as well as in the town. The Cardinal-Arch-
bishop of Naples, Monsignor Riario Sforza, gave
political receptions in opposition to those of the
king's lieutenant. His residence was the rendezvous
of conspirators and reactionists. The cardinal himself, if he did not conspire actively, at least always
declined giving the Government the aid of that
salutary influence which, in virtue of his character
and office, he might have exercised, and constantly
kept aloof from association with those who were
anxiously considering by what means they might put
an end to the deplorable dissensions which were bath-
ing the country in blood.

But this was not all ; he went still further, sus-

pending *a divinis* every priest who had sung thanksgivings for those victories by which the cause of
Italian unity was advanced, or who had preached in
favour of the national independence. This suspen-
sion, an act of great cruelty, depriving of their livings
those on whom it was imposed, fell with particular
severity upon the poorer Catholic priests, from whom
it took away the right of celebrating mass, the only
means of existence possessed by many of them. The
consequence was that, in several cases, those who had
not conspired were compelled to do so, in order to
get the small allowance that enabled them to maintain
themselves in comparative poverty.

The priests, however, generally were opposed to the
Revolution. At Salerno, with the view of rousing the
popular indignation against the new Government, they
considered it advisable to stop a certain miracle which
I forget what good-natured saint, in testimony of the
interest that he still continued to take in the world
he had left, was in the habit of performing every year.
At Naples, indeed, they did not dare to go so far,
although they contrived to get up some new miracles
against Victor Emmanuel. One day, for instance, near
the Vicaria, seeing a great crowd assembled before a
chapel, the doors of which stood ajar, showing the
interior, which was splendidly illuminated, I looked
in, and beheld the fanatic mob, under the influence of

the wild excitement to which they had been roused,
crying, groaning, and stamping their feet. I asked a
devout old woman what it was that had roused the
multitude to such a pitch of excitement.

"It is," said she, turning fiercely to me, and
shaking her fists in my face, "that the Holy Virgin
has performed a miracle. The doors of the chapel
opened by themselves, and the interior, which the
moment before had been completely dark, suddenly
appeared effulgent with a blaze of dazzling light!"

"And what does that mean?" said I.

"It means that the Madonna hates the Piedmontese!" replied the charitable old soul.

By what process of reasoning she discovered
any connection between the two events, I am unable
to divine.

Many newspapers which had taken an active part
in the conspiracies of the day, preached a regular
Bourbonist crusade. While some of the more able
journals, the writers in which were most distinguished for their ability, acted with a certain
amount of caution, others openly defended the
cause of the Bourbons, and even went so far as to
print articles in praise of the brigands, throwing out
at the same time the greatest insults and the grossest
accusations against the Government. The Radicals
and the Mazzinians, violently opposed to the lieu-

tenancy, joined the reactionary press in that un-
generous attack. Although they rarely confined
themselves to truth in their hostility to Victor
Emmanuel and his counsellors, the party of the
priests encouraged them in their dishonourable conduct. If a Republican paper, *Il Popolo d'Italia*, for
instance, forged one day some monstrous calumny
against the Government, the next day it was sure to
be repeated by the clerical press.

Among the other Neapolitan journals there was
a wretched microscopical paper, the name of which I
have forgotten, which, among other absurdities, once
announced to its readers the approaching arrival of
Francis II. This was at the period when perhaps the greatest'mistakes were committed by the chiefs of the National
Party. Opposition was prevailing in every direction,
and especially among the so-called Party of Action,
which was kept entirely in the background by the
conciliatory system adopted by the Lieutenancy. In
their desire to unite, by a common purpose and aim,
the two great political parties—consisting of the moderate supporters of Francis II. on the one hand, and
the equally moderate supporters of a united Italy on the
other—they deeply wounded the Garibaldian party,
the only one really spontaneous, popular, and buoyant
with life that was left in that corrupt and rotten
country; for although in this, as in every other

political party, there was great difference of opinion,
and occasionally chaotic confusion, yet, taken as a
whole, it presented a strong and compact body,
animated by a great vital principle of action. The
followers of Garibaldi were so powerful that it was
necessary either to crush them or to come to terms
with them. The Government found it impossible to
overcome them, and in neglecting, therefore, to con-
ciliate a party so formidable, it committed a great
fault.

How often have I seen the impetuous spirits of
the Garibaldians roused by some imprudent measure
of the Government into such fury that, in their indignation, they were prepared to brave any hazard, and
even precipitate the country into all the horrors of an
internecine struggle! The Bourbonists, of course,
artfully embittered the popular resentment, professing
to pity Garibaldi with heart and soul for the slights,
real or supposed, to which he was exposed. In their
endeavours to increase the general discontent, and to
create a fatal division among the Liberal party, they
even pretended to hold the most advanced opinions,
many of them carrying the pretence of Liberalism so
far as to assume the character of apostles of Mazzini.
And yet, in spite of all these intrigues, Naples did
not move, for the national heart was sound. With
the exception of two or three demonstrations, which

were not considered so important as to require their repression, the capital of Southern Italy passed through
the long period of one year of troubles and revolution
without, to all external appearance, losing for a single
moment its usual peaceful aspect.   Naturally gay
and noisy, the town presented no sensible change—
all that attracted the attention of the stranger being
the fact that the Italian colours were everywhere
exhibited.   In vain did the papers use the most
violent language; in vain did the priests distribute
secretly the proclamations of Francis II. and Chiavone;
in vain did they circulate in all directions Bosco's
cartes de visite, with his photograph, and a very
edifying quatrain, announcing *urbi et orbi* his arrival
shortly, *colla spada e colla face*—with sword and fire;
in vain had discontent spread wider and wider, until,
owing to the mistakes of the Piedmontese Cabinet, it
had become general—a misfortune which is the necessary consequence of almost every revolution—in the
midst of all these agitations, changes, plots, and conspiracies, the great body of the Neapolitan people remained
unmoved, and could not be roused to take any step
against those who were working for the unity of
Italy.

It is but an act of justice to say so much, especially as the estimate of the Neapolitan population
generally prevalent in Europe is by no means so

favourable, and, in my opinion, is scarcely fair to them.
There is evidently among the people of that city
much good common sense, which has saved them
from many a perilous situation. From the 25th of
June, 1860, when they were abandoned by Francis
II., up to the present day, they have bravely endured
many evils, and, in their collective capacity, have
rarely committed any remarkable act of violence or
rebellion. During this most terrible crisis they have
always conducted themselves with a unanimity and
wisdom, that, if there were any foundation for the
unfavourable opinion so widely prevalent regarding
them, could never have been expected of such a population. They have more than once manifested their
opinions not only as spontaneously, but also as pacifi-
cally, as the inhabitants of any constitutional kingdom
of Europe. In imposing their will upon their masters, they have done so without deeds of violence;
and, strange to say, it has always been proved that
right and justice were on their side. Their dignified
attitude after the forced concessions of Francis II.,
prevented the accomplishment of those dangerous
designs which were in contemplation, and saved the
country not only from a new 15th of May, but also
from the terrible reaction which would have been its
unhappy result, as the horrors of the 15th of July
fully justify me in believing. In the coldness with

which they regarded the Bourbon line of princes, the
Neapolitan population suffered the fall of Francis II.
Their enthusiasm consecrated the success of Garibaldi.
At a later period they baffled Mazzini by their determined opposition to his visionary and impracticable
schemes. They even dared, at one moment, to resist
the will of their beloved Dictator, when they insisted
on the establishment of a regular government, founded,
as they unanimously desired, on popular suffrage.
Since the annexation they have avoided every cause
of discord, they have discouraged every attempt at revolt, and they have continually opposed the efforts of
the revolutionary party, with a political tact which has
preserved Naples to the rest of Italy. When it was
necessary to be severe, I have not spared the Neapolitans; and when I can, with perfect sincerity, praise
their wisdom and self-command, it is with the greatest
pleasure that I render them the homage of my admiration.

Another element which greatly contributed to save
the country was the National Guard. It has been the
fashion to laugh at that institution, but, at Naples, any
insinuation against it would be badly received. There
the National Guard is composed not of those simple
burghers who, their heads foolishly turned topsy-turvy
by the mere idea of wearing a smart military uniform,
swear that the soldier's life is the ideal of human hap-

piness, but of the flower of the youth of the country.
They displayed the greatest earnestness and enthusiasm
from the beginning, and as a body of soldiers they have
always excited the admiration of every military man.
They constantly did their duty with admirable self-
denial.   When Naples was for a moment without
troops and police, both the gendarmes and policemen
having abandoned their post, and the Garibaldians
being engaged before Capua, at a time, too, when the
royalist army was within two hours of the city, the
National Guard undertook the defence of the capital,
and, great as was the danger to which they were
exposed, never flinched in the discharge of their
military obligations.   On duty night and day for
two months, they guarded the fortresses, the barracks,
the military posts, and the Government buildings.
They kept faithful watch over the city during the
silent hours of night, small bodies of them patrolling
the streets at regular intervals.   They were always
to be found at their post, and even after having made
their appearance before Capua, so active were they
in their movements that they were again seen on
Sunday at the parade before the royal palace.
During two months these twelve thousand youths
sacrificed everything—home, business, pleasure—in
order to secure the tranquillity of the town, which it
is only the simple truth to say had never been so

well guarded. Although a perfect host of adventurers,
many of them of doubtful or indifferent character,
had found their way to Naples at that time, nevertheless so effective were these volunteers in their watch
and guard, that not a single theft or offence of any
kind was committed.

These patriotic young soldiers subjected themselves, with uncomplaining obedience, to the severest
trials. When sent to the northern provinces of
Italy, they marched thither with the greatest alacrity.
When summoned, at a moment's notice, to proceed
against assassins and brigands, they met, fought, and
conquered them with unshrinking fortitude. Never
murmuring, never hesitating, never remonstrating,
they performed all the duties of soldiers with the
steadiness, resolution, and courage of veterans.
Commanded by a man of indefatigable zeal, General
Tupputi, they persevered in their noble task with
admirable self-devotion, no complaint being ever
heard from their lips, although, in order to secure
the safety of the city and its inhabitants, they were
at that time often called out for many days and
nights in succession. The state of feeling between
them and the regular army was everything that could
be desired. Far from feeling any of that jealousy
with which volunteer forces too often regard regular
troops, they took every opportunity of manifesting

their sympathy for the latter, associating with them
on the most friendly terms, and ever displaying the
utmost readiness to assist them in the discharge of
every duty. The Neapolitan National Militia, in
those days of trouble, exposed themselves to peril
over and over again with unhesitating alacrity; and
should it some day again be deemed necessary to
summon them to take the field against the enemies of
their country, they will assuredly, judging from their
past conduct, be found ready to do their duty like
veterans.

Order was thus successfully preserved, not only at
Naples, but everywhere throughout Southern Italy.
The National Guard, seconded by the good common
sense of the populations of the smaller towns and provinces, prevailed everywhere against those who were
desirous of fomenting tumult and disturbance. Since
the time of the reaction at Venosa and Melfi, the enemies of the great Italian cause have not succeeded in
rousing one single important district. It was said that
the brigands had proposed an attack against Cosenza
on the 13th of July, but they certainly never attempted such an exploit.

It is true that many small unprotected villages,
where the bandits had no serious opposition to dread,
suffered from their ravages; but this was at a time
when the district was under the lieutenancy of Count

San Martino, who, though not for want of ability,
failed in his task of pacifying the country. Following
out a system of conciliation, he was averse to making
war on the brigands, considering that they might be
more effectually subdued by moral force—an excellent idea, perhaps, in theory, but, in its application,
unfortunately too often proving a failure. At one
time he appears to have had an idea of carrying out his
plan by a combined system of moral and physical
force. He asked the central Government for sixty
battalions of regular troops, in order to make an
extensive and searching battue all over the Neapolitan
provinces. With this force he proposed to sweep
the brigands from the plains, and drive them to the
mountains, where, when they found themselves invested on all sides by the troops, he considered it
would be a matter of no great difficulty to bring them
to terms. Closely pressed on every side, threatened
by all the horrors of winter, utterly destitute of
provisions, tormented by hunger and cold, he concluded that it would be easy, by the promise
of their lives, and the assurance of providing
for them some honest means of livelihood, to
induce them to surrender. If this plan had
been anything better than it appeared in theory,
it would have been utterly impossible for the Government to spare sixty battalions from the northern

frontiers, for the purpose of attempting to carry it
into execution.

A precious time elapsed in useless negotiations and
discussions between Naples and Turin; and in the
meanwhile, reaction, with the aid of brigandage, spread
frightfully in all the southern provinces, a circumstance
at which, considering the state of Italy, there is
little reason for surprise. Times were very hard,
bread was unusually dear, no work was to be obtained.
While the brigands lived in luxury and ease, in which
they were enabled to indulge by means of violence
and plunder, many honourable and good men were
unable to procure the merest necessaries of life.
The priests, in these circumstances, incited the ignorant countrymen and villagers to robbery, assuring
them that it was for the sake of a holy cause, in
which, since the inauguration of the system of conciliatory measures, they did not even encounter much
danger. The clergy, too, in order to inspire with
greater self-confidence the unreasoning dupes whom
they deceived, had spread the report that Garibaldi
was dead, and that Francis II. was coming back
without delay. The police found upon Bourbonist
spies particular instructions regarding the false news
they were to spread throughout the country, to the
effect that Francis II. was on the point of crossing the
frontiers, that the Austrians would soon be on the

south side of the Po, and that the Emperor Napoleon,
yielding, after a long resistance, to the influence of
the clerical party, was now acting in common with
the enemies of Revolution, *the only means left to him
of saving his throne.*

On the person of one of these Bourbonist agents,
named Spadafora, arrested in Calabria, was found a
manifest announcing that Count Cavour, in consequence of his private correspondence having been
given up to Austria, had destroyed himself by poison,
and that the Piedmontese generals had been compelled to surrender Ancona to an Anglo-Russian
fleet, into whose hands all their material of war had
fallen; that every night such numbers of wounded
men belonging to the invading army from the North
were secretly conveyed from Naples, that ere long the
few who remained, being unable to maintain their
position, would be compelled, for their own preserva-
tion, to return to Turin; and finally, that before
September Italy would be entirely reconstituted, every
state in it being restored to the position in which it
was before 1859.

These and other absurdities of the same nature
were spread among the ignorant populations of the
country, and money was largely distributed, in order
to induce a more willing belief in such statements, in
which, unfortunately, they only too well succeeded.

In the distracted state of the country terror was one
of the most powerful allies of the Bourbons. If the
inhabitants of districts invaded by brigands had shut
themselves up in their houses when the aggressors
appeared, they would have been turned out of them,
their dwellings would have been ransacked, and they
themselves killed. Knowing that their only hope of
safety lay in submission, they at once yielded to the
aggressive bands, and even received them with welcome.

It has been said somewhere that the populations of
the Italian States never fraternised with the brigands—
a statement which, as far as the larger towns and bor-
oughs were concerned, is no doubt true, but it is also a
fact that the isolated and defenceless hamlets in many
instances surrendered at once to the invaders. The degraded mob of some localities did not hesitate even to
give assistance to the brigands, by pointing out to them
the houses of the rich. The National Guard of these
small places, consisting sometimes of only six or
seven men, were invariably disarmed without difficulty.

In one or two cases great cowardice on the one side
and boldness on the other assured the success of the
bandits in their expeditions. At Vallerotonda (Terra
di Lavoro) the National Guard were so completely
demoralized by terror, that they gave up a hundred

and sixty muskets to seventeen brigands! The invaded
districts had often no authority to look up to except that of the syndics, and these officials were
generally destitute of all real power. During the
period of conciliation the mayor of a place that had
received the brigands, if called to account for his
conduct, incurred no penalty more severe than that
of dismissal ; whilst, had he dared to refuse to admit
the Bourbonist bands, he would undoubtedly have
been burnt alive in his own house. Between the
two evils, it was natural enough that he should choose
the minor.

The proceedings between the municipal authorities
and the brigands were sometimes of an amusingly hypo-
critical character. After every house in a village had
been plundered and ransacked, a sort of arrangement
like the following was often come to between the
mayor and the chief of the assassins. The representative of municipal authority would beg to inform
Messrs. Chiavone and Co. it was now time for them
to go, as his duty required him to send for the Piedmontese. The representative of His Majesty Francis
II., thus warned, would graciously signify his assent
to the humble mayor's request, and decamp with his
followers. When the Piedmontese were at length
summoned, of course not a single brigand was to be
found, and thanks were returned to the syndic for the

energy and prudence of the measures by which
he had succeeded in defeating and routing the invaders.

When such was the policy of the authorities in
various districts, it is not to be wondered at that,
under the Lieutenancy, brigandage became almost
general throughout the Neapolitan territory. It has
been stated that at that time only five provinces out
of sixteen (including Beneventum) suffered from the
invasions of the brigands—a statement which, though
stamped with official authority, it is my painful duty to
contradict. If the importance of what the reactionary
party were pleased to call a general insurrection has
been grossly exaggerated by certain organs of a hostile
press, on the other hand, the Ministerial circulars, in
their too zealous eagerness, fell into the other excess,
by making statements very far under the truth when
they declared that the number of provinces overrun
by the brigands was so small. It may be that
they only desired to say that five provinces had
suffered more than the rest of the country from
the system of reaction fostered and protected by the
presence of the brigands; for it is a fact that cannot
be disputed, that when General Cialdini arrived
almost all the south of the peninsula was more or less
infested by these bandits. They were found in the
Abruzzi and in Terra di Lavoro, which was hardly

pacified by a brilliant expedition of General Pinelli.
They had invaded Basilicata and Capitanata—and
they had made their way also into the provinces of
Salerno, Molise, and Beneventum.

Even the neighbourhood of Naples itself was not
safe at that time. One band of brigands was roving
about the well-known hills of Camaldoli; another lay
hidden in the mountains of Somma, close by Mount Vesuvius; and a third between Mola and Cancello. The
latter fired almost every day at the trains running
along the line of railway; and when they captured any
of the railway guards, demanded very heavy ransoms
before they would restore them to liberty. On the
23rd of June, they attacked the station of Cancello,
which they plundered, carrying off more than seventy-
five ducats. Gennaro Ferrara, the master of a coffee-
house in the neighbourhood, who endeavoured to go
out to call for help, was taken and killed. A few
days afterwards the assassins entered the same shop,
and seating themselves quietly, asked for something
to drink, and were instantly served by the waiters
with every mark of respect; for it is needless to say
so great was the terror of the latter, that not one had
the courage or the presence of mind to call in the
police. When some customers asked one of them if
those fellows were not the murderers of his master, he
answered at once with what he no doubt considered

praiseworthy caution, that he did not know anything about it.

The brigands performed a deed of still greater audacity at Caserta, a place which is to Naples what Windsor is to London. The brother of Cipriano La Gala, the old felon, chief of a gang of bandits, and a Bourbonist general of much greater influence and importance than Chiavone, was confined in the prison of Caserta. The bandit, making up his mind to deliver him from his bonds, selected among his subordinates some men of resolution, directing them to assume the costume of National Guards—a uniform which he himself also put on. Under this disguise, the fearless brigand one night presented himself with incredible courage at the door of the prison, dragging a man after him by the collar. "Here," he said, "is a criminal I have just arrested and brought to be locked up." The keepers suspecting no treachery, the doors were immediately opened, and the supposed detachment of the National Guard, with their commander, were admitted. As soon as they were all within the walls of the prison, the brigands, falling upon the keepers, handcuffed them, and delivered not only Cipriano's brother, but also the other imprisoned felons, who, no doubt from inclination as well as gratitude, to a man joined the band. Some real National Guards, who by chance happened to be near at hand, alarmed too late, endeavoured to stop them on their departure from the prison, but without success. The band, after this adventure considerably increased, left Caserta, and once more retired to the mountains.

These pages would be extended to an interminable length if I were to transcribe all the remarkable facts concerning the brigands that have come to my knowledge. While I am writing this, I have under my eyes a very useful paper, prepared for me in the offices of the police at Naples—a catalogue of all the official documents preserved on the subject of the disturbances caused by the brigands, and a succinct view of their contents. I extract from this voluminous collection one or two pages, which, it is to be remembered, contain only a summary of the reports sent during the month of July, 1861, by the prefect of Foggia, about what occurred in the province entrusted to him. The real bearing of some important facts relating to the history of brigandage may be gathered from this document. If not a very elegant piece of literature, it is at least authentic, and is now for the first time given to the public.

July 1st.—*Casalnuovo.*—Murder committed by the brigands upon two men belonging to the farm called Finocchito. A band of brigands levy the following ransoms—upon Giuseppantonio d'Alessio

a sum of 2,000 ducats; Pasquale d'Elisi, 6,000
ducats; Gumaro Cono, 600 ducats; Francesco
d'Ondes, 500 ducats; Giuseppe Ferrecchia, 200
ducats, threatening to burn the fruits of the harvest if
these fines were not speedily paid.   From the Syndic
they requested a large supply of clothes, and a
remittance of 3,000 ducats, under the threat of burning his crop and his brother's.

July 3rd.—*Sansevero.*—Three brigands steal a
horse belonging to a cattle-dealer, after which they
attack a public mail-coach.

Torremaggiore.—The brigands kill some horses
belonging to a man called Tommaso Pensano.   They
impose a ransom of 400 ducats upon Stefano Cataldo,
and destroy a quantity of wheat, straw, and other provisions in a farm designated by the name of Ripalta.

July 5th.—*Sansevero.*—Four brigands seize Don
Ferdinando Parisi, and impose upon him a ransom of
60 ducats.   They release him for 30.   The same
day some disbanded soldiers steal horses and arms
belonging to a certain Don Paolo del Sordo.   Ten
brigands hoist a Bourbonist flag, and exact from
Don Luigi Trotta a fine of 300 ducats; they only
receive 48 ducats, but they make up the former sum
by stealing everything they can lay hold of.   Finally,
six other brigands deprive Don Antonio Gelanio of
some arms and many valuable articles.

Serracapriola.—Twenty-four brigands steal a certain number of horses belonging to Pasquale Carita.

Borini.—Six brigands carry away the muskets of a detachment of the National Guard.

July 6th.—*Biccaro.*—Five brigands steal all the stores and the horses of a farm belonging to Lorenzo Goduti, shooting indiscriminately at every one in their way.

Casalvecchio.—The most terrible brigandage prevails with all its horrors. Robberies, impositions, men carried away and ransomed—many of them shot.

July 7th.—*Torremaggiore.*—Three brigands steal many head of cattle belonging to Felice di Pampo and Pietro Inglese. Three other bandits seize Don Alfonso Ferrante, and levy upon him a ransom of 3,000 ducats.

July 8th.—*Cerignola.*—The brigands make a long resistance against the public authorities.

Castelnuovo.—Some brigands seize and carry away a certain Pettinario, and only release him on payment of 360 ducats, besides the surrender of many other things of value.

July 9th.—*Tenimento-di-Pietra.*—A band of brigands levy an enormous contribution upon one of the canons of the cathedral, Don Paolo Leo.

Torremaggiore.—Theft of a horse, and imposition of a ransom of 5,000 ducats on Don Vicenzo La Medica. Similar events occur at Lucera the same day. A ransom of 4,000 ducats is exacted from Don Tommaso La Medica, besides a large requisition of arms and ammunition.

Lucera.—Twenty brigands steal the cattle belonging to Giuseppe Montedoro.

July 10th.—*Ischitella.*—Invasions of brigands in several farms, plunder, assaults, &c. The National Guard arrives in time to disperse the aggressors.

Apricena.—A ransom of 1,000 ducats is imposed upon Filipo Fiorentino, and he is released upon payment of 336 ducats.

Sansevero.—A ransom of 4,000 ducats is imposed by nine brigands upon Pasquale Patruno, and he is released for 230 ducats.

July 12th.—*Carlantino.*—Invasion of that borough by a numerous band of brigands, who make the priests sing a thanksgiving in the cathedral in their honour. They proceed thence in another direction, laying waste the surrounding country with fire and sword.

July 13th—*Castelluccio (Val Maggiore).*—Some brigands attack and murder Don Michele Agresti in his own house.

July 14th.—*Sannicandro.*—The harvest on the estates of M. Eugenio Pisani is entirely destroyed, for not having paid the ransom the brigands had levied upon him. The loss is calculated at above 2,000 ducats.

July 18th.—*Foggia.*—The most ferocious brigand-age is carried on in the whole province. Excesses of every kind are committed.

Cerignola.—A considerable number of brood mares are stolen on the estates of the Duke of Bisaccia.

July 19th.—*Serracapriola.*—Don Aurelio Petroni is murdered by the brigands.

July 21st.—*Sansevero.*—Giuseppe Mannelli, Salvatore Codipietro, and some other brigands, burn the harvest of Don Francesco de Pasquale, and destroy all his agricultural implements, for not having made payment of a ransom of 2,000 ducats.

July 22nd.—*Sannicandro.*—The brigands lay on Don Vincenzo Vocale an imposition of 300 ducats. He can only pay 100—the brigands then plunder his house.

Sansevero.—500 ducats are levied upon Pasquale Petracchione, and he is only released after having paid 200. Four sailing-boats of Giovinazzo are entirely ransacked. The loss suffered by the owners is valued at no less than 2,400 ducats.

Montesantangelo.—Bartolomeo Scarano is murdered by some disbanded Bourbonist soldiers, on the ground that he belonged to the band of volunteers assembled for the repression of the reactionary movements at Vico in the month of April.

July 24th.—*Torremaggiore.*—Many horses are

o 2

stolén from M. Bocola. Don Pasquale Tusi is taxed
with a ransom of 1,600 ducats—the brigands besides
kill all the cattle in his farm-yard.

The list of the deeds of violence committed by
these armed ruffians does not go further for that
month. Troops having at last been dispatched, order
was not without difficulty re-established in the province. The importance of this official statement is
too striking to need any further illustration. Though
short and succinct, it is so clear that it saves me the
trouble of continuing further the monotonous narrative of the crimes committed by the bands of brigands,
either under the influence of political motives, or from
the desire of plunder, almost all over the old Neapolitan kingdom. The same story was everywhere repeated, only with the difference that in some places
certain bands distinguished or disgraced themselves
by more than usual violence. Such, for example,
was the case in Pricipato Ultra. On the arrival of
General Cialdini this province was found in all the
excitement and horror of a most savage reaction.
Driven from Terra di Lavoro by the skill and energy
of General Pinelli, the brigands had flocked round
Avellino with a sort of desperate and revengeful rage.
About sixty bandits, followed by a considerable number
of disbanded soldiers, and a host of peasants, recruited

among the scum of the country, and armed with
axes and scythes, fell one day, the 7th of July, upon
Montefalcione, with cries of "Viva Francesco II. !"
which were always the prelude of the most awful
deeds of violence.   They invaded Montemiletto,
Candida, Chiusano, and many other localities.   Avellino itself was threatened ; some suspicious-looking
persons, whose sinister countenances almost foreboded
scenes of violence and murder, having been observed
roaming about the streets.   The municipality were
almost permanently in council, that they might be
ready at any time to provide for the public safety; and
the governor, M. De Luca, a very clever and active
man, implored the Government to send some reinforcements of regular troops for the rescue of his
province, menaced on every side—a request which
they made with but little avail, for the Government
had few, if any, troops to spare.

In the beginning of the period of reaction the
country provided for its own defence.   One of the
captains of the National Guard, Carmine Tarantino, a
young man of thirty, professor of one of the royal
colleges,   and   the   Reverend   Arciprete   Leone,
syndic of Montemiletto, who had already lost his
father, his brother, and all his family in a preceding
engagement, where the brigands had been victorious,
marched, with only *five* soldiers of the line, and a

few National Guards, in the direction of Montefalcione, which, not being strong enough, they could not attack. Going back, therefore, to the town, they es-tablished themselves in the Palazzo Fierimonte. On the night of the 8th of July, Montemiletto was entered by the brigands, sixty in number, all well armed. They received, on their arrival, a reinforce-ment of four hundred peasants, and such support as they could derive from the sympathy of the mob.

This bloodthirsty multitude attacked the Palazzo Fierimonte to the usual cry of " Viva Francesco II. !" Tarantino and his companions, knowing that in such an unequal struggle they must die, but determined to sell their lives as dearly as possible, answered with a loud cry of " Viva Italia !" The struggle, a useless one, for it could lead to no beneficial result, was long and cruel. The mob set the house on fire, women and children, with horrible eagerness, bringing the fuel that was necessary to feed the flames. The front door, which was of oak, resisted the action of the fire for a long time, but the bandits, in their impatience, broke it down with axes and a sort of improvisated ram.

The scene of horror that ensued when the ferocious mob disappeared through the yawning breach into the crumbling edifice was such that one recoils from the task of describing it. Tarantino, the Arciprete, and some women and children who were in the place, were slaughtered with monstrous cruelty. One of the soldiers was shot, and two men who had cried " Viva Italia !" were dragged into the adjoining churchyard and there buried alive under a heap of putrefied corpses. Three other soldiers of the line were taken to Montefalcione, where they were ordered to shoot those of their brethren who had come to the relief of the invaded country. Two of them who refused were immediately shot. The third, pretending to accept the office imposed upon him, rushed against the Italians, as if with the design of attacking them, instead of which he entered their ranks, and though many a shot was aimed at him by the enraged reactionists, he escaped, as if by a miracle, unwounded. No fewer than seventeen persons were barbarously slain within the walls of the Palazzo Fierimonte. I shall not dwell upon the wanton ferocity with which these assassins committed the deeds of violence and blood to which they were incited by their commander. A certain Vincenzo Petruzziello, of Montemiletto, the man who killed Tarantino, was afterwards taken and shot in his turn. Before his death this felon chief confessed that his band was maintained with money that came from Rome—a statement which, with the other facts I have mentioned, is supported by an official memoir addressed by M. Ferrara, Vice-Governor of the Province of Avellino, to the Secretary of the Home Department at Naples, an unpublished document which I was allowed to peruse.

In the meanwhile, the Governor, M. De Luca, had left in the morning with the National Guard, and, having met the brigands not far from Candida, had defeated them. After traversing San Potito and Parolise, and re-taking Chiusano, he attacked Montefalcione, but was repulsed by the mob, who opposed their assailants with stones and boiling water. So furious, indeed, was their attack, that he was obliged to seek shelter out of the town in a convent, where he and his escort, closely besieged by the rebels, nearly fell into their hands. Luckily enough, however, he was delivered on the 10th by the Garibaldi Hungarian Legion * garrisoned at Nocera. In obedience to orders received from Turin, they had been sent with all possible speed to the rescue of that oppressed province, after the deliverance of the Governor of which they re-entered Montefalcione with him almost without a struggle. An act of violent

---

* This Hungarian Legion, first formed by Garibaldi at Naples, was recruited from those Hungarians who had deserted the Austrian Army in 1859, and who had taken part in the Sicilian expedition of 1860. Consisting for the most part of the division commanded by the Hungarian General Türr, it was placed under the immediate orders of General Eber, so well known as a soldier, and a literary man. After the disbandment of the Garibaldian Army, this Legion passed to the service of the Italian Government.

reprisal, however, took place, for thirty brigands
who had fortified themselves in a house were all
killed in the struggle. But it is only justice to
add, that such deeds of vengeance ceased with the
rage of the combat which had inspired them.
In that rural district where the whole population,
with very few exceptions, had risen in revolt—all the
Liberals having been either killed or expelled—the
only severe measure in the way of repression was the
death of five of the ringleaders, and the disarmament
of·the population and the National Guard of the
province, in whom, after the events that had taken
place, perfect confidence could no longer be placed.
On the advance of the Hungarians, four thousand
peasants and brigands fled from Montemiletto and
concealed themselves in the woods and mountains.
Nowhere was any resistance offered to the advance of
the troops, reaction being to all appearance completely
suppressed. The Governor, De Luca, went back to
Avellino on the 13th of July, preceding a detachment
of troops, who escorted a convoy of forty prisoners.
On his entrance into the town, he was received by the
grateful population with a regular ovation, a mark of
honour well deserved by one who had acted with so much
courage and decision. During these troubles General
Cialdini arrived at Naples as the new King's Lieutenant.

CHAPTER VI.

CHAPTER VI.

HENCEFORTH my task becomes an easy one, and I
shall proceed with greater speed. As the reader who
has had patience enough to follow my narrative may
have already formed a just idea of Neapolitan brigandage, I will no longer tire him by the narration
of a series of facts which present no other variety
than that of a change of names. It must be painful
to read of endless acts of violence committed on proprietors, and the infliction of heavy ransoms, the
payment of which was often enforced in blood on the unhappy residents of invaded villages. In addition to
these, their most frequent exploits, the only events we
read of in connection with the brigands are the disarmament of small detachments of National Guards, the sub-
stitution of the Bourbonist colours for the white cross of
Savoy, the conflagration of private houses, the throwing
open of prisons for the escape of felons, and finally their
precipitate flight at the first approach of the troops,

whom, even with a considerable superiority of numbers on their side, they rarely dared to meet. Such, with little variety, were the events daily happening during the period of reaction in Southern Italy. There are still, however, a few facts connected with the subject of brigandage, which I should not be justified in passing over altogether without notice.

One of these is the campaign of General Cialdini, whose march it is not always easy to follow. This distinguished general has displayed the greatest ability and courage in every duty he has been called upon to discharge. Although only forty-seven years of age, he has already attained the highest position a soldier can reach in Italy, having been invested with the first dignity in the military hierarchy, and having occupied the post of king's lieutenant at Naples. When he was only seventeen he was already fighting for liberty in the Romagne, and he has since taken part in the war in Spain, in the first Lombard outbreak in 1848, in the contest in the Crimea, and in the Tyrol in the year 1859. It was he, as all know, who defeated Lamoricière, and took Ancona, Gaëta, and Messina. In consequence of his disagreements with Garibaldi, his name was by no means so popular in the South as it might otherwise have been. When Cialdini came to Naples, the enterprise which he was expected to carry out to a successful issue was by no

means an easy one. The work that lay before him
was the destruction of brigandage in almost all the
provinces of Southern Italy, the annihilation of those
conspiracies in the capital which spread defiance and
discontent throughout the country, and the prosecution of the war with a vigour which would revive
public spirit, attach by the bond of obedience the
populations of the South to the new Government,
render the idea of Italian unity popular among the
lower classes, and make Italy a nation not only strong
and united at home, but trusted and respected abroad.
It was evident that the Peninsular kingdom could never
be a great and powerful state while the fair regions of
the South remained in a condition of chronic agitation,
while a desperate civil war was undermining the
prosperity of the provinces, and while the troops
of Victor Emmanuel were almost regarded as a foreign
garrison in a country which they occupied but could
not subdue.   This great task of the reconstruction of
Italy, hitherto far from being successfully carried out,
Cialdini was sent to effect.   He accepted the mission, devoting from the first day all his energies to
its accomplishment.   His proclamation to the Neapolitans was an able production.   In asking their co-
operation, he said that nothing could be done without their countenance and assistance ; and he announced his determination to strike at the root of the

matter by the total eradication of the whole mis-
chievous brood of agitators.

The consequences of this explicit declaration were
at once apparent. The fear with which the address
of the king's lieutenant struck the disturbers of the
national peace was of inestimable benefit to a government not yet firmly established. The noisy and
turbulent opposition considered it prudent to assume
the virtue of discretion, even though they had it not.
A few penny papers, it is true, still continued to
howl out their discontent with the new order of
things, but, with the sanction of the people themselves, their editors were arrested and fined, the journals were suppressed, and the restless concocters of conspiracies received a decisive blow. A Bourbonist
meeting, which was discovered at Posilippo,* was
followed by the arrest of twenty of their leading men
at Portici. In consequence of the well-conducted
perquisition which was immediately ordered, the
police were enabled to lay hold of no fewer than twenty
superior officers of the old army, together with a
great many influential prelates, several pontifical
Zouaves, and a few French legitimists, who, during
their residence in the country, had been doing much
mischief underhand. All these were taken to the

* The documents relating to this conspiracy will be found in
the second volume.

frontiers. M. de Christen was arrested; and a bold
decision, at the mere proposal of which everyone had
previously hesitated, was at once adopted; the greatest dignitary of the Neapolitan clergy was ordered
to quit the country, and the population who, thirteen
years before, had shed tears on the banishment of the
Jesuits, now hissed contemptuously after the carriage
in which their cardinal was departing.

The blow thus struck against the Bourbonist party
was a deadly one, but the party of action was still
left, strong, powerful, and dangerous, for it was a
popular one. Sometimes persecuted and sometimes
despised by the ministerial coterie, whose conduct in
respect to it was anything but wise, it was still in
vigorous life, increasing fast in influence and importance, thanks to the errors of the central power, and
to the general discontent prevailing among the population. The last elections had shown what influence
this party, in spite of the efforts made by the
Government to weaken and destroy it, still exercised
over the masses. The service they had rendered
under the dictatorship of Garibaldi was the great
secret of their power. Having always been in correspondence with the hero of Caprera, they pretended
that the task of continuing the work of regeneration
commenced by him was assigned to them. Their
opposition, therefore, to the authority of Cialdini is

easily understood. A party whose creed was composed of the most advanced political principles, could not be expected to accept willingly the idea of a military autocracy; and as Cialdini for the time was regarded by them as the personification of such a system, they were his most bitter enemies. In the course of events, however, a result ensued which no one could have anticipated, for these men finally became the General's most sanguine supporters.

Cialdini had, from the very beginning, sought their co-operation. Instead of dreaming of a reconciliation between reactionists and liberals, an idea which never could have been realized, he made an appeal to every true patriot, calling upon all the friends of Italy to join in the formation of a national coalition. Surrounding himself with men of the most advanced opinions, Garibaldians, and even republicans, he associated himself with them against the common foe, and was bold enough, when they hesitated to join him, to court their co-operation by making concessions. Thus, for example, notwithstanding the importance of the past services of M. Spaventa, their *bête noire*, who had passed ten years in prison during the tyrannical rule of Ferdinand II., Cialdini sanctioned the retirement of that eminent patriot. Again, when, moved by an unworthy spirit of faction, a demonstration was got up against the members of Parliament

who had supported the cabinet of Turin, Cialdini did
not make any attempt, at the time, to prevent what
was really a very harmless outburst; but when, a
little later, these agitators considered themselves
powerful enough, under the pretext of the national
defence, to form an armed legion of their own, the
general put a check upon what he considered an im-
politic movement, by condescending to accept their
co-operation for the good of the country, only, however, on the express condition that this armed body
should, at all times, receive their orders only from
him.   It is not to be supposed, however, that this conduct implied any unwillingness on Cialdini's part to
accept the services of the National Militia and of
volunteers, for, on the contrary, it was one of the
first acts of his administration to urge the national
armament on a greater scale than had ever been
attempted before. He ordered the mobilization of
two companies of National Guards for every district
of the country—companies which, formed by volun-
tary enlistment, proved to be an excellent institution,
and so popular, that many districts, instead of two,
were able to raise three or four of them. Fourteen
thousand men were thus gathered together for the
service of the country.   Whether there was any real
necessity for such an additional draft is very
doubtful, and, in all probability, the regular troops

would have been amply sufficient for the emergencies of the moment.

The organization of this military force was a measure prompted by a political consideration of great importance. The Government was anxious to prove to Europe that the army was not fighting alone, but that it and the people were united by a common interest ; and that so many troops had not been summoned forth to crush the so-called spontaneous movements of the population, but, on the contrary, to fight with them for the complete redemption of their country.

It was one great merit of Cialdini's that he was not indisposed to flatter the feelings of the people by paying homage to their favourite hero. When the municipality proposed to make arrangements for the solemn celebration of the anniversary of Garibaldi's glorious entrance on the 7th of September, the king's lieutenant was the first to applaud the idea. He even congratulated the town-council in the name of of his royal master, and in his own, "for," as he said in a proclamation issued on that occasion, "the arrival at Naples of the celebrated dictator, before whom a powerful army, and a dynasty which during successive reigns had made itself odious by its tyranny, had fled, was the most admirable event that courage and sagacity had ever accomplished, and one the consequences of which were amongst the most wonderful recorded in modern history."

Courage and sagacity! These two words are very
eloquent—especially in the mouth of one like Cialdini.
People are apt to admire in their fellow-creatures
the qualities they are conscious of in themselves.
Without meaning it, Cialdini, in praising Garibaldi,
was uttering his own panegyric. The man who, after
he had come to Naples, succeeded beyond expecta-
tion in the task he had undertaken, was, like the
great national chief, simple and straightforward, and
soon became almost as popular. Not to speak of the
people in general, who willingly submitted to him,
both the recalcitrant Bourbonists and the discontented patriots finally acknowledged his authority.
It is true that he did not succeed in entirely extirpat-
ing brigandage, for in a country like Italy, where the
bandits were almost universally befriended by the
peasantry, such an exploit was, we may venture to say,
almost impossible. How could a general ever be sure
that he had subdued an enemy who always lay hidden,
was constantly in ambush—at one moment buried in
the depths of a wood, the next showing himself
for an instant on an inaccessible mountain, and then
disappearing as if by enchantment as soon as the
exhausted troops draw near him? Foreigners have
very seldom examined this question with impartiality.
The French in Algeria, the Russians in the Caucasus,
and the English in India, with all their power, have

not found it easy work to maintain their respective empires in the midst of hostile populations.

General Manhès, it is true, was very successful in exterminating brigandage, but he was aided by the season in which he carried on his campaign, the depth of winter, when the brigands are unable to find shelter in the leafless woods, or food on the bare mountain sides. General Cialdini was compelled to act at a different season of the year, for it was neither convenient nor advisable to allow the country to be the prey of these lawless bands till the severity of the winter had driven them from the recesses where they concealed themselves. His first important measure was to interrupt the communications between the different bands, by entirely separating them from each other. To this end he ordered detachments of his troops to occupy that part of the country that lies between Avellino and Foggia, while, at the same time, by re-establishing regular communications with the Adriatic, he perfectly isolated the brigands of the extreme south.

By the adoption of these prudent measures he did not find it very difficult to destroy the bands that had taken refuge in Calabria, and particularly in the district of Cotrone, a noted nest of robbers in Southern Italy. The proprietors themselves, joining in the campaign, went at the head of their armed

peasantry in pursuit of the brigands, for, in that part
of the country, the internecine strife had proved but
the pretext for a socialist revolution. The poor had
risen against all who, being able to afford the luxury
of "tail-coats," were designated in these provinces by
the name of " galantuomini," and who were regarded
by these demoralized populations, in their ignorance,
as the natural victims of their rapacious instincts.
Hence the comparison between Victor Emmanuel,
the king " galantuomo," who, in their imagination,
was the sovereign of all who were respectably clad,
and Francis II., the king of the ragged, the monarch
of the Lazzaroni, whom they hailed with enthusiastic
vivas.

The brigands of Calabria had been tracked and
beaten by the landowners themselves, and those who
were lucky enough to escape could only find a refuge
in the impenetrable woods of La Sila. But in the
central and northern provinces, owing to the neighbourhood of Rome, brigandage had assumed a political
bearing, and was becoming more dangerous every day.
The thieves of Avellino, having invaded the province
of Beneventum, had taken possession of fifteen
abandoned hamlets, which they had converted into a
strong encampment. Colonel Negri, who had been
sent against them, succeeded only by the utmost zeal
and energy in the mission that had been confided to

him. By his activity the brigands were dislodged from their haunts and compelled to retire towards the mountains of Matese in the far north. General Pinelli—who, at the same time, with his flying columns, had made a regular battue in the vast plains by which Nola is surrounded—had succeeded in driving before him those pretended royalists who, though, in the moments of their greatest military ardour, they had never aimed at any higher exploit than that of shooting at railway trains, had yet been for a long time the terror of the country. After he had accomplished this task with his usual rapidity and bravery, General Pinelli, with a few Bersaglieri, embarked one morning with great mystery, and immediately set sail for the furthest eastern shore of the peninsula, where he landed. This young and dashing officer here began a series of rapid and daring operations, in which all the great military qualities by which he was distinguished were eminently displayed. The results of this brief campaign were highly important. By the vigour of the measures taken against the brigands, and the capture of four hundred who had committed, unmolested, every sort of horror, the inhabitants of that distant and neglected point of the peninsula were convinced that the Government was determined at once to put down reaction, whatever form it might assume.

In the sanguinary annals of this fearful struggle the brigands of this part of the country had acquired a sad celebrity for the horrid atrocities which they had committed. In those isolated districts, unprotected by troops, massacre, plunder, and incendiarism were everyday events. The savage character of the population is revealed in the following statement made in a letter written by a priest :—" Troppicione, his son, and Giovannicola Spina were killed—and they ate a piece of the flesh of the latter." Can this be true? some incredulous reader may be inclined to ask ; to which question I can reply by answering that I have not only read the statement myself, but have had it confirmed from many other quarters, with details of such atrocity that it is impossible to publish them.

If I refer to one other horrible story illustrative of the ferocious character of these Southern brigands, my object is to justify the severe measures of repression adopted by Government, which, though only resorted to in cases of absolute necessity, were yet often severely criticised by the enemies of Italy.

On the 7th of August some brigands, who had been summoned together by five canons and another priest, invaded Pontelandolfo, a little village in the mountains on the right side of Cerreto. Received

with shouts of joy by the brutal mob, they first
joined a religious procession; on coming back from
which they raised a great disturbance, in the course
of which they destroyed the municipal hall, the
police station, and the principal shops, committing
besides many acts of wanton and useless barbarity.
A septuagenarian, named Filippo Lombardi, whom
they struck down lifeless, was rescued from their
hands only by the devoted efforts of his wife. They
forced the house of the tax-collector, Michelangiolo
Perugino, and, after they had killed him, they set his
house on fire, and threw his naked body, which they
had barbarously mutilated, upon its burning ruins.
It was the unhappy fate of Pontelandolfo to remain
for some time in the hands of the savage mob, some
hundreds in number, by whom the village was kept
in a state of insurrection against the lawful authorities—a state of insubordination in which it was imitated by two other villages, Casalduni and Campo-
lettere.

On the 15th of August forty soldiers and four
gendarmes were sent against the brigands, who, on
the approach of the former, commenced their retreat.   ˙
Unfortunately, in their impatience, the soldiers im-
prudently attacked the brigands before they had got
far from the village. When news of this came to
Pontelandolfo, the mob of that place, joining the

bandits, soon obliged the Italian officer commanding
the detachment—Luigi Augusto Bracci, of the 36th
regiment—to take refuge with his men in a sort of
tower, from which he maintained a vigorous resistance
against his assailants.   After they had been besieged
for some time, a priest having told them that there
were some troops at Casalduni, they made a movement
in that direction in the hope of effecting a junction
with their comrades.

The information, however, was false, and had been
communicated with the intention of betraying them
into the hands of their enemies, by whom they were
suddenly attacked on both sides, the men of Pontelandolfo and of Casalduni, who were concealed in an
ambush, having united against them near the road.
Surrounded by superior numbers, they were all
killed, with the exception of one man, who hid himself in a hedge, and, ultimately making his escape,
brought tidings of the sad disaster to the quarters of
the troops.   When the particulars of this affair had
been inquired into, it was proved that, though the
soldiers opposed to them were only in the proportion
of one to a hundred, the ferocious peasantry were not
satisfied until each had obtained, as a trophy, a
portion of the flesh cut from the victims of this act of
treachery.

On the morning of the 13th, Colonel Negri, with

some troops, coming to make inquiry after these soldiers, was informed that they no longer existed. On demanding their bodies, he could obtain no information as to where they were to be found. The soldiers, then going themselves in search of their lost comrades, were horrified by the discovery of pieces of human flesh torn from their mutilated members, and suspended as trophies at the door of every house. The young officer, it was afterwards discovered, had been savagely tortured for eight hours before death mercifully delivered him from the hands of his enemies. When the soldiers learned these heart-rending details, we cannot feel surprised that, in their blind fury, they wreaked their vengeance on the villages that had been the scene of such a massacre, burning them both to the ground. "Justice has been done at Pontelandolfo and Cusalduni," was the laconic message sent by Colonel Negri to General Cialdini.

Some writers have raised their voices against these rigours, expressing the greatest indignation on account of the execution at Somma of some men who had helped the brigands in the above act of barbarity. Those who can palliate the monstrosities committed by such savages, not admitting the righteousness of the punishment sanctioned by military justice, I can safely leave to the calm and unprejudiced decision of

public opinon. General Manhès also burnt down
villages in carrying out his measures for the suppression of brigandage.

As the statements made by Colletta on this subject have sometimes been denied, I do not intend to
quote any passage from his work; but the following
extract from the history of Carlo Botta, the intimate
friend of the French general, is interesting, and—
somewhat abridging it, without omitting any material
fact—may be quoted with propriety at the conclusion of this chapter.

"Manhès employed four means of repression: he
ordered an exact census of all the brigands, district
by district; he completely prevented them from
coming in contact with the honest part of the population; he ordered the latter to be armed; and he
observed an inflexible justice. He ordered a general
concentration of the cattle, which, in the large
villages, were guarded by troops. Agriculture was
entirely stopped for a time, and the conveyance of
food into the country was prohibited, under pain of
capital punishment. Lastly, he armed the proprietors, and sent them in pursuit of the brigands, with
orders to bring them back, dead or alive. Throughout the whole country nothing was then to be seen
but a great chase, in which one set of men were
hunted by other men.

"Manhès was seconded by men as inflexible as himself, but who generally acted with less discernment, and often with arbitrary cruelty.   An old woman, not aware of the prohibition, was caught whilst taking some bread to her son, who was working in an adjoining field, and was immediately hanged on a tree.*   A poor girl was cruelly tortured only because some suspicious letters had been found upon her.   Mercy seemed to be a word unknown.   The lives of the Carbonari were never spared when any of them fell into the hands of their pursuers.

"In the meanwhile, such of the brigands as were not killed in action, or did not commit suicide, were destroyed by suffering and hunger.   Those who surrendered were brought before a special tribunal, composed of the prefects of the different provinces, and of some provincial magistrates; after examination by whom they were taken before the courts-martial appointed to try them, from whom they received sentence of death, which was immediately executed. Many are also said to have died of asphyxia in the horrid dungeons into which they were thrown."

Still, terrible as their fate was, this infamous and ferocious race richly merited the utmost punishment

* This old story was brought to light again, and reproduced by the clerical papers as a recent crime of Cialdini's soldiers.

that could be inflicted on them.   Compassion towards
such men would have been little short of a crime.
Many also, who, though not belonging to the bands of
brigands, were yet proved guilty of a certain complicity in their actions, suffered at this time the extreme
penalty of death—several of them men of wealth and
property; for, between the rich and poor, Manhès,
whose justice was ever impartial, made not the
slightest difference.

The narrative of some atrocious cases of repression
which follow, I decline translating. Those who are
anxious to feed on horrors, I must refer to the original
sources, where they will find a description of scenes
from the contemplation of which the mind gladly
turns. It is painful to read of long files of
human beings dangling from gibbets—of miserable
wretches dragged from the hands of the executioner,
to be torn and mangled by the infuriated peasantry
—of dungeons where the living were constantly sink-
ing under the influence of the deadly vapours, the
noxious fumes of which had already poisoned many
of their companions, whose lifeless bodies lay extended
beside them—and of the lingering tortures of those
who, left without food, often endeavoured to satisfy
their gnawing hunger on the corpses of those with
whom they had held counsel in life.

" Finally," I quote here the concluding words of

the chapter, " the heads and the members of the
executed, stuck at regular distances upon high poles
all the way between Reggio and Naples, remained for
a long time making people shudder with horror.
Many mutilated corpses were thrown up by the river
Crati, and its banks were strewed with the skeletons
of the unfortunates who had perished. By means of
such severity, incredible as it may appear, Calabria
became perfectly safe for travellers as well as for its
inhabitants. Communication between its most distant points was perfectly secure ; labourers once more
cultivated the land in peace ; and the country
assumed an unaccustomed appearance of prosperity
and civilization. This was the work of Manhès ; a
result for which, while many still hear his name only
with muttered curses, the majority of the population
will long continue to reverence and bless him as their
best benefactor."

The general who had acted with such relentless
energy had served under Murat ; and on afterwards
returning to France, was maintained in his grade by
Louis XVIII., who always showed him the highest
consideration. Ferdinand II. also received him many
years later with every mark of honour, and was in
the habit of saying—" It is to General Manhès that
Calabria is still indebted for her tranquillity."

General Pinelli's energetic measures against the

brigands of our days, though far less relentless and severe, were no less successful than those of the French general. The rigour of which this young Piedmontese officer has sometimes been accused has always been grossly exaggerated; the brigands having in more than one instance experienced from him a generosity which they seldom, if ever, practised. He was averse to the unnecessary shedding of blood, and never ordered an execution unless he considered it absolutely necessary. Those who surrendered always had their lives granted; and such as had not yet committed either robberies or murders were released. The hope of more merciful treatment than was usually accorded induced all the brigands who, after having been first swept from the plains, were afterwards driven to the heights of Gargano, Matese, Nola, Somma, Taburno, and La Sila, to surrender *en masse,* particularly the disbanded soldiers, the deserters, and those who had fled to escape the conscription.

Reaction was thus in time repressed. Its chiefs, who had been acting without any well-defined plan, were no longer able to continue the contest. They finally shrank from that attack on Naples which for a time they seemed to have been meditating, and which, indeed, would have been the wisest thing they could have done had they been sufficiently strong to make the attempt; for in that comparatively small

kingdom the power that possesses the fortress of
Sant' Elmo, and sits in the royal palace of Naples, is
able to keep the whole country under its sway.

Several circumstances, however, kept up the belief
that they had some such design in view. Some move-
ments broke out simultaneously, towards the end of
July and the beginning of August, in the provinces
of Bari, Foggia, and Salerno. Disorder. reigned in
Gioja, Viesti, and Auletta. Small bands of armed
men suddenly appeared in the neighbourhood of
Naples. Anonymous letters were sent to the King's
Lieutenant, threatening him with assassination. The
Bourbonists and the clerical press spoke even more loudly
and boastingly than usual. Some bodies of Pontifical
Zouaves, disguised with the red shirt of the Garibaldians, were embarked at Civita Vecchia. Reactionary
meetings were held at Rome and Marseilles, coinciding
with those held at Naples and Portici. They continued to issue proclamations, they threatened, promised, encouraged—leading people to believe that a
decisive blow was really about to be struck. Their
plan, however, if it was ever seriously entertained,
turned out a most ridiculous failure. Cialdini put
the fortifications of Naples in a state of defence; not
to bombard the town, as a reactionary paper sug-
gested, but in order to reassure its inhabitants. By
his order a few men-of-war were sent to cruise in the

bay, and to watch the neighbouring coasts. Some
extra patrols were appointed to guard the approaches
of the town. The increased activity and vigilance
displayed in these arrangements were sufficient to stop
the landing of the Pontifical Zouaves, and any attempt
to attack the town, or even a demonstration in favour
of Francis II., became projects which it would be
impossible to realize. In the very few hamlets where
the ringleaders of revolt had succeeded in exciting
some disturbance, reaction was crushed before it had
thoroughly raised its head. Discouraged every day
by some new defeats, thinned by numerous desertions,
the bands of brigands almost entirely disappeared ;
and the return of that state of security assured by
regular authority, was hailed with joy by the population, who began to hope that the coming winter
would sweep with its snow the few remnants of the
brigands from the mountains and the woods.

CHAPTER VII.

CHAPTER VII.

AFTER the indigenous bands of adventurers and fortune-seekers sent to us by the Bourbonist committees of Rome, Marseilles, and Trieste had been suppressed, a new enemy, whom the friends of liberty had hardly calculated on, rose in opposition against them. The cause of Italy was now complicated by foreign intervention. Naples became the rallying point of the legitimists, who, through the insurrection of the Southern provinces, hoped to be able to reconquer their lost dominion over Italy, to restore the dispossessed princes, and to establish the authority of those who still occupied their thrones. Such a design, if successful, would undoubtedly have tended to advance the cause of legitimacy throughout Europe, and perhaps have even enabled it to raise its drooping head in France, where, under every Government, revolution has always had the lead.

The moment was favourable for so bold an enterprise. In obedience, perhaps, to a superior necessity, the

Central Government of Turin was, by degrees, with-
drawing from Naples every trace of its former autonomy. Not only had the conscription been introduced, and a war-tax been imposed upon the population, but the Government was gradually assimilating
the institutions of Northern and Southern Italy—a
measure which was offensive to the municipal pride of
many Neapolitans of influence.

The Italian Government had just struck the last
blow at municipalism with a boldness at which we
still tremble when we think of all the dangers that
might have resulted from a step which involved the
suppression of the Lieutenancy of Naples, the transfer-
ence of the seat of Government from that most beautiful and important among the splendid Italian capitals,
and the reduction to the position of a provincial town
of that city that was but yesterday the head of the
largest kingdom of the peninsula.   Cialdini, too, had
been recalled, the only popular man, besides Garibaldi,
from the North, who, with the prestige of a conqueror,
had been more successful in his government of Naples
than any other ruler since the hero of the national
cause had resigned his authority.

The country then was in such a state of discontent,
that, to the enemies of Victor Emmanuel, the time appeared favourable for the trial of their strength in a
civil war.   A host of champions, accompanied with

the blessing of the Holy Father, invaded the country from every part of the world. The reception, however, which they received was so different from that which they had anticipated, that they lost all heart, and these expeditions, including those of Borjès and of M. de Trazégnies, resulted in total failure.

The following letter on the subject of brigandage, addressed by M. Rotrou,* the French consular agent at Chieti, to M. Soulange Bodin, the consul of France at Naples, one of the warmest and most devoted friends of Italy, gives a striking picture of the state of affairs in Southern Italy at this time:—

"Avezzano, September 15th.

" Monsieur le Consul Général,

"Brigandage has been lately losing ground in that part of the Abruzzi adjoining the Roman frontier. But we have no hope whatever of seeing it brought to an end, unless it ceases to receive recruits, money, and support from abroad. Chiavone has in his band men of every nation, French, Swiss, Germans, Neapolitans, formerly in the service of Francis II. and the Pope, together with the scum of the indigenous population.

* I am indebted to M. Rotrou for much valuable information which has already found its place in this book, as, for instance, in the chapter on the first movements in the Abruzzi.

"It is said that, after some severe engagements
that took place these last days, Chiavone, according
to his old custom, repaired to Rome. There can be
no doubt that the peasants are, in general, rather
well-disposed towards the brigands, and that they
show a certain readiness to help them ; but they are,
in reality, little inclined to take part in their adventurous life. Although they greet their successes,
when they are not themselves the victims, and sometimes supply them with food, it is more out of fear
than sympathy.

"The middle classes, who have not yet been quite
reassured, are not altogether persuaded that the old
system has been for ever destroyed. We have experienced as yet only the evils of revolution. The
Government has not been able, up to the present
moment, to accomplish any important improvements.
What is now taking place is only the natural consequence of the system of demoralization carried on by
Ferdinand II., during these last twelve years, with a
resolution and perseverance worthy of a better cause.
Since 1848 he has had but one thought, one end—
that of rendering a return to constitutional government impossible, by the complete degradation of the
middle classes. The state of abjection to which they
were designedly reduced, and the licentiousness encouraged among a still lower class, ended by depriv-

ing the former of all confidence, and by destroying
in them the consciousness of their strength.

"On the other hand, the return, without transition, to constitutionalism, was rendered now so much
the more dangerous, inasmuch as they had endeavoured, during twelve years, to destroy everything likely—even in the most remote way—to favour
its re-establishment. The lower class, accustomed to
recognize the rights of the king alone, saw in him
their supreme ruler, above whom there was no other
authority. The consequence was that laws, in their
untutored imaginations, were only the expression
of the will of a master, generally favourable to them,
but always inflexible to the better-educated classes.

"In 1860, when the Bourbons made a desperate
appeal to the same constitutional institutions, in order
to save their falling throne, they took care to explain
to the masses that the unsettled state of affairs was
the result of the violence of the middle classes, who
desired again to re-conquer the power of trampling
upon the privileges of the people, thus to revenge
themselves for their long sufferings. It is very easy
to understand the eagerness of the falling monarchy
to defend, by every possible means, those whom it
considered as the safeguard of its independence, and
as its protectors against the hated tyranny and
insatiable avidity of that intelligent class which it re-

garded as its constant and most bitter antagonist. We
cannot wonder, therefore, if the lower classes looked on
the revolution with great discontent, but, on the
contrary, must be astonished when we see how little
they stirred in defence of a cause that the Bourbons
had so eagerly contrived to identify with their interests and sympathies.

"Whilst Ferdinand II. left to the common people
an almost unbounded liberty, he adopted towards the
middle class a system which could end only in
the destruction of their energy, and in erasing the
consciousness of their civic duties and obligations.
Every one was pitilessly confined to his native place,
and it was only with great difficulty that a few were
allowed to visit occasionally the chief town of their
province.

"The magistrates were chiefly selected from the
middle class, or at least among those of its members
whose opinions were as servile as their incapacity was
notorious. Communal elections had been long suppressed, as in fact was everything that was likely to
recall to the minds of the Neapolitans the recollection
of liberal institutions.

"Even the reading of the official newspaper was at
last prohibited in every place of meeting, and parents
were no longer permitted to send their young men to
the great centres of the kingdom to finish their edu-

cation. In every locality the well-off families had
entirely ceased seeing each other, in order not to
excite the suspicions of a police ever ready to take the
alarm. Persons belonging to this class were often
punished as if they had been infamous criminals, and
their personal liberty was continually threatened.
The only freedom which they enjoyed was that of
superintending their own private affairs.

"The Cabinet of Turin was little aware of this
state of things, and judged of the Neapolitan provinces according to the ideas which it had formed
of Naples itself, which were precisely the reverse of
the true ones. At Naples strength and vitality were
the characteristics of the middle class, whilst in the
provinces it was only among the people that these were
to be found. It was consequently to the latter that they
ought to have spoken, explaining to them that they had
never enjoyed genuine freedom under the Bourbons;
that, moreover, they had never been in possession of
any guarantees for the continuance of such liberty
as they enjoyed; but that such guarantees the Italian
government had just given to the people, enabling
them to exercise their rights in common with the rest
of society. They ought to have made them understand how they had been systematically cast aside,
and to have pointed out to them the evils that had
arisen from such a state of things, leading to the

neglect of their most vital interests. In a word, they ought to have adopted such measures as would have led them to the conviction that they were, in point of fact, entering on a new era of justice and freedom.

"The numerous causes of discontent were still further increased by the distress that was the natural consequence of a series of bad seasons. Wheat was very scarce, and Indian corn, which constitutes the principal resource of the inhabitants, had failed entirely. It would now be necessary to set immediately in action some great work of public utility—as, for instance, the construction of railways and common roads. The want of communication is in this country the source of incalculable evils, the consequence of the system adopted by Ferdinand II. If the Government had a year ago undertaken these great works, they would have gained for themselves immense popularity throughout the whole country.

"Counter-revolution, however, not having succeeded, notwithstanding all the circumstances in its favour, it will not be able to gain or to preserve the mastery of the situation by keeping up the agitation.

(Signed) "ROTROU."

Great as was the discontent generally prevailing, Chiavone did next to nothing on the Neapolitan territory. He moved about, carrying devastation where-

ever he went; but he never succeeded in establishing
himself anywhere. His rare successes during the
partial invasions which he made of some parts of the
country, were immediately followed by a precipitate
flight into the dominions of his Holiness.

One of the expeditions previously referred to is
worthy of record, on account of the rather peculiar
circumstance that it was under the leadership of a
gentleman of aristocratic connections, M. Alfred de
Trazégnies, a nobleman of Namur, allied to the Mon-
taltos,* to General St. Arnaud, and to Monseigneur
de Mérode. Deceived, perhaps, by clerical falsehoods,
by which he was led to believe that, in following the
example of Chiavone, he was acting in a praiseworthy
manner, he set out for Naples in a comfortable carriage, which he left on reaching the frontiers. During
his march into the interior he came unexpectedly
upon a badly guarded Italian post, which he at once
attacked. The troops thus suddenly disturbed, being
few in number compared with their assailants, effected
their escape by boldly fighting their way through
the ranks of the enemy. The brigands, baffled in
this enterprise, rushed next against the village of
San Giovanni Incarico, which they plundered with
savage ferocity, robbing and killing the helpless

* Count Montalto is Italian Minister at Brussels, and married a cousin of M. Trazégnies.

inhabitants, insulting the women, and burning the
houses to the ground.   Incited by their example,
M. de Trazégnies committed excesses that in a calmer
moment he would surely have disavowed as disgraceful to one occupying the position that he did.   Unfortunately for him, Italian soldiers came up to the
rescue of the unhappy villagers, though not until
their homes were almost entirely desolated, and,
falling on the brigands, seized the young nobleman
while he was in the very act of firing, with his own
hands, a house into which he had broken.   When it
was announced to him that, seized, as he had been, in
the very act of insurrection, he was to be shot
instantly, he could hardly believe it ; but without a
moment's delay, and with scarcely any formality, the
sentence of military justice was carried into effect.
His back was ignominiously turned against a wall—
the position in which it is usual to execute brigands—and at the moment when, still confident in
his belief that they would not dare to put him to
death, he turned his head to speak to the soldiers, a
bullet struck him, and he fell dead.   His body was
shortly afterwards given up to a Franco-Belgian
deputation which had come expressly from Rome to
claim it.

Borjés, the Spaniard, the leader of the other expedition into the Southern provinces, was still more

unlucky. Among the documents seized upon him were found the instructions given to him at Marseilles by General Clary, and his journal written by himself, containing a curious record of the organization and objects of the brigands.

José Borjès was a Catalan, who, during the civil wars of his native country, had acquired a great reputation for bravery and energy. Such a man was considered a great acquisition by the leaders of the Bourbon party, by one of whose committees he was enlisted in France. The paper found, among other documents, on him, containing the orders of the Bourbonist General Clary, is now among the archives of the Italian Foreign Office. According to the instructions contained in this paper, Borjès was to take the lead of the national movement among the population of the Two Sicilies, deceived and oppressed by the Piedmontese Government. He was particularly directed to proceed to Calabria, with the view of re-establishing in that province the legitimate authority of Francis II., for which purpose he was to embark for any point likely to afford him a safe landing. After making all necessary civil and military arrangements, he was to offer an amnesty to all political delinquents who would acknowledge the authority of their legitimate king. If victory should crown his exertions he was directed to treat all prisoners of war with the greatest consideration and indulgence.

The document containing General Clary's instructions is followed by another with some special commands from the Prince of Scilla, among which is a recommendation à la Dowb.—"Prince Scilla recommends his faithful servant Lampo Lampo "—an ex-convict !

Borjès' journal is preceded by a very important letter* to General Clary, from which we learn the nature of the perplexities into which the Spanish adventurer fell, from the very beginning of his expedition, when, having left Marseilles for Malta, he intended to sail from the latter place with a handful of his countrymen, and land in Calabria. The letter is as follows :—

"MON GÉNÉRAL,

"After a great many troubles, and no end of difficulties, in trying to get some arms and ammunition, I have at last succeeded in procuring about twenty muskets. Another obstacle, however, then presented itself, how to get these articles out of Malta. The fact is that suspicions—how originated I don't know—were floating about the island, and the news-

* This letter, as well as Borjès' journal, was written in French.

papers talked of our expedition even before we had given any indication of our intention to depart.

"At last, on the 11th instant, I got on board a sort of 'speronara,'* with my officers, and we sailed at ten o'clock in the evening, abandoning ourselves entirely to God's mercy. When we were at a short distance from the shore of Brancaleone, we were surprised by a dead calm, which prevented our advancing any further. We decided, therefore, upon landing there; and on the evening of the same day, which was the 13th of the month, having got a little nearer, we landed at night-fall, and found ourselves surrounded by the most perfect solitude. Alone, without a guide, I bent my steps towards a feeble light that I could perceive in the distance, and after making my way over a most dismal country, reached the hut of a shepherd. By a providential chance we had fallen upon an honest man, who guided us to a place called Falco, where we spent the night.

"The following day, the 14th, at five o'clock in the morning, we set out, still under the guidance of our shepherd, and arrived shortly at the little town of Precacore, where we met with a rather friendly reception on the part of the inhabitants, who, with the curé at their head, came to meet us, with shouts of 'Viva Francesco II.!' This first success inspired

* Small Sicilian sailing craft.

B 2

me with a good hope for the future, in which, alas! I
was too soon deceived.

"In the meanwhile, some twenty peasants having
consented to follow me, with this microscopic army I
resolved to advance into the country.   Two villages
were close at hand, Sant' Agata and Caraffa, and I
bent my steps in the direction of the latter, having
heard it was the best-disposed of the two.   It was
then three o'clock in the afternoon, and I was just
passing the outskirts of Sant' Agata, when I was assailed by a detachment of some sixty mobilized National
Guards, who opened at once against us a deadly
fire.   At the first shot my new soldiers fled in every
direction, and I found myself once more alone with
my officers.   Having succeeded, however, in gaining
a strong position, I resisted the attack of our assailants for upwards of an hour and a half.

"Some time afterwards, the National Guards
having retired, I received a parliamentary from the
inhabitants of Caraffa, inviting me to enter their town.
I refused, and fortunate it was that I did so, as they
had prepared for me a snare, into which, had I ac-
ceded to their invitation, I must undoubtedly have
fallen, and have met with certain death.

"From the few people who had come over to me
during the engagement I learnt that there was a band
of brigands close by, commanded by a certain Mittica,

regarding whose whereabouts the monks of the convent of Banco could give me every direction. I hastened, therefore, to the convent with all possible speed, for I was informed that Piedmontese troops had been sent for at Gerace. The venerable abbot of the sanctuary of Banco directed me to Natile, which I only reached, after a wearisome march, in the afternoon of the 15th. Before I entered the village I sent for a barrister of the name of Sculli, to whom I was directed. I was treated by that man with every sort of consideration, and he took me to a place near Cirella, called Scardarilla, where Mittica was encamped with about a hundred and twenty men, most of whom were armed. I saw at once that Mittica had not entire confidence in us, suspecting we were enemies. He plainly told me that he could only condescend to place himself under my orders after the first engagement we should have, as that would give him an opportunity of judging me. I was therefore kept in captivity with my officers during three days, a great misfortune to us, for we lost thus much precious time. In the meanwhile, before I could exercise the power of a commander, I was compelled to obey.

" During that time Mittica told me that he had resolved to attack the small town of Plati, which was occupied by a considerable force of National Guards, but very few Piedmontese. During the night of the

16th, accordingly, we marched against that town.
Although the attack was to be directed on three
different points, only on one side was there any possibility of success, and that was the position Mittica
had reserved for himself.

"At twenty minutes past four the signal was given
for the attack, and the action began by a sharp fire.
If advantage had been taken of the first moment of
alarm, perhaps the town might have been easily
taken by storm, at least, I could certainly have made
myself master of it, but at that time I had no power,
and was merely there *en amateur.* The garrison,
which had been strengthened the day before, without
our knowledge, with about a hundred Piedmontese,
made such a vigorous defence, that it became perfectly useless to continue the attack, and we considered it prudent to retire. At half-past ten, accordingly, we began our retreat, none of our men
having been injured, while the enemy had several
killed and wounded.

"We then advanced towards Cimina, with the intention of disarming it, as we were anxious to secure
a few muskets. There we learned that four hundred
Piedmontese, who had landed the night before, together with the troops quartered in the neighbourhood, and the mobilized National Guards, were on
our track. We therefore decamped at once, flying

in the direction of the mountains. Although it was
raining in torrents we did not pause in our march
until we reached the top of the mountain. On the
18th, at six o'clock, we resumed our march, directing
our steps towards the mountains of Catanzaro. We
had not proceeded far before we unfortunately fell
into an ambush that had been prepared for us by the
enemy, who was trying to outflank us. We hurried
back again, but it was only to fall into another snare.
However, after a smart action, we succeeded in
extricating ourselves from that dangerous situation.
But the enemy still continued to harass us, and
we had to pursue our march, beset by numerous
difficulties, which so impeded our progress that it
was the 19th before we arrived, early in the morning,
in safety, at the Piano di Gerace. I was then alone
with my officers, and Mittica was following in the
rear, with only forty men, the rest having been disbanded. We descended the hill, and continued our
retreat until we had arrived within an hour's march
of Giffona, where, being utterly exhausted, we halted,
in order to get some provisions. Unfortunately, however, being unable to procure any, after a few
minutes' rest we were again compelled to set out.
While we were in this miserable position, Mittica and
his men deserted us. We stopped again on the
mountain called Il Fendo, panting for breath; but

being driven away by some armed mountaineers, we
were forced still to wander for some time, until, at
last, we found a secluded spot, out of the reach of
our adversaries, where we obtained shelter. We remained there a few hours, and then, at five o'clock
in the evening, resumed our march, taking the direction of the Cerri, which we reached after twelve
hours' march. When we halted at La Serra di Cucco,
near the village of Torre, an old private of the ex-
Neapolitan Rifles came up to me, offering his services,
*and this is the only partisan I have as yet found in the
country.*

"On the 21st of September we crossed the mountain of Nocella, and, after a long march, I arrived at
Sermstretta, opposite La Sila, which I hope soon to
reach."

The journal which now follows, bearing the date
of September 22nd, continues the narrative :—

BORJÈS' JOURNAL.

"September 22nd, 1861.—Caracciolo, partly on
account of the fatigues of the expedition, and
partly owing to the insinuations of a certain
Maura, came to me at two o'clock, saying that
he had made up his mind to go back to Rome.
I did all that was in my power to change his resolution, but with no avail; and at six o'clock he asked

me for two hundred francs, and then left with the man who has mostly contributed to his desertion.[*]

"September 23rd.—From the mountain of Serrastretta, I went to that of Nino; but I stopped on my way at a shepherd's hut, where I ordered some food to be distributed among my men. The shepherd, who was a bad one, sent word to the troops, and we had them instantly at our heels. They searched the bushes in every direction, but fortunately did not notice a corner where we had taken refuge; and we have been thus miraculously saved, for at four o'clock in the afternoon they seemed to have completely lost the scent, and had removed to some distance from us. After a modest repast, consisting only of some potatoes cooked in cinders, we cautiously left the bushes, and began to make our way towards the mountains of La Sila. The country we are in is better cultivated, but less wooded. There is a great quantity of game, and plenty of cattle.

[*] This Caracciolo, a Neapolitan officer, set out alone for Naples. He was arrested on his way by the National Guard. He has confessed and openly declared, in a letter that has since been published, that he enlisted under the orders of Borjès, in the hope of finding in Calabria a numerous Royalist army; but seeing that all the Bourbonist supporters consisted of a band of brigands, he was disgusted, and resolved to abandon the Spanish adventurer. As to Mittica, who is not mentioned any more in this journal, he was killed by the Italian soldiers and the Calabrian patriots, with the few men who were still with him.

"September 24th.—From the mountain of Nino I drew near the valley of the Asino, which I found swarming with people. During the present period of the year the almost nomad inhabitants are concentrated in this spot to reap the potatoe crop, and to feed their cattle in the surrounding pastures. A brook runs across the valley from the north side, and on its left bank the ground rises in a very steep ascent; but after half an hour's walk the path gets wider, and the hill slopes gently down. When I had reached the top, a merciful Providence enabled me to hear the distant sound of a bell. I stopped, as I was sure that I should find a shepherd's house on my right. I left the path I had followed till then; and it was fortunate I did so, for a few minutes after about a hundred and twenty Garibaldians came forth, and put themselves in ambush, waiting for our passage. Meantime we arrived safely at the shepherds', and were well received by them. We found a refuge in a secluded spot, where we spent the night, and at daybreak we took our departure. Guided by one of the shepherds, we next arrived at Espinarvo, or, as it is here called, Il Carillone.

"September 25th.—Once arrived at the mountain of Espinarvo, I stopped to give my officers a day's rest. From a muleteer of Taverna, whom I met there, I obtained the promise of a few provisions on the following day, for which I paid him beforehand. The muleteer sent us instead a detachment of Piedmontese, who soon made us decamp from our position. As they could not overtake us, however, we had nothing to complain of besides the fatigue caused by our hurried flight.

"At half-past eight in the evening we arrived at a shepherd's on the mountain of Pellatren. The mountain of Espinarvo is in many parts covered with very rich pasture, upon which a great number of splendid cattle find sustenance. The surrounding plain is covered with pine and other fir trees, called here Carillone. The soil is uncommonly rich and fertile. The temperature, however, is very cold, and, extraordinary as it is at this time of the year, we have already experienced a very severe white frost. If some of the trees were cut down and the land cultivated, the temperature would doubtless become milder.

"September 26th.—At daybreak I resumed my weary march across the mountains, and arrived at Ponte della Valle, a narrow little valley extending from east to west, in which we saw a number of cattle. Although the people were armed they did not attack us. When we were just leaving the valley, however, on our way to the mountain of Colle Deserto, five armed men came up to us, asking

who we were. We said we were friends, and they
left us in peace. After we had reached the top of
the mountain, we descended its declining slopes without meeting with any obstacle, and, having crossed
the valley of Provale, were about to ascend another
mountain, when we perceived a sentry at about three
hundred yards distance, in front of a peasant's cottage. A peasant, whom we asked why the man was
on guard there, told us it was the sentry of a detachment of two hundred Piedmontese troops who had
that very morning already explored the mountain towards which we were bending our way, This information made me entirely alter my plans, and we
immediately retraced our steps, marching for four
hours, with the intent of avoiding the enemy—an end
in which I completely succeeded. Being informed,
however, on our arrival at Nieto, that there were
more than fifty National Guards there, ready to check
our advance, we were compelled to hide ourselves in
a wood till dusk, when, with the aid of a guide, we
proceeded to the mountain called Corvo, on which
we spent the night.

"The mountain of Pellatrea, which we left on the
morning of the 26th, is fertile and well cultivated.
The rich people of Cotrone send their cattle to
these pastures. We ate a sheep at a farm belonging
to the captain of the National Guard of this town,

Don Chirico Villangiere. If he could only get hold of us, how he would be revenged on us!

"The little valley of Ponte della Valle is traversed by a torrent which, overflowing its shallow bed, makes the country somewhat marshy. If it was properly drained, it would soon become the most perfect garden of the world. It produces flax in great quantity, and affords abundant pasturage to innumerable cattle. The mountain of Colle Deserto is well wooded. The southern side is capable of producing good wine if its cultivation was attended to. The small valley of Rovale, while it is equally fertile, appears to me more salubrious. The valley of Nieto, which is about fifteen leagues in circumference, is one of the most delightful in the world. Gardens, sheepfolds, rivulets, cottages, large residences with drawbridges, and at short distances groves scattered here and there, make it one of the most enchanting summer abodes I have ever seen. With the women moving about with baskets filled with cheese, fruit, or milk; the men at work with the plough or the spade; shepherds leaning against the trunks of the willow-trees, singing, or playing on the flute or the bagpipes, it appears a perfect Arcadia. The mountain of Corvo offers nothing interesting except the beautiful pines which clothe its sides and crown its summit. The southern part, however, would, if well cultivated,

largely repay the exertions of those who undertook its
tillage.

"September 27th.—We started this morning in
the direction of the mountain of Gallopane, and arrived
there at nine o'clock. The only provisions we could
get consisted of a bit of hard bread and some onions,
given to us at a miserable house on the verge of the
forest. Learning afterwards that the man who lived
there was a National Guard, we ascended, for fear of
being tracked, to the top of the mountain, where, my
men being utterly exhausted with hunger and fatigue,
I was obliged to halt. We had not been there a
quarter of an hour when, seeing a young fellow apparently watching us, I gave the alert to my comrades,
and we started off again. We had advanced about
two hundred yards, when Captain Rovella, who was
marching in the van of my little column, made a sign
to stop. Learning from him that he had seen fifteen
National Guards advancing in our direction, I put
myself immediately in ambush with my men; but
when the Nationals came within musket-shot, they
saw us and stopped. Seeing they did not stir, after
we had waited in the bushes for half an hour, I
thought perhaps they were but the vanguard of a
strong body, and fearing a snare, I resolved to abandon my position. I set off, therefore, wandering
about in the woods without guide, having no other

notion as to where I was going except that I was
marching northwards. At five o'clock I found myself on a little mountain called Castagna di Macchia.
Utterly exhausted by so many hardships, and full of
anxiety for the future, I sank down, not knowing
what to do, nor where to go, when, no doubt through
the intercession of the holy soul of the pious queen,[*]
that providence which never forgets us, showed itself
in the shape of a shepherd, who, coming up, offered
us a shelter for the night, with such provisions as his
cottage afforded. We had scarcely entered the hospitable little house—the first time we have been
under a roof since our landing—when a most fearful
storm burst forth. How fortunate was it for us that
we had such a shelter, and a night's rest, which contributed greatly to restore our exhausted strength!
We did not fail to thank the Almighty with all our
heart for this evident proof of His protection.

"The mountain of Gallopane is well cultivated, but
only in some parts, though the whole might be turned
into very valuable land, capable of supporting a large

* This mystical allusion refers to the late Queen of Naples,
the first wife of Ferdinand II., and the mother of Francis II.
She was a princess of the House of Savoy, and grand-aunt of
Victor Emmanuel. During her short life she gave such proofs
of extraordinary piety and devotion, that she was considered as
a saint. Whether this supposition was right or wrong, the
court of Rome has lately settled the question by solemnly
canonizing her.

number of people. La Castagna di Macchia is a
mountain covered with picturesque old chestnut
trees. Numerous sheep, cattle, and horses are fed on
its green hills. The poor people in this neighbourhood are favourably disposed towards us.

"September 28th.—At half-past eight I left the
shepherd's cottage in order to establish myself under
a sort of shed at about a quarter of an hour's distance. Two lads, our guides, promised, when they
left us, to bring us in the evening a reinforcement of
twenty men, who they knew would gladly consent to
follow me. It is now nine o'clock in the morning,
and God knows what may still happen within the next
twelve hours.

"'Twelve o'clock.—No news of the enemy. We
have had a great treat—some potatoes boiled in plain
water.

"Nine o'clock in the evening.—The twenty men
promised in the morning have not yet made their appearance. I am half afraid that, if not imaginary, very
likely they do not trust us.

"September 29th, six o'clock A.M.—A messenger
from Prince Bisignano's agent came here to ask some
proofs of my identity. I handed him two of General
Clary's letters, and I am now impatiently waiting
the result.

"6.45 A.M.—I am informed that the enemy is in

pursuit of us ; news which, coupled with the distrust displayed towards us by these mountaineers, who, by-the-bye, are the greatest thieves in the world, oblige me to leave my refuge and go in the direction of the forest of Muzzo, where I am to meet the messenger of this morning.

" 9.20 A.M.—The messenger is come, but I must go with him to meet the agent himself at Castellone.

" 10.30 A.M.—I found him surrounded by about ten men ; he treated me very politely, and after the exchange of a few words gave orders to assemble as many peasants as were to be had, with whom we set off towards Territorio di Roce, before reaching which, however, they had all disappeared. The Serra di Muzzo is covered all over with very valuable timber. Some parts of it, which are in a perfect state of cultivation, are fertilized by a great many springs of limpid water. Territorio di Roce is a very healthy country, of mild temperature. Here and there are some beautiful specimens of cork trees, which, if cultivated on a large scale, might become the source of great wealth. The system of agriculture is generally good, though it might be immensely improved.

" *Territorio di Roce*, September 30th, 5 P.M.—A confidential messenger informs me that the enemy, in order to surprise us, has surrounded the woods of Macchia and Muzzo. Seven of the peasants who

were with us yesterday, having been captured, have
revealed our position to the enemy; we have consequently to decamp at once. The proprietors of La
Sila being very hostile to us, we shall be obliged to
retire in the opposite direction.   -

"10 P.M.—We have gained the forest of Ceprano,
only at an hour's distance from the enemy's encampment, but instead of being on the south side we are
to the north. We are in a pitiful state, shoeless and
footsore, and know not how we are to get out of our
miseries. Some peasants, whom I asked if they could
provide us with a few boots, brought rough, heavy
brogues which hurt our feet. Nevertheless, we paid
dearly for them.

"October 1st, 6 A.M.—We received some white
bread, ham, tomatoes, onions, and a small quantity of
wine—a rare treat in this country.

"1 P.M.—Seven National Guards were seen
taking position at Serra del Pastore, opposite to us,
whilst about twenty others reconnoitered La Serra
del Capraro. After half an hour they retired in the
direction of Roce, whence they had come.

"10 P.M.—The National Guards have assembled
to-day at Roce. They stole some sheep from the
farms of Prince Bisignano. These proprietors of La
Sila are anti-royalists, the only reason being that if
the king were restored to his throne they would no

longer be able to rule absolutely over their tenants.
The two districts of Rocc and Castiglione, however,
are very royalist, and therefore I can trust them.

" October 2nd, 6 A.M.—They report to us that the
authorities are arresting those who took part in the
revolution of last March.

" 7 A.M.—A spy informed me that the commanders
of the forces we saw yesterday were the sons of Baron
Mollo and Baron Constantino ; and that the body of
irregulars under their orders was entirely composed
of their own tenants.

" 8 A.M.—I am informed that yesterday all the
forces now at Cosenza were called out to march
against me ; but having learned on their way that a
royalist band had beaten a detachment of troops, they
had gone in another direction to their rescue. I
know not what truth there may be in these reports,
but, though I am daily employing a great number of
agents, I have not yet met in this country the smallest
royalist band. The National Guards of Rocc have
sent this morning a despatch to Cosenza, but its contents are not known to me. It is certain, however,
that there are no troops in the former. Yesterday they were obliged to have the guard mounted by
unarmed peasants. Besides, a Piedmontese general
having died, they could not gather fifty men to
accompany his body to the grave.

"5 P.M.—I don't know anything as yet of the reinforcements the agent had promised me. I am much afraid that they may turn out rather a well-intentioned wish on his part than a reality. I am told that on the 22nd they arrested two of our men, who were taken to Cosenza. As they were bearers of some medals and gold, I fear they may very likely turn out to be the unfortunate Caracciolo and Marra.

"5.20 P.M.—The National Guards have arrested at this moment the family of Prince Bisignano's agent, who had been conferring with me. Royalism in this district is sometimes real fanaticism. Unfortunately, however, this favourable disposition is checked everywhere by fear. Yet I feel convinced that if a landing of two thousand men could be effected on four different points, five hundred in the province of Catanzaro, and the same number in each of the provinces of Reggio, Cosenza, and the Abruzzi, the Piedmontese domination would soon come to an end. The rich, with very few exceptions, are liberal almost everywhere, * and, in consequence, hated by the masses. It was by order of the sons of Baron

---

* I call the attention of the reader to this confession, which is very significant, as it emanates from Borjès himself. The educated and more civilized classes of the population are for Victor Emmanuel, whilst it is only the ignorant and abject that side with Francis II. As to his belief that two thousand men would have restored the fallen King's domination, it is not worth refuting.

Mollo that sheep were stolen from Prince Bisignano's farms, and killed and distributed among the National Guards in the house of their captain.

"7.30 P.M.—Notwithstanding the resolution I had taken to leave to-night, I yielded to the entreaties of the agent, who begged me to remain here a little longer, to wait for the arrival of eight men, who have murdered a National Guard, and, they say, a liberal priest. What horror !

"October 4th.—The eight men I was waiting for did not come. It is reported that the Piedmontese have disarmed eighty National Guards who had refused to march against us; and the same men now ask to be admitted among my followers. Having strong suspicion, however, that the Piedmontese might have invented all this in order to entrap me, I have declined their offer.

"10 A.M.—I hear of different messengers who are shortly expected, and of various Royalist demonstrations which are hourly to take place; but I attach little credit to these reports The National Guards pillaged yesterday five country-houses, two of them belonging to M. Michele Capuano, in which, among the property stolen, were more than fifteen tons of figs, representing a value of at least seventy ducats. The enemy, believing we are in the district of La Sila, scours and searches in vain all the surrounding country.

10 P.M.—They came to tell me that a Royalist
band had disembarked at Rossano. This is a mere
illusion. From my encampment I can see the flames
devouring the country-houses of Baron Collici and
Baron Cozzolino, both of very bad political opinions,
as the latter gave more than sixty thousand ducats
(about ten thousand guineas) to the revolutionist
party. It is not known what Baron Collici gave, but
his contribution also must have been very large.

"October 5th, 6 A.M.—We take up our quarters
at the forest of Pietra Favulla, from which we command the woods of Pignola.

"9 P.M.—The brigand chief, Leonardo Baccaro,
arrived from his mountain retreat of Serra Peducci,
where I had sent for him to know whether there was
anything to hope from that quarter. I am sorry to
say that his answer, like that of many others, was a
negative one. 'Let us have but a small army,'
said he, 'and all the country will rise in arms like a
single man. Without that, it is useless to hope.'
And I believe he is right. All these people anxiously
desire their own king and the autonomy of their
country; but the idea that their houses will be
burned down, and their wives and children imprisoned, prevents them from making an attempt to
free themselves. If they but knew their strength,
they would exhibit greater resolution. It is a pity

they are not aware of that, for a harder-working or
more sober population I have never seen in my life.
Had I disembarked here three weeks sooner, I should
have found about the Carillone a thousand and sixty-
seven Bourbonist soldiers, with two hundred horses,
a force which would have been enough to show them
that their cause was not lost. The presence of these
troops would have roused their drooping spirits.
Unluckily, when I arrived, it was too late. The
Neapolitan soldiers had already dispersed, some
even giving themselves up to the enemy, and others
enlisting in the ranks of the mobilised National
Guard. The loss of time at Marseilles and at Malta,
on account of the many obstacles thrown in my way,
has been a serious blow to our cause, without calculat-
ing the dangers of my present position in an unknown
country, deprived of support."

The journal is continued in the same style, describing the movements of the bandits from place to
place, the sufferings they endured, their perseverance
under every difficulty, and their devotion to him
whom they regarded as their legitimate king. "If
it be the will of God that I should succumb,"
says General Borjès, "then I shall give up this
journal to Capdevila, so that it may be for-
warded to General Clary or Scilla ; and if Capdevila

also should share my unhappy fate, he ought to give
it to Major Landet for the same purpose.   I am very
anxious that these pages should meet the eyes of his
Majesty, in order to prove to him that I die without
regretting a life which I may have the honour of losing at any moment in the sacred cause of legitimacy."
The further movements of the band under Borjès
are minutely described, but are of no particular interest till they arrive at the wood of Lagopesole, where
they come in contact with Crocco and his band.   The
journal then continues :—

"October 19th, Wood of Lagopesole, 2 A.M.—
We arrived, not without many difficulties, at the
wood I have above mentioned.   The rain did us a
great deal of harm ; the by-ways we were obliged to
take making us waste a precious time.   We were no
less than eight hours advancing a distance of four
miles.   It still rained very hard, and at 3 o'clock P.M.
some of my soldiers informed me that Donatelli Crocco,
with a thousand partisans under his orders, was eight
miles further on.   I sent him a letter by Capdevila,
accompanied by two soldiers, to see if we could agree
and act together ; but I doubt very much whether I
shall succeed in this mission, for the greatest disorder
prevails everywhere.   It is a great misfortune that I
should not have three hundred men under my orders

to enforce my commands. If I had such a number how much brighter would be the prospect we should have for the cause of his Majesty!

"4 P.M.—We changed position, but did not leave the wood. They tell me that the Piedmontese are in very small numbers down here, though they cannot precisely state how many, but it is known they have with them two pieces of artillery.

"October 20th, 6 A.M.—Nothing new, except that the night has been an exceedingly cold one.

"10 A.M.—I am informed that the authorities do here what is generally done wherever I go—viz., imprison and vex the royalists.

"October 21st, 2 A.M.—The two soldiers who had left with Capdevila* are come back alone, and with no letter from him; but they bring me word to join the band, and we are preparing to do so as soon as we have taken our modest morning meal.

"10 A.M.—We set off to join the band and Capdevila, who, by-the-by, never came back, and is, as I am told, at the wood at Caporsola (Lagopesole).

* This Capdevila was a Spaniard, who had served with Borjes in the civil wars of Spain. In Basilicata he was wounded in the foot, and being obliged to stay behind, he hid himself in the wood of Lagopesole, where he was taken on the 9th of January, 1862.

"3.30 P.M.—We met a part of the band, but not the main body, which is still to come with its chief.

"October 22nd, 6 A.M.—The chief of the band arrived last night, but I have not yet seen him. He is gone to see his paramour, whom he keeps in one of the deep caverns of this wood, to the great scandal of his followers.

"8.30 A.M.—The chief has turned up at last. I showed him the written instructions I had received from General Clary, but, notwithstanding these credentials, I see that he does not trust me, or is not disposed to give up the command. I fear that I shall do very little with this man. However, I might still have a chance. He tells me we have to wait for the arrival of a French general, who is presently at Potenza, but will very likely be here to-morrow evening, when we shall decide upon the best course to follow.

"2 P.M.—The chieftain disappeared without leaving any information as to his intended where-abouts. They give him the title of general. I have forgotten to say that, having proposed to take with me five hundred infantry and a hundred horses, he flatly declined my offer. In vain did I tell him I should be able with that force to keep the field ; he would not listen to me, saying that double-barrelled shooting guns were not fit for a campaign against regular troops.

"October 23rd, 8 A.M.—M. de Langlois came with three other officers, giving himself the airs of a general, but in fact looking and acting like a fool. I did not oppose him, in order to see how far his impudence would go; but observing that the more I kept aloof the more his insolence increased, I threw off every consideration for him, and summoned him to exhibit the instructions he was boasting he had received. The tone in which I made this demand silenced him instantly, and he merely said they were verbal and not written ones. Carmine Crocco, the chief of the band, is certainly a shrewd fellow, but up to the present moment he has taken very little trouble to assemble his scattered forces. What a pity I have not five hundred men to enforce obedience!

"October 24th, 6 A.M.—Nothing new. We remained the whole day in the same position.

"October 25th, 6 A.M.—Three shots have announced to me the presence of the enemy.

"7 A.M.—We engaged with the enemy at a distance of about a hundred yards. A sharp fire went on between forty Bersaglieri and twenty of us. I held my position for upwards of an hour.

"8 A.M.—The enemy having succeeded in turning our flanks, we left those who were attacking our front, and threw ourselves upon a party who were trying to effect a diversion in our rear.

"8.30 A.M.—Great loss. My best officer, the only one whom I could entirely rely upon, Major L. Landet, fell dead, struck by a musket shot, on the field of battle. His musket and four hundred piastres he carried with him fell into the hands of the enemy. The latter stripped him of everything except his shirt. At the same time one of the four Calabrians who followed me, a man called Domenico del Rustico, was seriously wounded at a moment when he was so near me that the ball which struck him would have undoubtedly reached me had he not intercepted it.

" 2.30 P.M.—The enemy retired under cover. During that time I sent my wounded Calabrian to the surgeon. I have decorated two men of my own band for their gallant behaviour this morning. The cavalry officer, Captain Salinos, is missing, and I don't know as yet whether he is killed or not.

" October 26th, 6 A.M.—We occupy the same wood. Captain Salinos is still missing. I believe he is dead.

" 8 A.M.—Crocco, who, as I have already said, is very sharp, is seeking every pretext in order to gain time and avoid what he had promised, that is, to organise and enlist new bands of insurgents. I cannot understand this man. There is one thing, however, which is very plain, and that is, his venality, which is beyond all expression.

"9 A.M.—I am told by de Langlois that Crocco received a letter from a priest, promising a free pardon if he gave himself up to the authorities with his band. I should not be at all astonished, considering the sums of money and the quantity of booty he has somehow obtained, the manner in which he is led by the concubine he always drags after him, and, above all, the mystery in which, in all his relations with me, he always wraps himself, if he were meditating some act of treachery. Our engagement of yesterday rather increased my suspicions, for, when the enemy began the attack, he got the first start, but, on coming within a certain distance of the foe, turned back, and when I expected to be supported by him on my right flank, I found that, on the contrary, he was engaged in an attack in the rear. I must say, moreover, that neither Crocco Langlois,* nor any of the Neapolitan officers who are with us, stood the fire of the enemy. Alone with my own people and two men of Crocco's, I bravely

* This Langlois was a native of Brittany. I am told that Borjès does not speak very highly of his character. The end of his adventures, however, shows that he was not deficient in audacity or coolness. Instead of going back to Rome by the Abruzzi, after the destruction of the band, he went straight on to Naples, where he succeeded in staying a few days unmolested by the police, after which he embarked for Civita-Vecchia. He had assumed the command of the band, and there exist many proclamations signed by him.

withstood their assault, for which I paid dearly.

"October 27th.—Captain Salinos has just now reappeared in good health. The enemy have shot[*] a poor fellow named Nicola Falesco, a married man, with five children, whom they seized while he was bringing us some provisions. His widow came to implore assistance, and in the name of his Majesty the king I have assigned her a monthly pension of nine ducats. The day before yesterday the enemy burnt all the cottages and farms that were on the verge of the wood.

"October 28th.—From the same wood, 7 A.M.— I drew up the band in line of battle, to determine the number of our rank and file, and to endeavour to give a military organization to the whole.

"7.30 A.M.—In the execution of this purpose I was strongly opposed by Crocco, who is decidedly against any military discipline. He says that we can

---

[*] It must be understood that I do not answer for all the assertions made by Borjès. I shall not even attempt to contradict all his pretended victories, nor his statements about the exaggerated losses inflicted upon the Piedmontese. Nor do I always answer for the correctness of the names of the various localities, in almost every instance badly spelt, and very often illegible. It is, above all, as a sincere confession and a genuine picture of political brigandage as it is, taken from life, if I may so express myself, that this journal, with its characteristic simplicity, constitutes a remarkable and unique document, which in course of time will become very valuable to the historian.

form two companies, but he thinks it useless to make any attempt to organize them before the arrival of a reinforcement of one hundred and thirty, which we have long been waiting for in vain.

"10.30 A.M.—De Langlois comes to tell me he had last night a long conversation with Crocco, the result of which was that the latter declared he would always oppose every attempt that should be made for the purpose of giving his band anything in the shape of military organization. 'If I admit anything of the kind,' said he, 'my power is gone, whilst, as long as I am in these woods, I am the undisputed master. Nobody knows every corner of them better than I; nobody is a match for me in giving the slip to the enemy. What should I do if I were in an open country? Moreover, my men give me the title of general, and I have myself created many a colonel, major, and others, who, like me, would lose their rank if I were to yield on this point. Besides, having never been more than a corporal when I was in the regular army, I do not understand anything in the military line.' This man, it is evident, will never listen to my voice. 'He fears that the result of any change would be to deprive him of his influence, and of the unlimited power which he at present possesses of satisfying his desire for plunder.

"October 29th, 7 A.M.—De Langlois informs me

this morning that he was talking last night for
more than two hours with the nephew of Bosco,* who
appears to be the only one who enjoys Crocco's unbounded confidence. He (Crocco) said that, as the
condition of serving the legitimists, he should require
a regular commission, signed in the name of King
Francis II., entitling him to the full rank of general,
with many other promises besides for the future,
which he has not yet explained, and a considerable
sum of money in addition. It appears that Langlois
told him it was not in our power to grant all these
conditions, but his opinion was that the best means
of obtaining such a rank would undoubtedly be
not to oppose the introduction of military organization among his men. Crocco and his band have
stolen a great amount of money, which, of course,
they are anxious not only to retain in their posses-
session, but also to increase by favour of those
unexpected circumstances which occur during the
progress of a partisan war. If we favour their
wishes, they will consent to aid us in the cause of
royalty ; if not, they will carry on the war so far as
they find it conducive to their own interests, as,
indeed, they have hitherto done.

* This Bosco pretended to be the nephew of the general
of Francis II. of the same name. But the real Bosco denies
this disgraceful relationship.

"12 P.M.—I am informed that yesterday four National Guards of Livacanti (?) barbarously shot a poor woman called Maria Teresa de Genon, because her brother-in-law is with us.

"9 P.M.—A few marauders have come in this moment, who report that they had just met with a National Guard, who had fired at them. They retaliated by rushing at him, and after a few shots killed and disarmed him.

"October 30th, 9 A.M.—We are still at the same place. A few moments ago we had an alarm, and Crocco's men ran away like sheep. I stood with my officers in their way, endeavouring to stop them, calling them cowards, but with no avail.

"10.30 A.M.—We have changed our position, but still remain in the same wood.

"5 P.M.—De Langlois tells me that Crocco's father is in communication with General La Chiesa, and that the latter wrote a letter to Crocco, inviting him to come forth with his band. The latter, it appears, said that it was rather the general who ought to come first to us. La Chiesa then replied: 'If they give a sum of six thousand ducats, and a fixed allowance of thirty-six ducats more per month, I will put the province into your hands. Now that reaction has broken out, the best thing I can do is to make the best of it!'

"Though I have not a sum of six thousand ducats

in my power, yet I authorised de Langlois to assure
La Chiesa that, as soon as he succeeded in putting a
large town into our possession, he should have them.
As I never entirely trust de Langlois, I made him
understand that I did not quite believe the truth of
this extraordinary statement, for the simple reason
that Crocco had never, in his conversations with me,
made the slightest mention of it. De Langlois, however, said in reply that Crocco wanted to keep it
secret, in order to derive alone all the benefits
of the affair—adding that Crocco was very jealous
of his power, which he would not willingly give up.
' Very well,' said I, ' tell him to make our cause
triumph and I have no objection to it—I shall be
myself the first to recognize his authority. But I am
well aware of one thing, namely, that Crocco's ambitious
projects may be frustrated at any time. Everybody
has admired us since our gallant behaviour during the
engagement of the 25th; and I don't think I am mistaken in saying, that the day I shall think it convenient
to raise my voice, Crocco will lose all his influence.'
However, now I am decided to wait to see the
result of all these intrigues, in order to avail myself of
the advantages chance may elicit in our favour. If
I had a few thousand ducats with me, three hundred
men, and some good officers, how soon I should become master of the situation !

"October 31st, 7 A.M.—Croccohas handed over to me a letter from the chief of a band, who says that he puts five hundred men at my disposal. If he does not alter his plans, we are to join them to-night without fail, and to-morrow we shall proceed to the formation of the first battalion.

"November 1st.—Yesterday we set out for the wood of Ariusa (?) di Potenza. On our way we went along the Serra Tocopo-Palese (?), which runs from north to south. On the outskirt of the woods we came to the river Serra del Ponto, and we arrived towards two o'clock in the morning at the above point.

"November 2nd.—Nothing new, except that we are once more without provisions. They say we shall get some by-and-by, but in the meanwhile it is growing late and the soldiers are exhausted.

"November 3rd.—Nothing new.

"11 A.M.—We leave the wood for Trivigno, a little place of 2500 inhabitants, four miles distant.

"1.30. P.M—We arrived at Trivigno, but were received by a hostile population who had taken up arms against us.

"3.30. A.M.—After a struggle of two hours we stormed the town. It is my painful duty to state that the most absolute disorder prevailed among our soldiers, especially among the chiefs themselves. *Thefts, murders, and many other blameable excesses, have been the only results of this attack.* I have no authority whatever.

"Nov. 4th, 6.30. A.M.—We leave Trivigno, and go to Castel Mezzano. We intend stopping there two hours.

"3.30 P.M.—We continued our march, taking the direction of the wood of Cognati, where we arrived at 7 in the evening. I am told that Crocco, de Langlois, and Serravalle have made at Trivigno the grossest exactions that can be imagined. The aristocracy of the place had sought for a refuge at the town-hall, and these three men were not ashamed to go there at once to levy upon them very heavy ransoms. Moreover, they allowed their people to run riot about the town, threatening the inhabitants with death and fire if money was not instantly delivered to them. Having questioned de Langlois on this matter, he told me that the mayor of the town had given them no more than 80 ducats, the only sum that could be collected.

" November 5th, 6.30 A.M.—Order is given to form our column and to start for an unknown destination.

" 11 A.M.—We met eight National Guards, whom we took with us as far as Calciano. We halted there, *and the houses of Royalists as well as Liberals were plundered and ransacked in a savage way!* They even, as I am informed, brutally murdered a poor old woman, whose sad fate was shared by three or four harmless peasants.

"5.30 A.M.—We reached Garaguso, where we met a long procession of citizens, led by the old curate, with the Holy Cross in his tremulous hands, who had come forth to implore that peace and mercy which I am truly willing to grant them. God grant that the others may follow my example.*

"Alas! I shall not attempt to say anything of the scene of horror which took place, when, overpowered with indignation at the sight of the disorder which I was unable to restrain, I withdrew from the wretched village.

"November 6th, 10 A.M.—We set off this morning to attack the town of La Salandra, guarded by a hundred Garibaldians and a detachment of Piedmontese. As soon as the enemy perceived us they took up their position on a little elevation, from which it seemed that it would be impossible for us to dislodge them. When I arrived at about a hundred yards distance, I sent on Major Francis Foms with half a company, who succeeded, notwithstanding the ruggedness of the ground, in dislodging the enemy from their position. When we had obtained possession of it, the latter, retreating before our advancing column, occupied a few houses a little further on, in the vain hope of being able from them to oppose a stronger resistance; but when they saw that I was ready to

* From this point the present MS. is written in pencil.

attack them from behind, they retired in great disorder, leaving the town entirely defenceless. Divining
their intentions, I lost no time in falling upon them;
and we killed twelve of their number, took their
colours, and made several prisoners. On our side
we had only one casualty, that of the chief Serravalle,
who was slightly wounded in the head. The town
was then pillaged. (Salandra is a place of about two
thousand inhabitants.)

" *Terra di Cucariello*, district of Salandra, November 7th, 2 P.M.—Serravalle has died this moment from
the consequences of his wound. They beg me to write
to his Majesty to give orders for the construction of a
stronghold in this place.

"November 8th, 3 A.M.—Having drawn our soldiers up in line of battle before leaving the place,
Crocco ordered Don Pinno Spazziano to be shot in
one of the rooms of the Town-hall; after which, we
set off in the direction of Craco, where we arrived at
three o'clock in the afternoon.   The whole population
came out to meet us, in order, by this act of respect,
to avoid the devastation of their village.   I am
sorry to say, notwithstanding, that the village was
savagely plundered as soon as we were the masters of
it.

"November 9th, 6 A.M.—We left Craco and advanced in the direction of Aliano (both villages con-

taining from one to two thousand inhabitants). At
two o'clock in the afternoon we met a body of National
Guards, at whom we rushed impetuously. They
could not stand our attack, and retired into a neighbouring wood. Not, however, until our cavalry had
killed four of them and captured one prisoner, whom
I soon after ordered to be released.

"7 P.M.—We arrived at Aliano, the population of
which, led by a priest carrying the Holy Cross, came
forth to receive us in procession, shouting 'Viva
Francesco II.!'" But this did not prevent the usual
disorders during the night—a state of things which
would indeed be astonishing, were it not that
the leader of the band and his satellites are the
worst set of ruffians and thieves I ever came across
in my life.

"November 10th, 9 A.M.—A sentinel told me
that the enemy were concentrated on the Alcinella.
I went out instantly to see if this report was true,
and I ascertained that there were at least five or six
hundred. I called up my men, four hundred in
number, and drew them up in a line in front of
the enemy, waiting to see what movements they
contemplated, before I adopted a plan. Soon after
I had an opportunity of discovering the inexperience
of the Piedmontese commander, and thinking I could
take advantage of this favourable circumstance, I

addressed a few encouraging words to my men, promising them an easy victory if they would but strictly
obey me. I then advanced towards the enemy's outposts. When I got near a little chapel, which is but
a hundred yards distant, on the east side of the village,
I sent on Major Francis Foms with the first company, instructing him only to display half his force as
skirmishers, and to bring the rest up in the rear, in
order to protect them, always keeping the road that
runs from Aliano to the river. At the same time I
ordered the Lieutenant-Colonel in command of the
second company, to occupy an elevation formed by the
ground on the right side, and thence vigorously to
attack the enemy on their flank. This movement was
executed with admirable precision, whilst the first
company was attacking the front. As the bed of the
river is here very wide, I placed the cavalry in the rear
of the first company, with orders to cross the river,
to take up their position on a sort of little islet planted
with olive trees, and then to attack the enemy in the
rear. I took with me the rest of the infantry, and
advanced in column between the two wings, ready to
protect them in case they required assistance. The
impulse of the two companies was so strong that the
enemy could not resist it, and I hoped at that
moment to see the cavalry advance and thus prevent their retreat; but, to my great disappointment,

instead of following my orders, they had all
alighted from their horses, and were amusing themselves by shooting under cover at such a distance that
their fire could not have the slightest effect upon the
enemy. This circumstance rendered our success very
doubtful. However, I charged the fellows with my
men. Making them rapidly advance with me towards
the centre of the river, where I had once more the
superiority over the enemy, I succeeded in dislodging them from their former position. But the Piedmontese got hold of a mill placed rather in a good
situation for defence, and there they stood ready
again to dispute with us the ground.   I then
detached a section from the main body under my
orders, leading it to the back of the mill, whilst the
two other companies were directed to take it in front
and on the flanks. This unexpected movement was
so rapidly executed, that the enemy did not wait for
the attack, but evacuated his strong position before
we could reach him. Unfortunately, however, the
ruggedness of the mountainous ground between the
mill and Stigliano favoured the Piedmontese once
more, for, making a desperate effort, they charged us
with the bayonet. The first and second company
stood the attack very firmly for more than ten
minutes, during which interval I was enabled to
come up with the reserve.   From that moment

the rout of the Piedmontese was complete. They
disbanded themselves in great disorder, flying into the
woods on both sides, and leaving, besides their dead,
five prisoners in our hands. We killed about forty of
them (?), among whom was an officer who had displayed the most heroic bravery whilst leading his
men to the bayonet charge. The five prisoners took
service with us (?). We then halted at about a mile
from Astagnano,* so exhausted, that we left the enemy
unpursued, not being able to go onward after them.

"Strange as it may seem, in this affair we did not
suffer any loss; a piece of good fortune which was
more like the result of a miracle than the effect of
mere blind chance. Lieut.-Colonel Augustus Lafond
was struck a little above his right eye by a blow from
the muzzle of a gun; a soldier had his head grazed
by a ball; and these were the only casualties we had
to lament. After an hour's rest a messenger, despatched to us from Astagnano, came to say that the
population were awaiting our arrival, and that they
begged us to hasten it as much as was in our
power.

"Encouraged by these friendly declarations, I drew
up the troops and we set off. As soon as we reached
the approaches of the town we saw a long procession

* Probably Stigliano (5000 inhabitants), the only important
place they have succeeded in occupying.

of monks and priests, preceded by the Holy Cross
and various sacred banners, advancing towards us.
An immense crowd lined both sides of the road,
among whom were many carrying the white flag of
the Bourbons, who made the air resound with cries
of ' Viva Francesco II. !' Amidst all that enthusiasm
we made our triumphal entrance into Astagnano,
strictly enjoining every soldier not to commit any
disorder, and making a distribution of money
among them, before we had them billeted about the
town, in the vain hope that, having thus satisfied
their cupidity, they would perhaps be restrained from
committing excesses. Apparently animated, however, by an evil genius, they began as usual their deeds
of violence, and with the view of restraining them, we
were obliged to have two of the ringleaders shot on
the spot, the only mode by which we could hope to
make our authority respected.

"*Astagnano*, November 11th.—We have spent a
quiet day, though we have been very busy in enlisting about three hundred men from the neighbouring
villages; with these new recruits we number now
seven hundred well-armed men.

"November 12th, 9 A.M.—We left Astagnano
with the intention of going to Cirigliano and Gor-
goglione to disarm the National Guard. At the first
of these two places we stopped nearly two hours.

We set off for the latter at 1.30 P.M., but had hardly got near the beginning of the ascent which leads to it, when we were told that the enemy was not more than a mile off. Seeing that my position was greatly endangered, I ordered Major Foms to go forward with the first company, whilst with the rest of our force I occupied the towering points of the surrounding hills. These dispositions made, I waited for the enemy with my lines drawn up in fighting order. After a quarter of an hour I could perceive the head of their column, at least twelve hundred strong, slowly and cautiously advancing between the two villages, with the evident intent of getting possession of the road that lies in the centre of the valley; but it was too late. Seeing at a glance all the advantages of my position, I boldly faced the enemy with my front. He durst not accept the engagement. After evincing great hesitation, he tried to out-manœuvre me, but failing also in that, he withdrew at nightfall without even exchanging a shot. We did not wait long before we took our departure in our turn, setting off in the direction of the wood of Montepiano di Pietrapertosa.

"November 13th, 6 A.M.—Leaving the above wood, we proceeded towards Accettura, reaching its highest point, notwithstanding Crocco's opposition. I gave the signal to halt, and, to prevent any disorder or surprise, I ordered the troops to remain where they were, until I had sent out a few men to get the necessary provisions for the day. These were very liberally supplied by the neighbouring villages, and distributed among the men. The clergy, covered with their sacred ornaments, and bearing the image of our Saviour, came to pay me their respects, requesting me and my officers to attend the celebration of the Holy Mass. I thanked the good priests as best I could, but, though few things would have given me greater pleasure, I was not able to avail myself of the kind offer. I told them, however, that I hoped, with the help of the Holy Virgin, I might soon be able to do so. In the meanwhile, a sentry gave the alarm that the enemy were fast approaching ; I accordingly dismissed the servants of God, and hurried off to my battalions. I took up my position at Guransi, which we reached about mid-day.

" 2 P.M.—The enemy is in sight. I made the drummers beat the 'générale,' and the bugles give the signal for the attack, but again the enemy retired and took up a strong position.

" 6 P.M.—I fell back to the wood called La Macchia del Cierro, where we put up for the night.

" November 14th, 6 A.M.—We started for Grassano, which we reached by ten o'clock. I had the men billeted about the place, but no sooner was this done,

than their unworthy chiefs went out robbing, plundering, and laying waste everything that came within
their reach.

"2 P.M.—The enemy making a movement, we
were at once in arms ready to fight.   Though twice
our number, they did not appear very sanguine as to
the result.   A few shots, however, were exchanged
between our outposts during the rest of the day.

"8 P.M.—Seeing that the enemy did not stir, I
placed some sentries for the night watch, and retired
into the town with the troops.

"November 15th, 7 A.M.—The enemy occupies
still the same position.

"8 A.M.—I recalled all the sentries and outposts,
and we went to Santo Chirico, where we arrived at
eleven o'clock.   I left one of the officers on guard
at the residence of the captain of the National Guard,
for the protection of his property and his family.   He
felt greatly indebted for this, and I was glad to see
that some order had prevailed on that particular
spot.

"3 P.M.—We left Santo Chirico with the intention
of attacking the village of Longli (?) ; but when we
arrived within a mile of it, we halted for the rest
of the day.

"November 16th, 6 A.M.—I made a reconnoissance
in order to ascertain my position, and found that it

was a very strong one. I sent out the fourth
company against the left of the village, the
first against its right, and the third against its
centre. The rest of the infantry I kept under my
command on the high ground facing the village on
the right of the new road. I distributed my so-called
cavalry between my right and left sides. When the
infantry reached the bridge, which is situated at the
foot of the ascent, the enemy made a heavy discharge
of musketry, and wounded a man belonging to the
first company. Nevertheless, they continued bravely
to advance to the attack. The enemy, seeing our
firmness, retired in haste, taking refuge in a palace
close at hand, but a great portion of them fell into
the hands of our soldiers. The captain of the first
company attacked the palace, setting fire to bundles
of straw and burning pitch which he had collected
around it. The enemy, not knowing what to do,
and some of them driven to despair, tried to throw
themselves out of the windows. All of a sudden,
however, the signal for retreat was sounded. I do
not know the traitor by whom it was ordered, but
already our columns had begun to fall back, and our
success consequently remained incomplete. Two of
our wounded were left in the village, and we had to
lament two deaths, besides a few wounded. When the
action was thus unexpectedly terminated, we marched

towards Pietragulla, which was also occupied by the
Piedmontese, and we arrived at 3 P.M. Having re-
connoitred the position, I sent on, against the right of
the town, the third and fourth companies, the fifth and
sixth, with part of the cavalry, against the left,
and the first and second against the centre. The
enemy, strongly entrenched behind a wall, opened
a deadly fire against us; but Major Don Pasquale
Marginet, now lieutenant in the second company,
dashed forward with admirable courage, followed by a
few men, and, as quick as lightning, took possession
of the first houses of the town.

"The captain then followed up instantly with the
rest of the company, and, with the exception of the
old Ducal Castle, where the enemy sought a last refuge, the town was stormed and taken in the twinkling of an eye. We had four killed and five wounded, or more correctly, between these two affairs,
nine wounded, Lieutenant Laureano Carenas being
among them. The action once over, I hastily retired
to a house, in order not to witness the scenes of
disorder and horror which it is not in my power to
prevent, owing to the lack of a sufficient force to
make myself obeyed and respected. I fear Crocco,
who *has been robbing and plundering all this time,
must be scheming some treason.**

* Evidently there is a gap here. One naturally wonders

"November 19th, 10 A.M.—We formed our lines in order to start for the wood of Lagopesole, where we arrived at four o'clock in the afternoon. Crocco disappeared soon afterwards, saying it was only to get some bread; but I am afraid it was to find out a place where he could conceal the large quantity of booty, and the considerable sums of money, he had obtained by violence during this expedition.

"November 18th, 1 P.M.—We are still in the same wood, and Crocco is not yet come back with the provisions. This doubtful conduct has been the cause of our losing, in less than three days, nearly three hundred and fifty men, or, in other words, half our force.

"4 P.M.—We raised our little encampment, and transported our head-quarters to a position a mile further on. Crocco is still absent.

"November 19th.—Crocco has arrived, but has not yet shown himself in my presence.

why Borjès and his band, after having stormed Pietragalla with so little trouble, if we can believe his own account, should have left it so suddenly. Official and more reliable documents do not, however, leave any doubt to be entertained about that. The heroic resistance of the inhabitants of Pietragalla is well enough known. From the castle, where they had strongly barricaded themselves, they entirely repulsed the reactionist band, inflicting upon them a loss of more than forty men. And it is worth noticing that the National Guard *alone*, without the help of the regular troops, was enough to defeat Borjès's partisans and Crocco's bandits.

"12 A.M.—Crocco has summoned everybody around him, after having fired many shots in the air. I went up the hill to find out what the firing meant, and he said that it was the signal for rallying, to be ready to march against Avigliano, a town of 18,000 inhabitants. On my objecting that this was a mere impossibility, considering how much stronger were the national forces assembled there, he bluntly observed it was an irrelevant remark, as we could not draw back, and were bound to go somewhere. To this I answered that nobody was more eager to advance than myself, and I was therefore ready to follow him. He was pleased to find my answer so very satisfactory, and declared that we should soon be off. He then retired to speak with some men, whom he ought never to have seen or consulted. After a few moments he came back, and everything being ready, we raised our encampment and set off. After a certain time had elapsed, hardly believing that Crocco, notwithstanding what he had said, would really persevere in such an absurd plan, I asked a man whom I met on the road in what direction we were going. 'To Avigliano,' was his brief answer. It was enough, however, for me. I had acquired the certitude that that faithless ruffian was leading us into a snare. Whilst absorbed by a thousand sad reflections, excited by this discovery, our cavalry major came up to me, saying: 'We are going to attack a pretty town, general.' 'We are then really going to Avigliano?' said I. 'Yes, general,' replied the other. 'Well, major, all I can do is to protest with all my power against such an enterprise.'

"3 P.M.—Arrived in sight of Avigliano, Crocco signified to me I had now to make all the necessary dispositions for an immediate attack. I indignantly told him that, since he was doing everything in his power to compromise the success of our cause, he might take himself any such steps as he thought convenient, as I would not on any account assume the responsibility of an enterprise which could not possibly succeed.

"He then ordered the town to be attacked by the whole of our forces, without leaving a single man in reserve. The action once begun, he put himself in safety, and I remained to witness what was going to take place. The redoubt, which is on the left side of the town, was stormed by the first company, supported by the second, but they could not take a chapel which is in advance on the same line, and which protects the approaches of the town towards the centre. The right was assailed by the rest of the band, but their efforts were checked by a stone wall which protects the western portion of the town. To crown all, the night came on, and with it a thick dark fog, accompanied by a cold drizzling rain which was unbearable.

"Crocco gave at last the signal for retreat, and we repaired to a little village called Paolo Duce, where, without food of any description, wet to the skin, shivering with cold, and with no straw even to lie upon, we spent a horrid night, surpassing in misery the worst we had as yet endured. These hardships, added to the preceding disorders, contributed to reduce to a very small number the already limited force of our band. During the whole night I could never find out what had become of Crocco.

"November 20th, 5 A.M.—I ordered the reveille to be beaten, and passed the muster. Ninco-Nanco voluntered to be my guide, an offer that I accepted immediately. After half an hour's march, they told me that Crocco was staying at a country house situated at about two hundred yards off the road where we were. He has sent me word this very moment (8 o'clock) to stop. I accordingly gave the signal to halt, in the hope of seeing him, but in vain, as he has not come.

"9 A.M.—Ninco-Nanco, Donato, and some other officers, announce to me that Crocco has left us altogether. I assembled all the officers and asked them what they intended to do, assuring every one that I was firmly resolved to persevere to the last, if they would but follow me.

"Bosco, replying in the name of his brother officers, was interrupted by one of them, who said that
nobody in the band would submit to the orders of
Spanish officers; and that, moreover, having been
appointed by General Clary to command only in the
province of Basilicata, I had no right to exercise such
authority in any other part of the country. Although
far from in any way resenting the freedom of the
officers under my command, I called upon them all to
resign the various posts of authority which they held,
as I did myself, in order to show that it was from
devotion, and not mere personal interest, that we
were serving the cause of the king. De Langlois
stood aloof during all this discussion, never saying a
single word. I understood at once that he was the
soul of the conspiracy, and, therefore, I told the men
of the band to settle the question among themselves,
promising to adhere to their decision. The
result was that all their own officers were put at the
head of the companies, and de Langlois assumed
the chief command. Not a word, however, with regard to this proceeding was communicated to me, and
I only knew the new dispositions by seeing de Langlois arrogating to himself the entire direction of
everything, without even consulting me. In a word,
I had been altogether dismissed.

"November 21st.—Last night de Langlois sent

his orderly to tell me to be ready to leave early next morning; but it is already eight o'clock, and we are still in the wood of Lagopesole.

"8.30 A.M.—We have set out, but where we are going I know not.

"9.30 A.M.—We halted at a glade in the forest, from which we can discover Rionero.

"10.45 A.M.—We resumed our march for Santa Lauria (?), where we arrived at 1.45 P.M.

"November 22nd.—We set off this morning at half-past six, in order to reach Bella before mid-day. There we stopped, and de Langlois mustered the troops. I, being at the rear, did the same. De Langlois came to me to ascertain whether I meant to take the command in the attack on the town; but I told him in reply that, as he arrogated to himself the right of superintending everything, he must also make the necessary dispositions for the attack. He did not make any remark, but went off and made the arrangements which he considered necessary for the ensuing movement; but they were such as to prove to me that he had never been a soldier. In proof of this I may state that, although it is now more than four hours since they commenced their purposeless attack upon this position, they have not yet been able to get at it. I am confident that if we had advanced against it in a soldier-like manner, boldly storming it, it would have fallen into our hands in a quarter of an hour.

"4.30 P.M.—The town has been set on fire on two different sides—an untoward event, which does not in the least relax the vigour of the resistance with which the inhabitants meet our attacks.

"6 P.M.—One of the streets of the town is in our hands; the centre and the north side are still in the hands of the revolutionists. What is in our power is being recklessly burnt down.

"November 23rd, 6.30 A.M.—We went out of the town, or rather that part of it which we had succeeded in taking, an operation during which one of our lieutenants was severely wounded. We formed, our ranks facing the east, and at a few yards from the enemy.

"8.30 A.M.—We are marching towards our fellow-soldiers scattered here and there near the south part of the town.

"10 A.M.—Crocco, who has reappeared since yesterday, is occupied in burning the country houses on the west side.

"11 A.M.—We are going to Muro.

"12 A.M.—Some shots being heard from the van-guard, the infantry gave the alarm, and asked the cavalry to proceed forward. I could soon perceive that our companies were wrongly directed, from the ignorant manner in which they were scattered in different positions.

"1 A.M.—I reached the top of the mountain of Serra, and thence beheld the dispersion of all our men. Hearing shots near a tavern, I proceeded there to ascertain the cause, and met Crocco and Ninco-Nanco flying at the utmost speed to which they could put their horses. Nevertheless, I went forward, though I had no instructions to do so, to see if I could ascertain what was the exact number of our enemies, and in that moment I perceived de Langlois, alone, cowardly sheltering himself from the fire of the enemy. I inquired where our captains were, but received no answer from him. I continued my way with the remaining officers, and some men who had joined me, and in a few moments discovered the enemy. The party with me being exposed to their fire, one of my soldiers was killed by a musket shot. I discovered from the movements of the enemy that on the left they were yielding, but the right, defended by a wood, was still maintaining its position. Our soldiers, when they perceived the intention of their officers to move forward, took to flight, abandoning the wounded, the fruit of their robbery (*sic*), their provisions, and their fire-arms, and retired as quickly as possible before the National Guards, who were advancing from Balvano.

"After this first battle, the success of which seemed very doubtful, we crossed a little river at the foot of a mountain, where de Langlois again formed the ranks, an operation which he did not now find very difficult, as the enemy had not dared to pursue us. We descended afterwards the river (probably the Fiume di Muro), which flows from north to south, and after marching one hour, met a company of forty-seven men, of good appearance, and, judging from the orderly manner in which they marched, well disciplined. They placed themselves at our head, and we followed them, arriving at Balvano at nine in the evening. The town was entirely illuminated, and we were almost deafened on our entrance by the shouts of the people crying aloud—'Viva Francesco II.!'*

"The bishop, some priests, and the remainder of the National Guard shut themselves in the castle, a place of such strength that it cannot be taken. The National Guard said to us they hoped we would respect property, and they would not fire upon us even if we fired on them. Their captain had an interview with Crocco. Don Giovanni and de Langlois

* It is to be observed that the National Guard, that is to say, the Liberal party of Balvano, had been sent to Muro, where they had already obliged the band of Crocco to retire, but the latter, driven back, took possession of their abandoned city. This is not the least curious episode of the campaign.

went to the castle. I do not know what they did, but I know, and write it with sincere pleasure, that during the night the town was kept in perfect order.

"*Balvano*, November 24th, 7.30 A.M.—We ascended a mountain, and continuing our march, reached in the afternoon Ricigliano (Principato Citeriore), where we were received by the people bearing olive branches in their hands.

"11 A.M.—The most extraordinary disorders are taking place in the town ; I dare not give any details, so revolting are the horrors committed.

"November 25th, 6 A.M.—We formed our ranks, an operation which takes some time—but whether to march, or with any other object, I know not.

"8.30 A.M.—Crocco has given orders to send forward the vanguard, because the enemy is before us.

"9 A.M.—I heard a general fire of musketry going on, but after it had continued about five minutes it began to slacken, and soon ceased altogether. The National Guard are retiring. A hundred Piedmontese hold a good position, from which they do not seem inclined to move.

"12.45 P.M.—We formed our ranks in order to reach a miserable shelter at five minutes distance, where we spent a wretched cold night.

"November 26th, 7.30 A.M.—We are pursuing

our march over very high and cold mountains. At twelve we descended towards the valley, where we met a force of forty soldiers, who, after preparing to fight us, yielded to our first charge, and were obliged by our cavalry to shut themselves in Castellogrande.

"10.30 P.M.—We continued our march in the direction of Pescopagano, where we arrived at a quarter to four. We invested the town, but the resolution of our soldiers seeming to be doubtful, Lieut.-Colonel Lafond and Major Fonis addressed them. 'We give no commandment,' they said, 'but if you consent to follow us, we shall take the town.' A hurrah was returned; our troops rushed to the assault, and in a few minutes became masters of the position."

[Five lines which occur at this place in the manuscript are scratched out.]

"November 27th, 5 A.M.—I sent Captain Martinez to Crocco, in order to let him know that it is time to wake the soldiers, but he paid no attention to my words.

"6 A.M.—Hearing no roll, I called myself on Crocco. Seeing him speaking with somebody in the street, I bowed to him, and immediately after told him we ought to leave the town as soon as possible, in order to prevent our losing a considerable number of men. At that moment a bugler happening to pass, I

gave the order for a sudden reveille, which Crocco
forbade. I begged of him again to order the usual
call, but he still refused, and, standing for a moment
as if immersed in thought, turned away. I did the
same, foreseeing the danger that must be the consequence of military operations so conducted. The
result of all this has been the loss of twenty-five men,
according to some—of forty, according to others. We
have undoubtedly lost a considerable number of our
infantry, and even some cavalry.* The failure of payment, the prevailing disorder, and the opposition of
some men of influence will now cause the loss of our
entire band.

"4 P.M.—The enemy of whom I was speaking is
still in sight, but dares not attack us.

"5 P.M.—We entered the wood of Monticelio,
where, although we were without any provisions, not
having so much as a loaf of bread, we fixed our
camp.

"November 28th, 7 A.M.—We made a halt in the
middle of the wood, still destitute of provisions. The
band is gradually dissolving.

"12.30 A.M.—We are ready to resume our march,
but I do not know whither we are bound. If their

---

* Thanks to the volunteers of l'escopagniic, whose conduct was admirable. After this fight one may say that the band
of Crocco was reduced to nothing.

direction does not suit me, *I had better go to Rome.*

"3 P.M.—What a sad scene! Crocco has assembled his *ancient chief robbers,* and has given to them his old comrades. All the other soldiers are violently disarmed, their rifles or percussion guns being taken from them. Some soldiers have taken to flight; others are crying; they ask to serve only that they may be enabled to earn their bread, and would gladly give up their pay. But these assassins are inexorable. The soldiers have been given into the custody of some brigand chiefs, by whom they are discharged without food, after having had none for two days. All this had been arranged beforehand, but had been purposely concealed from me. Some soldiers kissed my hands, and said: 'Come back with a small force, and you shall always find us ready to accompany you.' For my part, I asked Crocco to save these poor men; I gave them all the consolation it was in my power to give, weeping myself, like them, all the time.

"November 29th.—We have marched the whole night.

"November 30th.—We are tired after a long march, and stop.

"December 1st.— *   *   *   *   *   *   "

Thus ends the journal of Borjès. The remainder of the manuscript only contains the names of places.

There is also the draught of a letter, addressed on the
26th to General Clary, giving, without any additional
details, an account of the last battle, terminating
with some short narratives of no interest. I think it
unnecessary to add any commentary to this terrible
journal, the authenticity of which is beyond doubt.
The original is at Turin, in the Foreign Office, where
it may be perused by those who are curious respecting such documents.

The retreat of Borjès into the Papal States was
almost as difficult an enterprise as the restoration of
Francis II. He felt, however, no hesitation in entering upon it. It is now quite impossible to follow his
track. For some time he was completely lost, and
no one knows in what direction he was proceeding.
We find him again in Terra di Lavoro, near the
frontier of the Roman State. On the 4th of December he was in the neighbourhood of Pescasseroli. He
could proceed to Rome by two ways—either by the
mountain and the valley of Rovelo, or by the usual
high-road of Avezzano; but the snow constrained him
to take the last. At about two miles from Avezzano,
he turned suddenly in the direction of Capelle and
Scurgola. He was under the necessity of passing
through this last village at ten o'clock at night, not
far from a post of National Guards.

" Who's there ?" cried the sentinel.

" Friends !" answered Borjès.

And· he passed on without hindrance, the sentry being totally unsuspicious of the prize within his reach. He was even able to pass Tagliacozzo without being detained by any one. Taking the advice of his guide, he answered the sentinel on duty at the entrance, " We are *castagnari* (that is to say, bearers of chestnuts), going to Santa Maria." Borjès, thinking himself already safe, stopped, and there gave his soldiers some hours of rest.

It is now my painful duty to relate the circumstances of Borjès' tragic death. His fearless audacity and almost constant good-fortune had enabled him to pass in safety through the continental part of the old Neapolitan kingdom in all its length, although surrounded by a hostile population, thousands of National and Mobilized Guards, gendarmes, soldiers sent out against him in every direction, hidden in ambush on his way, concealed in the woods, lurking among the hills, and guarding the villages where he was thought likely to pass. Ever ready to fight, bold and prompt in his movements, vigilant and full of courage, he had succeeded in making his way through many provinces, sleeping during the night in the mud or snow, and often fasting almost the whole day. He had thus reached the Abruzzi, and was nearly touching the limits of that territory, where he would have been safe under the paternal protection of Pius IX. The good-fortune which had so long attended him forsook him almost at the moment when his perils and difficulties were about to cease. At the entrance of this promised land, in the very last village beyond the Roman frontier, he was taken and killed.

We are indebted for all the details of this important capture to the report of the gallant officer, Major Franchini, who was the chief actor in it. The following document, containing an account of the manner in which the fearless and adventurous Borjès was taken, was addressed to General Lamarmora :—

" *Tagliacozzo*, December 9th.—On the 7th, at half-past eleven at night, a letter of the *sous préfet* made me aware that Borjès, accompanied by twenty-two of his men on horseback, had succeeded in crossing Patcano on his way to Scurgola. On the 8th, at half-past three in the morning, by another letter from the major of the gendarmes, I was informed that on the previous evening, at seven o'clock, the same men had passed through Cappelle, and everything seemed to prove that they were proceeding towards Scurgola and Santa Maria al Tufo.

" Having received this information, I immediately despatched some soldiers, commanded by a serjeant, to Scurgola, in the hope of finding them again, sending others at the same time to Santa Maria, under the command of a corporal, to inquire whether the brigands had arrived there. But they had already received information regarding the steps we were taking, and had passed over Tagliacozzo and Santa Maria on their way to Lupa, a farm belonging to Signor Mastroddi. I was then certain of the arrival of the band, and, taking about thirty Bersaglieri with me, the first I met with, and Lieutenant Staderini, the officer on duty that day, two hours before daybreak I went on the track of these wretches. On my arrival at Santa Maria, I heard more of the brigands from the patrol which had been ordered out by me, and also from the peasants. I rested in this village a very short time, and then, aided by the marks of their footsteps in the snow, proceeded in pursuit of them.

"It was about ten o'clock in the morning when I reached the farm Mastroddi, where I observed nothing indicating the presence of the brigands, when suddenly, at fifty yards from it, on the other side of the way, I perceived a man running away. I went after him, and soon overtook him. On accosting him, the Bersaglieri following me, the bandit pointed his musket and fired at me. The shot fortunately did not go off. I immediately fired the first barrel of my revolver at him with the same negative result;

but a second shot, which I directed at his head, killed
him on the spot. ' My Bersaglieri came round
me, and, with their bayonets, killed five men
found outside.   We then surrounded the Cascina,
but the brigands fired at us from the windows, and in
their turn killed five of my soldiers.   In the sharp
engagement which now took place, the brigands
defended themselves with great fury.   After half
an hour's contest, I summoned them to surrender;
otherwise, I assured them I had decided to set fire
to the house.   They refused to surrender.   Wishing
to spare the lives of my brave soldiers as much as I
could, I gave orders to set the place on fire, on seeing which the brigands surrendered unconditionally.
Twenty-three muskets, three swords, seventeen horses,
many important papers, fell into our hands, besides
three Italian banners with the cross of Savoy, which
they, no doubt, occasionally displayed, in order to deceive their pursuers.   General Borjès himself and his
other countrymen, a list of whom I have included, were
now prisoners.   I had them brought with me to Tagliacozzo, where they were shot at four o'clock in the afternoon.   May this example be useful to all the enemies
of our king and country !   Several National Guards of
Santa Maria, and their captain, who had followed
me, behaved well.   I shall send to the governor of
this province the proposal for medals and rewards.

Lieutenant Staderini showed himself a man of honour, full of intelligence, coolness, and courage. All the Bersaglieri have very much distinguished themselves. I send you a list of the rewards which I think ought to be granted to my soldiers, with all the papers and the interesting correspondence found on General Borjès and his company. They may be very useful to the Government.

(Signed) " MAJOR FRANCHINI."

It is fortunately in my power to add certain other details respecting the death of Borjès. When he was taken in the farm, he consented to surrender his sword into the hands of Major Franchini alone, saying to him, " Well done, young major !"

The prisoners were tied together two by two, and sent to Tagliacozzo. During the journey, Borjès was generally silent, smoking the whole time, only repeating now and then, " These Bersaglieri are really very fine soldiers." He also addressed Captain Staderini in these words: " I was just going to tell Francis II. what miserable criminals are the only supporters of his cause—Crocco being a knave, and Langlois a brute." He expressed his regret at having been arrested so near the Roman territory.

Franchini did his best to obtain some revelations from the prisoners, but none of the Spaniards spoke.

x 2

"Were you to inflict torture upon me, you should not get a single word in return," said Borjès, whom nobody, however, thought of torturing; "you had better thank God that I did not get up this morning one hour earlier—I should now be in the Papal States, and would soon have come back again with a new band to put down the rule of Victor Emmanuel." These words are given in the second report (unpublished) of Major Franchini.

At Tagliacozzo, Borjès and his men were shut up in a barrack, where they were asked for their names. A Spaniard, Pedro Martinez, asked for some ink and paper, and only wrote these three lines : " We are all ready to die ; we shall meet again in the valley of Josaphat —pray for us !" They were all confessed in a chapel, and soon after conducted to the place of execution. " Our last hour is come," said Borjès. " Let us die like men !" He kissed his companions, and asked the Bersaglieri to aim straight at his head. Then falling on his knees, he began singing with his countrymen a Spanish litany, the others joining in the chorus. The litany was interrupted by a discharge of musketry, and ten Spaniards fell to the ground. Then came the turn of the Neapolitans, among whom, however, there was still one foreigner, who is reported to have exclaimed : " I ask a general pardon from everyone !"

Such was the end of Borjès and his companions.

Only one of them, Augustus Capilcorta, being ill, had been left on the way. Borjès had given him sixteen Napoleons. This poor man lived for one month in a grotto in Basilicata, where the National Guard went in search of him. All the depositions made confirm the account I have given. As I said above, all the Spaniards avowed that, seduced by the false arguments of committees and newspapers, they expected to have been met in Italy by a standing army, whilst they only found some brigands, obliged to flee and look for a refuge, like themselves.

The execution of Borjès has been blamed. M. Victor Hugo exclaimed: " The Italian Government sends the royalists to death. But how are they to be distinguished from brigands? How can they be justly declared innocent of murders and robbery, which they commit like the others ? Borjès had always lived with Crocco, and fought with him side by side. The law must be executed, and it runs thus : ' Anyone who shall be taken fighting against the government is sentenced to death.' This law was made only against brigands, for brigands only used to mix in this civil war. Not a single honest Italian, not one officer of the last king, not even a single man with whom the leaders of reaction would have shaken hands in public, was to be found in the bands of Crocco or Mittica. Why, then, did Borjès, a stranger, come with these

assassins? Was his life to be spared because he was
a Spaniard?"

The Neapolitans would have violently protested
against this injustice. Such is the truth of this statement, that when, at a later period, at the request of
Prince Scilla, General Lamarmora consented to the
exhumation of the body of Borjès, which was transported to Rome, there was a cry of indignation from
all the neighbouring villages. They protested against
this measure at Caserta, Naples, and Turin. The
excitement prevailing amongst these populations
admitted of no distinction between royalism and
brigandage.

After the execution of the Spaniard, the band of
Crocco was dispersed. Having vainly attempted to
effect a junction with him, Cipriano La Gala made
his appearance on the heights of San Martino, in the
province of Avellino, but a brilliant expedition, directed by General Franzini, succeeded in putting him
down. He appeared again in Terra di Lavoro, on
the banks of the Volturno; it was, however, only for a
short time, and since then his track has been completely lost. Perhaps he had already succeeded in
safely arriving at the Quirinal, or—who knows?—
the Vatican!

At the same time, also on the limits of the
Roman States, brigandage was losing intensity.

A fresh expedition of legitimists, stopped at its beginning at Alatri, showed how miserable and exhausted were these bands, how weak their supporters. Another attempt made in Sicily proved a failure, and only succeeded in reanimating in that island its past hatred against the Bourbon family, and its faith in the national cause.

In the spring of the year 1862, there were still, however, some bands in the Gargano, in Capitanata, on the shores of the Adriatic. But on the other hand, Zambro, Turri-Turri, and Codipietro were already forgotten or dead, and other parts of the kingdom were quiet. Such was the state of things at the beginning of General Lamarmora's administration. Both governor of Naples and commander of the sixth *corps d'armée*, he made himself exceedingly popular amongst the Neapolitans on account of his good sterling *Piedmontese* quality. Full of reserve, strongminded, vigilant, bold if required, strong, never boasting in vain, he kept, nevertheless, Naples in his hands, and did not make a display of his power. He alone could have succeeded in such a task after the conqueror of Gaëta and Castelfidardo. Moreover, General Lamarmora first dared to take the great measure which frightened so much all his predecessors. He ordered a conscription of thirty-six thousand men, and it was carried out almost everywhere with

the warmest enthusiasm.   For the first time since
Naples existed, it witnessed young recruits joyfully
joining their banners, exclaiming—" Long live the
King !"

If we now think what Italy was towards the end
of 1860, with Francis II. at Gaëta, brigandage
strongly organized almost everywhere, Civitella del
Tronto and Messina yet under the sway of the Bourbons, three standing armies—that of Francis II., that
of Garibaldi, and that of Victor Emmanuel—the
country in revolution, the finances exhausted, the
authorities unrespected, France uncertain, Austria
threatening an invasion, the Pope fulminating his ana-
thema ; and if we afterwards consider that Piedmont,
amidst all these difficulties, has not only succeeded in
resisting Papal maledictions, Austrian revengefulness,
French hesitation, and revolutionary impatience, in
conquering Messina and Gaëta, in totally destroying
the power of Francis II., in discarding that of Garibaldi, and capturing fresh batches of foreign brigands;
moreover, that it met, resisted, and conquered whatever opposition arose from Neapolitan municipalism,
that, even at that most dangerous moment, it persevered in its idea of annexation and unity at any
price, exposing to misrepresentation the characters of
those most distinguished statesmen, Nigra, Ponza di
San Martino, Farini, and even more—Cavour ; that

it became unpopular by gradually taking away from the Neapolitans their autonomical government, and even their supremacy over the southern provinces, by reducing a capital of half a million inhabitants to the rank of an unimportant chief district, by suppressing the lieutenancy and its petty splendour, just when it was growing popular on account of its being occupied by Cialdini; that, notwithstanding all these faults, Piedmont was able to obtain all it aimed at, as if by miracle, without producing any agitation in the towns—pursuing with relentless energy brigands all over the country, overpowering everywhere not only Bourbonists, but Mazzinians and Garibaldians, when they openly opposed the Government; and that, in the midst of such troubles, it succeeded in carrying out the conscription with the utmost enthusiasm, the whole population applauding the new recruits who rallied round those glorious Italian colours, the symbol of the independence of the nation, which have already led to victory the worthy descendants of the ancient masters of the world—when we take all these things into consideration, to what other conclusion can we come than that the star of Italy is in the ascendant?

END OF THE FIRST VOLUME.

www.ingramcontent.com/pod-product-compliance
Lightning Source LLC
Chambersburg PA
CBHW031029120726
47905CB00007B/2108